# SLIPPERY TIMES

NICHOLAS DE KRUYFF

Copyright © 2021 by StoryWell Publishing

All rights reserved. No part of this publication may be reproduced, distributed or transmitted in any form or by any means, without prior written permission.

Story Well Publishing
2637 Northgate Blvd
Fort Wayne, IN 46835
www.storywellpublishing.com

Publisher's Note: At Story Well we believe that every author deserves to have their voice heard, and by purchasing this book you have helped us continue to find new voices to bring to the world. Thank you for supporting us and our authors!

This is a work of fiction. Names, characters, places, and incidents are a product of the author's imagination. Locales and public names are sometimes used for atmospheric purposes. Any resemblance to actual people, living or dead, or to businesses, companies, events, institutions, or locales is completely coincidental.

Slippery Times/Nicholas de Kruyff -- 1st ed.
ISBN 978-1-952876-12-7

For Sarah. Thanks for stabbing me in the leg with an ice cream cone all those years ago.

# CHAPTER ONE

## -- SCARBOROUGH, YORKSHIRE. NOW --

Edmund Lovenight fumed.

He fumed at the universe, at his rapidly diminishing alcoholic buzz, his sketchy memory, and for good measure, life in general.

It was October, it was the middle of the night, it was raining, and it was miserable. Typical North Yorkshire. The fact the rest of the world was in the middle of October made it October$^2$ in North Yorkshire. Lovenight wondered if some temporal divot had situated itself over the northern English city and as a result every month became October. He wasn't far off the truth.

"I will not be trifled with!" he cried defiantly into the wind, as the North Sea answered him by blowing sheets of hard rain sideways into his face. He considered yelling back, but realized the wind would always win. Instead, he tucked his chin down into his double-breasted black velvet jacket, mumbled, and continued walking, looking for the damn retirement home.

A few short hours ago he had been at a swinging party in Soho attended by most of Hollywood's A list, several Chinese dissidents, the real Dalai Lama, recuperating *bon vivants*, and all one hundred of Forbe's List of the 'World's 100 Most Powerful Women'. He had left the party reluctantly because a trans-corporeal message materialized in his martini in the form of complex geometric patterns swirling around the olive. The message simply read COME IMMEDIATELY and it was signed LADY MONTIQUE.

He did the only thing he could when a summons from Lady Montique arrived instructing him to COME IMMEDIATELY: he left immediately. He hadn't time to change out of his glad rags into proper operative gear, hence the velvet jacket.

He did of course destroy the message by downing the martini.

The problem was he could not remember for the life of him where he was supposed to COME IMMEDIATELY to. It was a retirement home, certainly, a sort of industrial looking building trying to appear cozy by the addition of a few Japanese maples outside its magnetically locked front doors. The retirement home was in deepest darkest Scarborough, but that was all he could remember. No address, nothing else. And he'd be damned if he tried to look it up on the internet.

Literally, damned.

As soon as he typed on any electronic device, the electromagnetic parasites which kept constant surveillance on him would report it to his adversaries. If you'd been a professional rogue and chrono-operative for a secret society called the Outliers as long as Lovenight had, you had your fair share of adversaries, not to mention nemeses, enemies, and bowling partners.

A cab approached from up the coast road, its headlights illuminating the fat drops of rain pelleting Lovenight. He waved his hand frantically in the headlight beams. The cab stopped beside him.

He slid into the rear seat and said, "Well timed, my good cabbie. I'm looking for a retirement home."

"A little young for one, don't you think, sir?" the cabbie quipped, without turning around.

"What? No. Not for me." Lovenight sighed. "Look, just take me to a retirement home."

"Which, sir?"

"Any!" Lovenight snapped. "You're a cabbie, you must know

them all. Pick one."

"Have an address, sir?"

Lovenight regarded the back of the cabbie's head. "If I did, I would have given it to you."

"Why not look it up on..."

"No! No electronics. They're creeping death."

"Do you know what this retirement home looks like?"

"If arch-supports were a building, they would be this building. If geriatric vitamins were a building, they would be this building."

"Ah, you want the Leasuirex Shady Lane Retirement Home."

"That's it! Good man. Take me there, posthaste."

"Right you are, sir."

The driver started driving.

Lovenight settled back in the worn leather seat and checked his watch. Three in the morning. The party would really be getting started back in Soho. The Dalai Lama would be cracking (what he claimed) was the rudest joke possible on this plane of existence, while the Forbe's women tipped waiters with luxury German automobiles. If he could get back before the party ended he would able to get in on the after-party party. Lovenight didn't consider it a proper weekend unless he'd been invited to several after-party parties. That was the way to spend a weekend. Not roving around North Yorkshire looking for a retirement home that housed the oldest human on Earth.

In some remote part of his brain an alarm sounded.

Lovenight didn't like alarms. Alarms generally meant some kind of imminent danger. Alarms meant jumping out of windows or airplanes or something equally life-challenging. Alarms were bad. Alarms meant no hope of waking up in luxury suites. Alarms were to be avoided at all costs.

Internal alarms however could not be ignored. That made them even more dangerous.

Leaning forward, he said to the cabbie, "Ah, excuse me, I said I wanted to go to the Shady something something."

"Right you are, sir," the cabbie said cheerfully.

"But we're on the A1 heading towards Leeds."

"Right again, sir."

"Out of Scarborough and North Yorkshire?"

"Correct."

"But I thought Shady something something was in Scarborough."

"Oh yes, absolutely in Scarborough, sir."

Lovenight puzzled over the cabbie's response. He examined his directives to the cabbie, concluded they were clear enough, clarion really, and the fault must lie with the cabbie, which meant either the man was a lunatic, deliberately disregarding his wishes, or, more likely, something sinister was afoot. What Lovenight needed was further information.

"Ah, so we are heading towards Shady something something?"

"Yes, sir."

"Via Leeds?"

"Correct, sir."

"Yet the Shady something something is in Scarborough; you have said as much."

"It is, sir."

"Then why are we leaving Scarborough?"

"To get you to the Leasuirex Shady Lane Retirement Home."

The alarm in Lovenight's head flashed big red warning signs. Lovenight blinked them away and focused on the driver, one hand on the door handle. Better to be ready to jump out of the cab if things went sideways. Not being ready to jump could lead to nasty accidents.

"I feel like there's something you're not telling me."

"Oh, sir? How do you mean?"

"Well, I say 'take me to X', and you say, 'right you are', but then you take me in the exact opposite direction. Are you a Dadaist?"

"Don't know. Don't know what a Dadaist is."

"A follower of the Dadaist art movement."

"Oh? And what are they on about?"

"Well, they reject logic in favour of nonsense, intuition, and randomness."

"Sounds like a thirteen-year-old."

Lovenight considered this for a moment. "Yes, very similar."

"Sorry sir, I'm no Dadaist, nor Mommyist either."

Lovenight gripped the door handle tight. "You're not a

schizophrenic, are you?"

"No, sir. I had me shots."

Something about the cabbie's diction and cadence reminded Lovenight of the postwar films of the 1940s, the way people spoke back then. An alarm in Lovenight's head fired every synapse and neural pathway it could commandeer, leading him to an epiphany.

"Hold everything! What's your name?"

"Reginald Warrick, sir. But everyone just calls me Reg."

"Reg, I have a question for you, and I want you to think very carefully before you answer."

"I will endeavour to do my best, sir."

"Reg, are you dead?"

"Oh yes, sir. Most definitely."

"Mind if I take a look?"

"Not at all, sir."

Reg turned around. He had been dead a long time. Beneath his cap the round face was drawn and eyeless, the skin blackened and leathery, the cheeks sunken and stretched so tight Lovenight could clearly see each ridge and bump of the jawbone underneath. Reg's nose resembled a dried fig. Thin wisps of blonde hair dangled from beneath his cap. There was an astringent smell about him reminiscent of formaldehyde.

The moribund visage would have been horrible to behold except for one mitigating factor: Reg had a fluffy moustache that was as thick as Lovenight's ring and middle finger combined. A blond cookie-duster that could have graced the lip of any 70s network TV detective. It somehow made him affable and ridiculous at the same time.

"Reg, why didn't you tell me this before?"

"What sir?"

"This whole 'you being dead' thing."

"Never came up, sir."

"Who revivified you?"

"They never gave their name."

"And it never came up?"

"No, sir."

"Lots of things don't tend to come up with you, do they Reg?

Now listen, please give me a detailed account of where we are heading."

"Happy to, sir. We're going down the A1 to the M1, then straight to Heathrow."

"Ahh, see, there's an important piece of information."

"From there, we are taking a flight to Toronto, Ontario. That's in Canada, sir."

"Thank you, I know where it is."

"The Leasuirex Shady Lane Retirement Home is in a suburb of Toronto, called Scarborough. So you see sir, we have to leave Scarborough to get to Scarborough."

Lovenight struck his forehead with the back of his palm. Several more details surfaced in his alcohol-hazed memory. *Scarborough, CANADA; not Scarborough, UK. Of course!*

"Wait a moment, did you say 'we' are taking a flight'?"

"Yes sir," Reg said. "I'm to accompany you. All the way, the ma'am said."

"On a plane? You? In your state of...living-challenged existence?"

"Absolutely, sir."

Lovenight took his hand off the door handle and eased back in his seat. "Forget the after-party party," he said, "This, I've got to see."

# CHAPTER TWO

### -- GRAND RAPIDS, MICHIGAN. NOW --

Simon swung the censer from side to side, filling the wood-paneled basement with thick grey smoke, obscuring the velvet posters and causing Mark to cough uncontrollably. Something at the bottom of the censer rattled ominously.
"Not so much! My asthma," Mark complained.
"Screw your asthma, man! We're going for broke here!"
"You're going to set off the smoke alarm and I'll get in shit!" Mark took a dose off his inhaler and turned to Herb, who sat peacefully on the couch rolling a joint. "Herb, open that window, will ya."
"Wuss," Simon said mockingly.
Mark shot back, "It's Saturday night and we're hanging out in my basement. *Ergo est*, we're wusses. Thanks for stating the obvious."
Mark unfolded the legs of the card table he'd pulled from the crawlspace, then set half-burnt birthday candles (found in a junk

drawer in the kitchen) stuck in zucchini muffins (leftovers from a book club meeting held by Mark's mom) at each of the corners. That done, he turned to Herb who had forgotten what he'd been asked to do only moments before and had gone back to rolling his joint.

"Herb? Herb! Can you please open the window?"

"S'no problemo," Herb slurred.

Herb put the joint down and stood up. He walked slowly, methodically placing one foot firmly on the floor before raising the other, moving at a snail's pace toward the basement's only window. He walked slowly because he was certain the floor was about to decide it was *not* a floor and it no longer wished to be trod on. Floors like that were dangerous. They could suddenly slip and transmogrify into walls or tables or cabbages. They needed firm footfalls to constantly remind them they *were* floors and to mind their place.

"Hurry up, Herb! Jeez, what's the holdup?" Mark could already feel his bronchial tubes filling with whatever incense-crap Simon had put in the censer. He popped his inhaler in his mouth and sucked in measure amounts of prescription steroids.

"Herb's tripping balls," Simon explained, still cleansing the corners of the basement with thick sage smoke. "Got hungry before he came over. Only food in the fridge was two hash brownies."

"Jesus, Herb! You don't eat hash brownies because you're hungry, you eat them to get wasted!"

"It's alright. If he gets comatose, we'll get him a pizza and stick him in the corner," Simon said, capping the brazer. It stopped smoking immediately. "Help me light the candles."

"My mom's going to be back at 11."

"Don't worry, we'll be done before she gets back."

Mark nodded, then turned and watched Herb lumbering towards the window. "Herb, you okay?"

Herb mumbled something which sounded similar to 'it's cool' but had entirely too many P-sounds in it. In reality, Herb himself wasn't really sure what he had said. He just said it because he felt the need to acknowledge his friends were talking to him. Of a much more immediate concern was the dubious floor beneath him. He was intent on making sure it stayed where it was. So, he crept at his petty pace towards the window. An overly excited worm could have passed him.

While Herb's shuffling looked ridiculous to Simon and Mark, it was in fact, the only thing keeping them alive at the moment.

Herb opened the window. The sudden intrusion of fresh air into the smoke-filled basement made him cough violently for several seconds. Once the coughing subsided, he started his long, arduous journey back across the basement floor towards the card table.

Simon and Mark stared at him with blank expressions.

"If we wait for him we'll be here all night," Mark said to Simon. "What's next?"

"We need to draw a triangle-of-conjuration on the floor, to contain whatever demon we summon."

"What's a triangle-of-conjuration look like?"

"This is only a guess, but...a triangle?"

"Funny. So funny I forgot to laugh." Mark chalked out a triangle on the basement floor next to the Laz-Y-Boy. "How's that?"

Simon stared at the triangle. "It's purple," he said flatly.

"That was the only colour of sidewalk chalk I could find in Beth-Ann's toy box."

"She's going to kill you for going through her stuff."

"She hasn't used it in years. She'll never miss it."

They sat at the fold-out card table. Simon picked up the deck of tarot cards. "Light the candles."

Mark struck a match and lit the wicks. The smell of sulphur tickled their noses.

"What now?" Mark asked.

"We start the summoning."

"All right! Dungeons and dragons on steroids! Real occult magic! Herb, hurry up!"

"Can't," Herb mumbled. "Floor's tricky tonight."

Mark sighed. "Just start, Simon. We need to finish before my mom gets home."

Simon picked up the worn paperback. The cover, done in the style of Norman Rockwell, depicted a blissfully naive family gathered around a table covered with tarot cards. The title, *Pax*

*Arcana: The Handbook to Arcane Tarot Card Readings and Incorporeal Summonings,* was written in block letters. Simon flipped to a dog-eared page and began reading, "I invoke thee, Michael, Gabriel, Raphael, Uriel, in the name of all that is holy to protect us, your humble servants, so that we may--"

"Hurry, Simon. The candles won't last."

"--so that we may do thy work and stuff like that, blah blah blah, yadda yadda yadda. Amen."

With his eyes closed Simon shuffled the tarot cards, then laid the cards out in a Celtic cross spread.

"Wow, all major arcana!"

Mark's eyes roved from card to card. "The Hanged Man, The Tower, Judgement, The World. Something huge is going on!"

"I've never seen a spread like this."

"Herb, you gotta see this!"

"See, like Kurosawa, man," Herb said, still shuffling across the floor. "It's all perspective. Dude shot with multiple cameras. Total coverage. Unreal. Ever see *Yojimbo* or *Seven Samurai*? Far out!"

"Film majors," Mark scoffed, shaking his head. "What's the verdict, Simon?"

"Shut up, will ya? I'm trying to figure it out."

He read furiously for a moment, his eyes scanning the page. Finally, he put down the book and said in a hushed tone, "According to the *Pax Arcana* we have rent the veil between worlds and have summoned forth a vile and malignant force."

Mark and Simon glanced over to the triangle-of-conjuration. It remained empty.

"We did?" Mark asked, sounding unconvinced.

"According to the instructions."

"Shouldn't something have appeared then?"

Simon shrugged, considering. Mark did have a point. Normally, summonings summoned *something*. That was the whole point of summoning. There should have been a slobbering, foul-smelling, shape-shifting beast contained within the triangle, squirming and spitting and cursing in forgotten languages while scratching at the floor with its scimitar-like claws in a vain attempt to free itself.

Instead, there was, well, nothing.

"Perhaps it's invisible," Simon suggested.

"An unseen force?"

"Yeah, unseen. Like a poltergeist or something."

"How do you know it's there then, if it's invisible?"

Mark got up and walked towards the triangle-of-conjuration.

"Don't step inside!" Simon warned. "You could be possessed..."

Mark moved close to the chalk line without stepping over. "I don't see anything."

"Doesn't mean it's not there."

"Bogus."

"It's not!" Simon stood up, bumping the card table with his thighs, causing the candles to flicker. "Try throwing something at it."

"Like what?"

"Your slipper."

"I'm not throwing my slipper. What if there is something there? It'll get pissed."

Simon reached into his backpack and pulled out a sheet of paper. He crumpled it into a tight ball and tossed it. The crumpled paper arced through the space just above the triangle-of-conjuration, hitting nothing.

"Maybe it's crouching," Simon said.

"Crouching?"

"Yeah."

"Bogus," Mark reaffirmed.

Simon was about to object when the basement door swung open and a small figure stood backlit at the top of the stairs. Simon and Mark both screamed high-pitched, emasculating screams.

The figure descended the steps, its small form racked with laughter.

"You losers scream like little girls!" the figure said, waving away the smoke from her eyes. "What's that skunk smell? Are you guys getting high down here? YOU ARE! You're in so much trouble, Mark."

"Beth-Ann, get back upstairs!" Mark demanded. "You're not

supposed to come down when I have friends over."

Beth-Ann shrugged and said, "Wifi is down. I need to reset the modem."

"Fine," Mark said exasperated. "Do it and get out of here."

Beth-Ann walked smugly to the jumble of wires at the back of the basement and unplugged the modem, counted to fifteen slowly, on purpose just to annoy her brother and his friends, then plugged it back in. In that time Herb managed to reach the card table and take his seat, feet firmly on the floor.

"Good job," he said to no one in particular.

"Finished," Beth-Ann said.

"What're you waiting for, then? Get out of here."

"Ask me nicely."

"Beth-Ann!"

"Or I won't leave."

"Just do it, Mark," Simon said. "We've got shit to do."

"Language!" Mark snapped back. "Not in front of Beth-Ann."

"We've got *stuff* to do."

Mark, slightly mollified, turned back to his younger sister. "Please, Beth-Ann."

Beth-Ann, chin up, started to walk past her brother when she noticed the triangle drawn on the floor.

"Is that my chalk?" she said accusingly, her hand reaching out to erase it. "You don't get to play with my chalk!"

"Don't touch that!" Simon yelled, standing suddenly and bumping the card table a second time, causing a lit candle (zucchini muffin and all) to fall into Herb's lap. Startled, Herb jumped in his chair and for an instant both of his feet left the floor -- causing slippage. At the exact same instant Beth-Ann's hand brushed the chalk line, breaking it.

The air whirled above the triangle-of-conjuration; a shimmering, glimmering rushing of air, a blur, a tornado made miniature. Beth-Ann lurched, trying to back away from the contained storm, but could not. Something pulled at her. For a moment she fought against the unseen force, resisted it with all her strength, then she stumbled and fell completely into the triangle-of-conjuration. The diminutive maelstrom enveloped her. One instant Beth-Ann was there, then the rushing air snatched her away. The tornado

fizzled out, leaving behind a man in a black suit kneeling within the confines of the triangle.
Both Mark and Simon screamed again.
Herb squinted, "Uh-oh."

# CHAPTER THREE

-- GRAND RAPIDS, MICHIGAN. BEFORE --

Herb was fifteen years old the first time he disincorporated and slipped into the incorporeal.

Late one night, after smoking a doobie in the shed behind his house, he settled down in his bedroom, headphones on, listening to Santana's *Moonflower*. The music soothed Herb, allowing him to achieve a zen-like state. The longer Santana played, the deeper Herb sank into his transcendental mind-set. Then, halfway through 'Soul Sacrifice', his mind opened and swallowed the universe whole in one, big, psychedelic bite. Or maybe the universe had swallowed him. Whichever, he found himself free-floating three feet above his Star Wars bedsheets, as easy as a dandelion fluff on a spring breeze.

"Wild!" he exclaimed while regarding his transparent fingertips.

This was more than just astral projection or consciousness migration. This was next level. This was disincorporation, actually physically slipping into an incorporeal state. His bed was empty, the headphones lying on the pillow where they had fallen, Santana still grooving away while Herb's body, now incorporeal energy, drifted above, beyond the perception horizon of the corporeal universe.

His incorporeal stomach grumbled. A shimmering thought popped into his head, insistent and demanding: *munchies!*

He surprised himself by instantly translocating across town to Taco Haven, his favourite hangout. Pleased and delighted, he folded his legs, hovered in midair, and waited for the employee at the cash, whose name-tag read 'Greg', to take his order.

Delight soured into disappointment as he realized he simply could not get Greg's attention. He fanned his arms in the air. Greg entirely failed to notice, remaining fixated on a small brown spot on the counter he was attempting to scratch away with his thumbnail. Herb whistled. Greg itched his neck. Herb somersaulted in midair. Greg wiped his hands on his apron.

"Boy, save your flipping and twisting. You could set your johnson on fire and that taco-pusher wouldn't notice."

Herb looked around, but could not see who had spoken.

"Relax boy, you can hear me, but you can't see me, because I'm not there."

"Trippy," Herb said. "Never talked with a ghost before."

The voice chuckled, low and deep and bottomless. "I ain't a ghost, boy. I'm living and breathing just like you, here in Georgia, just outside of Atlanta. Name's Earl, what's yours?"

"I'm Herb."

"Good to know you, Herb."

"You too, Earl. Can I be honest with you, Earl?"

"Sure."

"Earl, you're freaking me out. How's it you're in Georgia and you can see me?"

"I can't see you, Herb. Even if you were right in front of me, I couldn't see you, but that's beside the point. I'm sensing you, Herb. I've got the perception, just like you. When a new perceptor enters the incorporeal, they make waves all up and down the electro-paradisiacal spectrum. That's where you are now. That's why burrito breath over there can't see you."

Herb tried to concentrate on what Earl was telling him, but the words were like half-eaten gummy bears: slippery and hard to hold on to. Their meaning kept sliding past his understanding no matter how hard he focused.

"Hey, Earl, man. Could you tell me what's going on, and use as few words as possible? I'm really high right now."

Earl's low chuckle rattled through his skull. "Herb, you got your smoke on? Well, I'll be damned and judged! All right, I'll help you out. Now, listen, first thing you gotta do is get back to a safe place."

"Yeah, good idea," Herb agreed. "How exactly?"

"All you gotta do is think it. Picture it in your mind and want to be there."

Seemed easy enough, so Herb thought of the *Rashomon* poster above his dresser and instantly he was back lying on his bed, Santana blazing out of the headphones. A smile cracked his lips.

"Earl, thanks man. You did it."

"No Herb, you did it."

"Okay, if you say. But how, Earl? I mean, is this some weird part of puberty no one ever talks about? Am I going to still like girls after this? I hope so, because I sure do like them now."

"Oh, hell. Let me explain it to ya."

Earl set about explaining to Herb what was happening to his fifteen-year-old body and mind.

"See, you gotta start thinking about the universe in terms of the 'corporeal' and the 'incorporeal'. The corporeal is everything you can see and feel and touch and hear, and everything that can see and feel and touch and hear you -- the breeze, heat, a cold beer, trucks driving by on the street, bears in the woods, molecules and atoms, the sun and moon and stars, gravity, electricity humming through power lines, all of it. That's all the corporeal part of the universe.

"Then there's everything you can't see or feel or taste or hear. Love, knowledge, an argument, consciousness, understanding, that uneasy feeling you get when someone's watching you, intuition, dark matter, dark light, quantum entanglement, that's all energy too, only it's energy that belongs in another state of being:

the incorporeal state. You feel me?"

Herb nodded despite only catching half of what Earl said. "Batting 500. Keep going."

"What you just experienced was your crossing over, disincorporating yourself. My first cross-over happened when I was around the same age you are now. It's normal, is what I'm trying to get at. Normal for us. Most people don't have perception. There's only a few of us with this gift."

"How many?"

"Jeez, boy, I don't know! A dozen or two maybe. We're perceptors. You're one of us now."

"Cool. Can I ask a question?"

"Shoot."

"What do we perceive?"

"Good question. Let me give you a for-instance. Imagine we're all just dots living on a ball. Just little dots on the surface of this ball called the 'universe'. All we can see is what's in front, behind, and beside us. Now, imagine us dots walk around the ball, eventually we'd end up right where we started. No matter how many times we walked around we still wouldn't come to an end. No finish line. Just more 'ball' stretching out in all directions forever. To us dots, the 'universe' would be infinite, even though it was just a ball, right?"

"But what if one of the dots looked up and saw something else?"

"Exactly, Herb! Now you're getting it. That's us, the perceptors. We're the ones who look up. And we just don't look up, we can get off the ball. We can slip out of 'reality' and go places no one else can.

"Now, here's where it gets tricky. The corporeal sometimes gets slippery. The ball becomes an egg, or a football, or a piece of toast, or whatever. We can see the change, but regular folk can't. We call it slippage. And us perceptors, we can, sometimes, persuade the corporeal not to change. We can keep the ball being a ball."

"You lost me, or maybe I lost me."

"Don't worry about it, Herb. Just realize things around you are going to get slippery sometimes."

"Cool. One last question?"
"Go for it."
"Who's holding the ball?"
Earl whistled. "That, Herb, is the million-dollar question."

# CHAPTER FOUR

-- GRAND RAPIDS, MICHIGAN. NOW --

His face was bird-like, with a long sharp nose and small, darting eyes. The top of his head was bald, smooth, and liver spotted. He wore a black suit two sizes too big. A thin string necktie gave him the appearance of a Southern US preacher. He squatted dead centre in the triangle-of-conjuration, his sinewy limbs ready to pounce, his small white teeth eager to pull flesh from bone.

Herb placed his feet firmly back on the floor. The corporeal universe reasserted itself. Reality stabilized. The air stilled. The floor, for the moment, seemed content to be a regular old basement floor again.

The man in the black suit regarded the shocked faces around him, then relaxed.

"I know the location of eight lost Faberge eggs," he said in a voice as smooth as buttered silk. (Not that anyone actually butters silk, but if they did, the man in the black suit's voice would have been that smooth.) "I'll give them to you, if you send me back."

Mark and Simon screamed again.

This was not the reaction the man in the black suit had hoped for. He frowned. It was a mighty frown, capable of moving armies to battle fronts.

"Beth-Ann!" Mark screeched. "What happened to her?"

"Don't listen to it! It's a devil, it's unclean!" Simon grabbed his friend and yanked him back. "It will tell only lies and twisted truths! It's the Great Deceiver!"

"You're thinking of Martin Poppelwell of East Chester, Maine," the man in the black suit said matter-of-factly. "Thoroughly unsavoury man."

"Beth-Ann! What happened to my sister?"

The man in the black suit turned a casual eye to Mark. "Your sister?"

"She was here a second ago, then...then...you..."

"I see," said the man in the black suit stroking his chin in thought. "You brought me here by a mercantile substitution--transference fuelled by an incredibly powerful singularity, a piece of universal errata. The substitution was this sister of yours. Well then, the solution is simple, don't you see?"

Mark and Simon shook their heads.

"Send me back and you shall have this Ruth-Ann."

"Beth-Ann."

"If you like. It's all one to me."

Mark, wild-eyed, glared at Simon. "You got to send him back!"

"Mark, I know you're upset..."

"I'm freaking out!"

"It's just, I don't know how."

"What?"

"I don't! The book only describes how to summon demons." Simon flipped through the *Pax Arcana*, turning the pages back and forth. "It doesn't say anything about un-summoning them."

"How is that even possible?" Mark screamed. "What're we going to do?"

While Mark and Simon shouted at each other and the man in the black suit watched, Herb quietly went about checking the nature of reality in the room, probing it with his perception. It was sort of like checking for seeds stuck in your gums after eating a sesame bagel. He prodded the couch here and poked at the black light poster there. Everything seemed solid again.

And yet there was a residual tingle after this slippage. An annoying, persistent tingle. It was like when bubbles get lodged in your nose after drinking a soda -- everything around you carries on the same, but you feel like your skull is being fracked. Some universal scale had been tipped towards...what? Herb didn't know, but he did know he had to find out what exactly had been tipped and what had done the tipping.

"Wow," he said to himself. "Trippy."

# CHAPTER FIVE

## -- GSTAAD, SWITZERLAND. BEFORE --

"Humanity yearns to be be controlled," Baroness Zamora mused as she strolled along the forest path. Her accent, which sounded like it originated somewhere along the remotest bends of the Danube River, added a touch of spine-tingling menace to her words. In truth, she could have scared someone out of their wits just by reading aloud a soup label.

"It's their dirty little secret, the hope buried deep in their hearts. Look at Marx's communists defending the world's proletariate, Plato's benevolent philosopher kings -- two completely different philosophies, yet each relies on a firm and controlling hand."

"Right on brand," Ken, her senior marketing strategist, agreed.

They walked the foothills outside of Gstaad, the early October snows coating the hiking trails. Ken glanced over his shoulder looking for the retinue of security personnel who must surely be following them, but could not spot anything out of the ordinary. Nothing but tall Swiss pines, like a scene from *The Sound of Music*. He half expected Julie Andrews to come running down the path followed by a gaggle of blonde-haired children...of course, if Julie

Andrews and the gaggle of children did come running down the path they would be ambushed, seized, and interrogated by camouflaged shock troopers loyal to Baroness Zamora and the Governance. If the baroness was in a good mood, she might even let them sing a song before doing away with them.

Brutally tough with a nostalgic side, that was the baroness.

Something glinted in the bough of a pine tree. The scope of a sniper's rifle, perhaps? Ken hurried to catch up to Baroness Zamora.

"Some will deny it," the baroness continued. "Some will claim to want less government control in their lives. They will write sweeping manifestos on their 'God given right' to pursue life and liberty. They will shoot firearms into the air every national holiday, yelling 'Look at my freedom, world! We're the best!' But in their hearts they simply want to go to work in the morning, a bar in the afternoon, and bed at night. It's our job to provide them with that. Simple, yes?"

"Simple in theory, complex in practice."

"Complex? Obviously!" she said with a hissing sneer. "That's why we delegate. Running governments, that's what underlings are for! *We* must keep our eye on the big picture. We remain the all-seeing eye in the pyramid, watching where this world is heading, making sure it continues to travel on the course we have set for it."

"Yes...super..."

The baroness faced her senior marketing strategist, taking a good look at him for the first time. "Why are you staring at that tree?"

"No reason, I, thought, I saw, something, sort of...assault rifle-ish. Mistake on my part." Ken forced himself to smile. "You were saying, baroness?"

"My point is we must be diligent if we're to maintain our position in this world. Any little slip up and we'll lose control of the whole mechanism, making us no more relevant than..."

"Contemporary jazz?" Ken suggested. "Betamax? A two-party system? Nutritional information on a bag of crisps? Backbenchers?"

"Absolutely! Backbenchers! Perish the thought." The

baroness stopped, once again regarding her senior marketing strategist with a disapproving eye. "Why did you kick that rock away?"

"Oh, it seemed a trifle...grenade-like."

The gap between the baroness' eyebrows narrowed. "Have you always suffered from these?"

"These?"

"Delusions of...ammunitions?"

"Only for about the past ten minutes."

The baroness nodded, her head cocking to the side slightly. "I understand. You're nervous, you hope this is going well."

Relief washed over Ken's face. "Exactly, baroness."

"It isn't."

"Ahh."

She took a step closer to him. "You're married?"

"Was. To a behavioural geneticist in our augmentation division. A cold fish, really, with no imagination. And no heart. And no genuine human emotion. Or empathy."

"So, you married a psychopath?"

"It was a physical thing," Ken admitted. "She left me last year to work on some project with our robotics, engineering, and logistic divisions. I asked her when she'd be back and she said she wouldn't."

"I see."

Ken waited for the baroness to say something else, but she didn't. She simply stood and stared at him with a sharp eye and keen interest. That stare felt like lasers strafing his skin.

He cleared his throat. "Uhh...I thought you'd like an update on our Beyond-Truth directive? That is, if you wanted an update...I mean there must be a reason you wished to see me. I have the update ready. Would you like to hear it?"

Baroness Zamora shrugged and said, "If you must."

"Beyond-truth is exceeding our wildest expectations--"

"Tut-tut," Baroness Zamora interrupted, wagging a finger at him. "Hyperbole."

Ken began again. "Beyond-truth is exceeding our expectations."

"Go on."

"We shortened the news cycle from twenty-four hours to five minutes, trimmed soundbites down to three seconds, reduced stories down to 14 characters. The result: no substantive content can get out. At present, we can create scandals in seconds. We can manufacture theories and opinions from the most patchwork of details, theories and opinions so ludicrous they scored over 9.8 on the wackadoodle metrics. Our grip on the current zeitgeist is complete! People only believe what we tell them!"

"Sorry," Baroness Zamora said with a smile. "But, I think we'll go in a different direction from here on. It's all very interesting, but maintaining world domination must become simple, elegant, foolproof." Her smile became predatory. "Controlling humanity must come from the inside, not imposed from the environment."

Ken tried to speak but found he could not. Unseen fingers constricted inside his throat, collapsing his windpipe. He fell to the ground, gasping for air.

Baroness Zamora waited until the senior marketing strategist stopped moving, then removed her trans-kinetic hands from the body. She had all the information she needed.

"Now, let's see the progress his ex-wife has made," she said to herself, and walked off back down the ravine.

The bark around a dozen trunks bulged as the camouflage shock-troopers peeled themselves away and stalked after her, assault rifles held at the ready. Two troopers split off from the rest of the platoon to dispose of the recently deceased senior marketing strategist. *It's always prudent to have backup,* she thought. It was the reason dozens of contenders for her position were rotting in unmarked graves, while she was still walking.

# CHAPTER SIX

## -- TORONTO, CANADA. NOW --

Lovenight approached the yellow line painted on the floor. The sign in front of him read, WAIT BEHIND LINE UNTIL CUSTOMS AGENT IS CLEAR. In one hand he clutched a duty-free gift bag, in the other a carry-on purchased from a store inside Heathrow. He began whistling. The family of four in front of him, all dressed in Hawaiian shirts and sporting second degree sunburns, moved off after having their passports stamped. He advanced, still whistling.

Whistling was something he did when he was nervous. Mainly because he figured it made him look nervous, so people would think *Oh, he's whistling, only a complete idiot would whistle if they were nervous, so he can't really be nervous: he's just a complete idiot.* Lovenight was a big fan of reverse-reverse psychology.

He handed his passport to the female customs officer who promptly slid it through a scanner. The customs officer had relaxed brown eyes, contrasted by blonde hair pulled back and lassoed into a torturous ponytail. The tension of her hairdo pulled the skin on her forehead tight as a drum. Lovenight developed a tension headache just looking at her.

"Purpose of visit to Canada?" she asked crisply.

"Oh, you know, a vacation I suppose. Just an impulsive getaway sort-of-thing."

"Where are you staying?"

"In a hotel...or with friends, you know, whichever happens. Probably a hotel, a really nice one close to the action, where ever the action is in...what city is this again?"

The customs officer looked up and regarded him, her eyes taking in the double-breasted black velvet jacket, the scandalously tight Italian leather pants, the silver cufflinks, and his vintage Beatle boots. Everything about him seemed aggressively affectatious, yet at the same time, mildly harmless.

"Sir, is everything all right?"

"Sure. Of course. Fine. Tickety-boo. Thanks for asking. Why are you asking, again?"

"Because you seem...please stop whistling."

"That could be a problem."

"Please."

"Don't think I can."

The customs officer paused, trying to decide what to do. It was obvious to any thinking person if they wanted to deal with Lovenight they would need a warehouse full of patience and be prepared for long bouts of obstinance. He wasn't a mule, obviously. He wasn't a threat. He was just silly. And in the end, would it really be worth it?

The customs officer stamped his passport and declaration form. She was in no mood to have precious minutes of her life wasted by this individual.

"Cheers," Lovenight said, and whistled as he strolled through baggage claims and straight out into the terminal.

Half a kilometre outside of the airport, Lovenight stopped the completely underwhelming rental car just before the onramp to the highway, unbuckled his seat belt and leaned over to unzip his carryon bag. Several drivers behind him honked in frustration.

"Dude, what the hell?" one of them yelled, leaning out of his window.

Lovenight flipped him a very rude finger gesture which the driver mistook for the peace sign.

"No one has any patience, these days," he said to himself.

"Quite right, sir," Reg said, still disassembled and stowed away in the carry-on. "The world would be a better place if we all had a moment to sniff the daisies...or petunias, or nasturtiums...whatever you have growing in your garden, really. Roses, of course, and lilies..."

As he mused about different floral aromas, Reg unfolded himself, his femurs reconnecting to their corresponding hip sockets with a dry click. Lovenight did his best not to watch, but found himself repeatedly sneaking looks at the dead cabbie. When he helped disassemble Reg in the Heathrow parking garage, dislocating bones from their sockets under the cabbie's leathery skin, and then packing Reg in the carry-on, he couldn't help but marvel at the corpse's resilience. Reg was similar to one of those naturally occurring mummies who occasionally turned up in bogs or on frozen mountaintops. Just a bag of bones that snapped together in seconds, really.

"Reg, may I ask you a personal question?"

"Absolutely, sir," Reg replied while fiddling with his patella, trying to position it in just the right place.

"What keeps you together?"

"A sunny disposition, I suppose."

"Not that."

"How do you mean, sir?"

"I mean with a living individual such as myself, it's all tendons and ligaments and so forth. But with you, being...uh...a...life-challenged individual, what is it?"

"From what I understand it's something called Necronominal Probability Placement, or N.P.P."

"Necronominal Probability Placement?"

"Yes, sir. It has to do with inertia. Are you familiar with the concept of inertia, sir?"

"Out of the past twenty-four hours, I've spent five hours in the back of your cab, four hours in a waiting room, and seven hours in a plane -- in *economy*. My ass knows all too well the meaning of inertia."

Reg regarded him with a dower look. "Steady on, sir. No need for strong language."

"Pass me the vodka bottle in the duty-free bag."

"Very good, sir. Just let me pop my humerus back in. There. Here you are."

"You were explaining Necronominal something something?"

"As I understand it, N.P.P. works with the bone's natural inertia on a necro-quantum level. The bone's sub-atomic particles want to be in the position they had in life, so necro-quantum mechanics uses their natural disposition to *be* together to *keep* them together."

Lovenight spewed out his mouthful of premium French vodka, almost dropping the bottle. He took a swig to replace his loss, then said, "Reg, that's ridiculous."

"What is, sir?"

"Mixing quantum mechanics and necromancy."

"Well, that's how Professor Bohr explained it to me, sir."

Lovenight spit another mouthful of premium French vodka. "Niels Bohr? The excruciatingly famous quantum physicist?"

"Oh, you know him, sir?"

"I'm asking the questions here! How could you possibly know Niels Bohr?"

"I had the honour to be his personal driver when he was in London."

"When was that?"

"During the War, sir. I was in the Army Service Corps as a driver. He would travel to all these big, mucky-mucky, secret conferences, tube alloy boys and so forth. Nice chap, really. Loved talking about physics and all the little quantum bits. Wicked necromancer and cricket player as well. Not many people know that. He'd come off the pitch after scoring 400 runs, people patting him on the back and congratulating him, while he'd shake his head, smile this wry smile, and say, 'It's all an illusion. Time is an illusion. Space is an illusion. Perception is everything.' You want to veer left here, sir."

Lovenight swerved, merging with the traffic heading east.

After a moment of silent reflection, he exploded into a series of expletives which would have made the Marquis de Sade blush.

"You're telling me Niels Bohr was a necromancer?"

"One of the finest, sir. He was the first to pinpoint the source of trans-chromatic elemental particles leaking into our universe from the inflation-zone. I was in the pub with him one night when he worked out the fuzzy mathematics of it on a napkin, reconciling quantum mechanics with necromancy." Reg chuckled. "Good times, those."

With a sharp crack, Reg snapped his skull back in place atop his spine. "There we are sir. All done. I can take over driving now if you want."

Lovenight slammed on the breaks, stopping the car in the middle of the highway. A chorus of horns and squealing tires erupted behind him, followed by the sound of crunching metal and shattering glass. Miraculously, no one hit the completely underwhelming rental car.

"About bloody time," he said to Reg. "I need to do some serious drinking before meeting with the Lady."

Lovenight checked his wristwatch and his sobriety. Both were questionable.

He hadn't changed the vintage Hamilton Ventura to local time yet, so by his best estimate it was somewhere near six in the evening. In regard to his sobriety, he still could get out of the car and walk by himself, but he no longer dreaded the looming meeting with Lady Montique. *Perfect mental balance,* he thought. *If only humanity could achieve and retain this level of consciousness and inebriation, ninety-five percent of the world's social problems could be solved over the course of a holiday weekend. Of course, that would be one helluva bar tab.*

The rental sedan was parked in front of the Leasuirex Shady Lane Retirement Home and Long-Term Care Facility, a squat, red-bricked building with benches and shady trees.

Lovenight sauntered up to the driver's window. "You coming,

Reg?"

"Don't you think my condition of moribundity might be noticed, sir? Compromise the mission, it might?"

Lovenight took a moment to look at the seniors near the entrance, some stuck in wheelchairs, others holding onto walkers. He shook his head.

"Reg, you'll fit right in."

"Fair enough."

The receptionist behind the desk put down the phone and smiled. She had a pronounced overbite which made her face appear slightly goat-like. "Can I help you?" she asked.

Lovenight smiled. "I'm looking for Lady Eleanor Montique."

The receptionist scrunched up her eyebrows. "Who?"

"The meanest, oldest, most demanding battle-axe you've got trapped in here."

"Ah," the receptionist smiled tightly. "Room 216."

# CHAPTER SEVEN

-- LEASUIREX SHADY LANE RETIREMENT HOME, SCARBOROUGH, ONTARIO. NOW --

Lady Eleanor Anastasia Firth Montique sat upright in the mechanical bed, the nurse call-button pinched between her bony fingers, her withered thumb repeatedly clicking away to no avail. The wretched nurse must have been on break or some-such foolishness. She would have words with those responsible as soon as she could ascertain who exactly was responsible. Whoever they were they would rue the day they crossed her, rest assured of that!

In the meantime, she clicked away.

Faded black and white snapshots dotted the walls behind her, mostly of Lady Montique at upper-class social events -- fox hunts, debutante balls, state dinners, garden parties, parliamentary openings, and the like. If someone looked closely, which no one ever did, they would recognize titanic historical figures in those pictures, most in various states of inebriation. Churchill and Picasso appeared particularly wasted in one shot, while a young and comely Lady Montique frowned mightily in the background. That frown could have cracked walnuts.

No one ever looked closely at those pictures because no one ever came to visit her, not on their own accord. No one liked being in a retirement home. Not the staff, not the visitors, and certainly not the residents. Retirement homes where places were people waited to not be people anymore.

Lady Montique was not surprised however when the door swung open and Lovenight and Reg strode into her private room. She had summoned Lovenight, after all. If anything, she was a little surprised how long it had taken him to arrive. Her lips thinned.

"Did you bring tea?" she demanded in a voice as ridged as her spine.

"Tea?" Lovenight asked.

"Yes, tea, you cretinous imbecilic donkey! Tea!"

"Now look..."

Before Lovenight could finish his sentence, Lady Montique produced a small caliber pistol from beneath her comforter and levelled it at him. Lovenight, wisely, shut the hell up.

"The most admirable parts of the British Empire owe, in one way or another, a vast debt to tea," she began. "It has fortified and comforted us for two hundred years. Milk, sugar, lemon -- you can discern oodles regarding an individual's character from how they take their tea. How do you take yours, Eddie? Oh, yes, you don't! Because you neglected to bring any! *Tu ergo*, cretinous donkey!"

Lovenight scowled and put up his hands. "Okay. I'll get you tea."

Lady Montique lowered the pistol to her lap. She placed the call-button down and turned to Reg. "Reginald."

"My Lady Montique," Reg said, doffing his cap and adding a little bow. "Good to see you, ma'am. I brought him, just as you asked."

"Never state the obvious, Reginald."

"Yes, ma'am."

Lovenight glared at the corpse. Reg shrugged.

"You never told me you knew Lady Montique personally," Lovenight said, accusatorially.

"It never came up," Reg answered.

"There you go again..."

"Tea!" Lady Montique reminded them sharply.

After fifteen minutes of frantic activity -- which consisted of finding a personal support assistant, begging them to make tea, threatening them with the good Lady's wraith if the water wasn't heated to precisely seventy degrees Celsius and allowed to steep for three minutes, finding suitable china, putting it all on a tray, putting the tray back and finding a silver platter instead, then rushing back without spilling a drop -- Lovenight returned to Lady Montique's room and placed the tray next to her bed.

She looked down the length of her nose at it.

"I'll pour, shall I?" It must have been a rhetorical question because she was already reaching for the teapot. Lovenight walked over to the visitor's chair, sat, and smoothed out his lapels.

Lady Montique regarded him with a steely eye. "Tea?"

"Please," Lovenight said cautiously.

Lady Montique poured him a cup, then addressed Reg. "Tea?"

"Oh, no thank you, ma'am." he said, cap in hand. "Can't, you see. Dead and all."

"Right then," Lady Montique said turning back to Lovenight with a stare sharp as broken glass. "How do you take your tea?"

"Ahh, milk and sugar."

Lady Montique frowned. "This is Earl Grey."

"Of course. Ah, lemon then?"

Lady Montique arched her right eyebrow. "You don't sound sure, Eddie."

"I'm sure...ish."

"Donkey!" Lady Montique shouted, flinging the teacup at him. Lovenight ducked. The cup sailed inches over his head and hit the wall, exploding into shards. Judging from the amount of indents and scrapes covering that particular section of wall, other operatives must have failed the Tea Test.

"It's taken black, or with a little sugar if the drinker is a milksop! Only philistines and donkeys drink Earl Grey any other way! Reginald!

"Yes, ma'am?"

"Fetch someone to clean that mess up."

"Right away."

Reg stalked out, not because he was angry, but because being dead caused a fellow to stalk. It went with the territory.

Lady Montique shook her head once he was gone. "I'm disappointed, Eddie, I really am. The Outliers used to have such a fine class of operatives: refined, debonair, suave..."

"...people who knew what to take in their tea?"

"Exactly! Someone who knew the difference between a fish fork and a shrimp fork. Someone who cared as much about their appearance and manners as they did the Outliers. Alas, those days have gone. Now for operatives we have, well, you. Someone who dresses like a German cabaret host."

"How horrible for you."

"Don't be impudent. I wouldn't have summoned you unless it was of vital importance. And at 124 years of age, I believe I've earned the right to be cantankerous. Besides, there's nothing wrong with wishing there was a little more decorum in the world."

The old bat had a point. With a little more decorum in the world he, well, he wouldn't be in Scarborough, or Ontario, or Canada -- the cultural home of lumber jackets, work boots, and cabin socks. Yech.

Reg stalked back into the room with a nurse who had all the warmth and demeanour of a drill bit. The nurse snapped on a pair of latex gloves and began picking up pieces of broken china.

Lovenight turned to Lady Montique. "I don't mean to rush you..."

"Then don't!" Her withered hand grasped the tea cup firmly. Her sips were short and silent.

"You would not have summoned me if the situation wasn't dire," Lovenight said. "That is, if there is a situation, which I don't know, because I haven't been briefed. I can only assume there's a situation, unless, this is some kind of wild reverse psychology designed to mess with the Governance, which would be truly epic, if there was no situation. So I have to ask, what's the situation with our situation?"

"Dear Eddie, consciousness is a precious gift: don't waste it."

"Too late, I'm afraid."

Lady Montique cleared her throat, producing a sound

reminiscent of wind chimes had they been made of chicken bones. Eventually she said, "In the last forty-eight hours we have lost contact with our entire network. Our hive-mind sleeper cells, the gravitational rescue teams, all surveillance on the perceptors, ether ninjas, bone wraiths, void accountants, everyone."

Lovenight felt a hollowing in his stomach. His stomach always hollowed when dangerous, illegal, time-consuming work loomed in his near future. He had become an operative for the Outliers precisely because there was so much downtime. Now, he feared he might be called upon to save the world or something equally taxing. The thought of it made him yearn for several very dry martinis consumed in rapid succession.

"At this point in time..." Lady Montique paused as the drill bit nurse exited the room. "The entire Outliers fellowship consists of the three of us in this room."

"Well, then," Lovenight said, standing up. "It's been a good run. I wish you both luck in your future endeavours. I think I'll take my severance and retire to a nice, luxury beach resort somewhere, something with palm trees and turndown service. I do love the little mints they leave on your pillow at night."

"Donkey!" Lady Montique screeched, her small caliber pistol suddenly aimed directly at Lovenight's pelvic region. "You're by no means dismissed from duty. Quite the contrary. Your services are deemed essential until further notice."

Lovenight raised his hands, his eyes fixed on the open muzzle pointed at his nether-parts. "Let's not go off half-cocked."

"Begging your pardon, sir," Reg said, tapping Lovenight on the shoulder. "Something's wrong."

Lovenight swung his gaze from the pistol aimed at his nethers to Reg and back to the pistol. His mind wrestled with the two directives, trying to decide which was more pressing. After a few anxious seconds he decided he needed more information. "Can you be a little more specific, Reg? Something's wrong in an *oh-dear-the-pillows-don't-suit-the-drapes* sort of way, or an *Armageddon-is-nigh, death-is-imminent* sort of way?"

Reg sniffed the air. His cookie-duster moustache bristled. "The walls, they're the wrong colour."

In a desperate effort not to assault his undead driver,

Lovenight pressed his fingertips to his temples and said in a restrained voice, "What does the colour of the walls have to do with anything?"

Reg merely pointed.

The paint on the walls moved.

Gone was the institutional grey. In its place was a vibrant scaly pattern which oozed and flowed over the entire room -- crawling up across the ceiling and dripping down over the floor. Each scale scintillated, constantly shuffling between different hues and tones as if they couldn't decide exactly what colour they wanted to be. It's like a drunken chameleon staggering across a tie-dye shirt, Lovenight thought.

On some unseen cue, the scales began pulsing hypnotically, and somehow, menacingly.

"Bugger," Lovenight said.

# CHAPTER EIGHT

-- GRAND RAPIDS, MICHIGAN. NOW --

Having absolutely no indication from the paperback edition of *Pax Arcana: The Handbook to Arcane Tarot Card Readings and Incorporeal Summonings* on how to dismiss a demon once summoned, Simon had to improvise. He held a birthday candle out before him as if it was a flaming scimitar and said in a commanding voice, "Hear me, o demon! You will return to us Mark's little sister, Beth-Ann!"

"You don't have to shout," the man in a black suit said, still kneeling in the middle of the triangle-of-conjuration. "My hearing is perfectly fine."

"Silence, devil! And return her to us at once! I compel you by all the Heavenly Host, all the cherubim and seraphim, by the archangels Micheal, Gabriel, Raphael, and Leonardo!"

The man's small black eyes peered intently at Simon. "I think one of those is a painter, or a samurai turtle."

"I summoned you and you have to obey me," Simon said, but didn't sound very sure of himself. "Now, return whence you came and bring us back Beth-Ann."

"No!" Mark said. "Beth-Ann first!"

"Look," the man in the black suit said in a reasonable tone which was somehow infinitely annoying. "Do you even know how summonings work? The basic rules I mean? You're the ones in charge of the entire procedure. You summoned me. You're the potter and I'm the clay. Now, if you want me to return to 'whence' I came, you're going to have to send me there yourself." He smiled an infuriatingly reasonable smile.

Simon nodded for a moment before replying. "And, how do I do that?"

The man in the black suit let out a loud sigh and shook his head in exasperation.

Mark jumped to his feet. He waggled a recriminating finger at Simon. "This is all your fault. You're the one who thought it would be a good idea to meddle with forces beyond our control. Forces! Beyond! No control! Look where it's got us! Herb? Hey Herb! Herb, where are you going?"

Herb put on his jean jacket, grabbed his army-surplus backpack, and stumbled up the stairs. (The backpack contained a hash pipe, several varietals of premium sativa and hashish, a change of clothes in case he decided to stay overnight, the pocket edition of *History of Film,* a dozen individually wrapped granola bars, his water bottle, and a toothbrush -- everything he needed to save the world.)

He said over his shoulder, "Going for help. Hang out, back soon." He did a little two-step at the top of the stairs, and with that he vanished.

Both Simon and Mark's conscious minds came up with the same rationalization to explain why Herb was there one instant and gone the next.

Each assumed they had blinked at the very instant Herb rounded the corner, thus their optic nerves didn't actually observe Herb leave their field of vision. And of course, if the optic nerves didn't see it, they couldn't relay the information on to the conscious minds. Satisfied this explanation fit well within their perception of reality, their conscious minds went back to dealing with the other matters at hand.

Simon and Mark's subconscious minds knew this assumption was wrong. Simon and Mark hadn't blinked. Herb had winked out of reality, and the fact their high-and-mighty conscious minds refused to acknowledge factual information provided by their own optical nerves was proof of incompetence in upper management. Soon they would be believing such lunacy as trickle-down economics and the value of juice cleanses.

Both Simon's and Mark's subconsciouses sunk back into the dark underbrush of their respective psyches and brooded, waiting for a time to pounce.

"Never mind Herb," Mark said. "What're we going to do with him?" He stabbed his finger at man in the black suit.

"If I might proffer a suggestion," the man in the black suit said, holding out his hand to Simon. It was a thin hand that looked quick to grasp. "Allow me to examine your tome of summoning."

Simon clutched the *Pax Arcana* to his chest, fearful of giving away the one weapon he knew worked. The man in the black suit sighed. He spoke slowly, gently.

"Simon, is it? Well Simon, believe me when I say I want to go back to 'whence' I came as much as you want me to. I want to get out of this basement and back to my life. And I just might be able to help you get me there by taking a look at your book. Now, please."

There was a long pause. No one moved for several, confusing seconds. A number of mixed emotions crossed Simon's face, starting with suspicion, then shifting into mistrust, moving rapidly onto frustration, anger, self-loathing, sadness, depression, and finally, indecision.

The man in the black suit sighed and shrugged his shoulders. "What do you have to lose?" he asked. "It's not as if it's doing you any good right now? You're sitting here in your basement, staring at me, with no back up plan, while your intoxicated friend has gone off to find more dried cannabis, and that fellow's mom is on her way home, and his little sister -- whom you substituted for me, I may remind you -- is missing. I say again, what do you have to lose?"

Mark said to Simon, "He's right. We can't fix this by ourselves. Give him the book."

Simon sagged a little, then tossed the *Pax Arcana* over to the man in the black suit who plucked it out of midair and began rifling its pages. His speed and intensity were frightening. His eyes darted over the words, consuming their meaning in nanoseconds.

Mark shook his inhaler and then took a deep breath. The action caused him to cough violently several times. Simon fidgeted. Both waited anxiously for the man in the black suit to say something.

"Anything?" Simon prodded.

"Enough," the man in the black suit said. "I'm trying to read."

"Okay then."

Minutes went by. Mark paced back and forth by the Laz-Y-Boy. Simon watched the man in the black suit intently, taking note of every page and paragraph he lingered on. A slick, oily film covered the boy's foreheads as their adrenal glands pumped a torrent of hormones into their blood streams.

Just as the glands ran dry and were about to send for takeaway, the man in the black suit closed the book and looked up at Mark and Simon.

"It can be done," he said after a pause you could drive a truck through. "But it will take time to set up."

At that moment, from upstairs, came the sound of a door opening and closing.

"Hello sweeties! I'm home!"

Mark's mother was home.

## CHAPTER NINE

-- LEASUIREX SHADY LANE RETIREMENT HOME, SCARBOROUGH, ONTARIO. NOW --

"Parlour assassin!" Lady Montique shouted.
"A what?" Lovenight asked.
"A pan-universal being made up of non-dense matter," Lady Montique explained. "Its individual quanta contain less mass than Planck-weight. Consequently, its corresponding cells in millions of universes must coalesce in order for it to feed."
"So, this thing is one individual existing in different universes?"
"Correct."
"And those gauche scales covering the walls, the ceiling, the floor..."
"That's its outer membrane; its skin, if you will."
"And we're..."
"Inside it."
"Hang on! This pan-universal bunch of hippy vomit choose to coalesce...*as your room?*"
"Donkey! Not a room, a parlour! A parlour assassin! That's

what it *is* and what it does. It solidifies around its intended target, traps them, then slowly digests them. Those scales are at present extruding gastric acids and digestive enzymes. Soon, everything in here will be dissolved, including us, unless we can find a way out..."

Lovenight dashed over to where the door was, or rather where it had been moments ago. He was about to grab the scale-covered lump he presumed was the door handle, but thought better of it. Instead, he held his hand an inch away from the scales. Heat radiated off them.

"The bloody thing eats through steel! Bugger!"

"Begging your pardon, sir. You're--"

"Not now, Reg! I'm trying to figure a way out of this!"

"Fairly important detail you're missing, sir."

"Not now!"

"Right you are."

Lovenight swirled, looking for a way out. The dresser, the ceiling light, every stick of furniture and piece of decor slowly blackened and bubbled where the scales touched them. Reg jumped up on Lady Montique's mechanical bed and gestured for Lovenight to do the same.

"Sir, if you'll just look down, you'll see you're being eaten."

Lovenight glanced down. The heels of his boots had dissolved.

"Zulch!" Lovenight cussed. "Bastard's trifling with my wardrobe!" He dove onto the bed, scrambled up the covers, quickly took off his destroyed boots, then tossed them to the floor. Scaly rainbows oozed over them until they were nothing more than misshapen lumps.

"Bastard turned my boots into unicorn poop."

"I did warn you, sir."

"Shut up, Reg!" Lovenight screeched. "No one likes an I-told-you-so."

"Fair enough. What's the plan, ma'am?"

"Escape from a locked room, I should think." Lady Montique fiddled with the remote control for her mechanical bed. She pressed several buttons, sending servos whirring. The footboard elevated drastically. "Blasted thing," she mumbled. "Which one was it now? Eddie, Reginald, look for the blowhole."

"The what?" cried Lovenight.

"It's how it breathes. Look for a dark hole, a kind of curvaceous tunnel leading to the interior of the beast."

"Perfect," Lovenight remarked drily. "I'm looking for a pan-universal orifice."

"Donkey!"

"Found it, ma'am," Reg said. "Directly beneath the headboard."

"Well done, Reginald. At least someone else is pulling his weight around here."

"But it won't do us any good, ma'am. It's only about the size of crabapple."

"Never you mind. Now, if I could just get this blasted contraption to work. Eddie, make yourself useful, won't you?"

Lovenight gripped the duvet, ready to fling it if the digestive scales came closer. What good a duvet might do against a being that existed across unfathomable dimensions he wasn't sure, but at least it was something. "Hurry!"

"Quiet, Donkey! And try not to breathe for the next minute or so. You as well, Reginald."

"Don't breathe as it is, ma'am."

"Quiet!"

They watched as Lady Montique stabbed and cursed at the buttons, frequently bringing the remote closer to her glasses, then farther away, then deciding the first position was preferable, then scowling when it wasn't. "Why do they print labels so small no one can see?" she mumbled rhetorically. After a particularly intricate series of curses and finger stabbings, a look of relief came over her face. Triumphantly, she held the remote high and flicked a small toggle.

The nightlight on her dresser came on.

"Confounded contraption!" she hissed.

"That's technology for you," Reg mused.

Lovenight quivered for a moment, apoplectic with outrage. "Am I the only sane one left in this world? We're dying and my fate is in the hands of an antediluvian spinster who can't figure out the remote! Press everything!"

"Donkey! Stop moving. Here we go!"

She pressed another button.

The bed, along with its occupants, vanished.

In its place a cloud of monarch butterflies fluttered. The swarm dipped and swooped, creating a roiling cloud of movement -- a blizzard of butterflies, obscuring everything within the room. Then, after a moment of chaotic swarming, the butterflies winked out of existence.

The parlour assassin brooded, as much as a pan-universal being with a bi-cellular brain could. Which was not a lot. In order for it to brood both brain cells had to be in a funk, and the only way that could happen was if things didn't go anywhere close to normal.

Things hadn't gone anywhere close to normal.

Normally, things it was sent to kill didn't turn into a swarm of monarch butterflies. Normally, things it was sent to kill flailed about a bit, cried, shook their fists, complained some, tried to bargain with it, then finally laid down and were absorbed by the friendly, scintillating colours rippling over its surface. That's how things went, normally. When that happened both brain cells were pleased and released pan-universal endorphins as a reward.

There would be no pan-universal endorphins today.

The parlour assassin considered the remains inside it. It had ingested dozens of pictures and frames, medicines, lotions, a dresser and nightstand, and oddly enough, a pair of Beatle boots. Nowhere near enough mass to justifiably claim it had ingested its target.

The brooding ceased as the two braincells came to a unanimous decision. The assassin would hang around for a bit, just to make sure the butterflies didn't come back.

"Quickly now! While it is distracted!" said the alpha

cockroach as it skittered across the scintillating floor. "This way, away from the horrible light!"

"The light! The horrible light!" the other two cockroaches echoed in unison, following along largely due to the social herd directives imprinted in their DNA. Above them a swarm of illusionary monarch butterflies fluttered, happy in their momentary existence.

One of the cockroaches, a male with very hairy antennae -- the texture of which strangely resembled black velvet -- felt he was being trifled with. Due to his contrarian mindset, he briefly flirted with the idea of going in the opposite direction. However, millions of years of evolution overrode his consciousness and he crawled after the alpha cockroach toward the only speck of darkness in the entire room.

Cockroaches hate light.

They can identify darkness, no matter how tiny, in the brightest of environments. This darkness was indeed tiny, a mere burnt-out pixel in the sea of colours surrounding it. As a few million butterflies popped like soap bubbles above them, the cockroaches reached the anus-shaped cavity.

"Into the blowhole!" the alpha cockroach yelled by forcefully expelling air out of several orifices on her abdomen.

The contrary cockroach wanted to yell *Now wait just a bloody minute! I'm not sticking my thorax in that disgusting opening!,* but instead he yelled enthusiastically, "Into the blowhole!"

With that the trio of cockroaches slipped into the smooth darkness. Their antennae waved about, scenting the way forward. A slightly cooler, fresher air blew past them. They moved deeper into the twisting airway. The darkness intensified; it comforted them, made them feel safe. The airway bent sharply, forcing them to climb up a chimney-like structure and through a tight bottleneck. The surface was smooth and fleshy, an easy climb for the insects.

"Darkness, blessed darkness!" they chorused. "Blessed darkness in the blowhole!"

The blowhole widened into a cavern, then narrowed into a tight sphincter which the insects scrambled up and out of. They stood on tile, cold and dusty. Narrow walls enclosed them. The insects felt safe. Despite this, the alpha pushed forward, dragging the meagre swarm behind her. Under normal circumstances the insects would have darted back to the safety of the shadows, but the alpha cockroach pulled something from its thorax and commanded, "Don't move!"

The contrary cockroach padded its feelers over the item: a piece of plastic with several soft pads which yielded when depressed. A name formed in the contrary cockroach's mind, a fearful name, a dreadful name.

"Remote!" it hissed through its specially adapted breathing orifice.

"Donkey," the alpha replied.

In an instant the entire world changed. The cockroaches' shells cracked, became liquid, as did their heads and thoraxes and abdomens. They grew, gathering mass, reconstituting themselves into humans while patterns of energy swirled about them.

In nanoseconds they were human again.

They stood in a supply closet next door to Lady Montique's room. Lovenight stared at his hands. Seconds before those very same appendages had been scent organs. He distinctly remembered smelling the floor with his fingertips.

"Ewwwwww!" he cried.

# CHAPTER TEN

## -- DESERT HIGHWAY, MEXICO. BEFORE --

Deep in the Mexican state of Michoacán, a man swung in a hammock next to a roadside coconut stand.

This was unusual for several reasons.

The first was its location. The coconut stand stood on a desolate stretch of highway somewhere west of Playa Azul along the Sierra Madre del Sur, a region known for its ongoing cartel wars. Often, criminals would wash up on the rocky shoreline, or at least bits of them would. The region was so infamous for its violence the Mexican Army refused to enter it.

Not exactly prime real estate for a coconut stand.

The second reason the man swinging in the hammock was unusual was the man himself. He appeared to be somewhere between thirty and sixty years of age, or perhaps older, or maybe younger. It was hard to tell with this man. Lean, of average height, he wore Hawaiian shirt covered in luminescent tiki idols. His shorts could best be described as desert island chic. His most striking feature was his grey hair which frizzed outwards, surrounding his head in a fluffy halo. The hair seemed to have a mind of its own. It would sway back and forth in unseen breezes even if no breezes were around, unseen or otherwise.

The third reason was the man's disposition. He appeared

completely at ease, swinging peacefully, not a care in the world. Considering his present location, this was akin to taking a nap in the middle of an alligator pit at feeding time.

Upon seeing him, Baroness Zamora smiled a smile that couldn't have been more toothy.

She pulled the pink humvee over to the side of the road next to the coconut stand. Humidity enveloped her as she exited the air-conditioned vehicle. She adjusted her sunglass, gold bangles dangling on her wrist. The air smelled tropical sweet.

The coconut seller got up, pushing his misbehaving hair away from his eyes. He shuffled behind the cart piled high with young green coconuts, trying to keep it between himself and the baroness. A wicked looking machete hung by a leather thong just off the side of the cart.

"*Dos cocos, por favor,*" Baroness Zamora said, pulling out a wad of cash secured with blue elastics.

The man's eyebrows shot up, completely disappearing under his mop of hair. He backed away, holding up his hands as if she brandished a katana in one hand and an elephant gun in the other.

"Away with ya!" he said in a heavy Glaswegian accent.

"*Dos cocos, por favor,*" Baroness Zamora repeated. "With straws. The two on the top will do nicely. There's a good fellow."

"Ya think I'm daft?"

"I'm in a bit of a hurry."

"Fine and well. Serve yourself, and off you go." He backed away until he was twenty feet from the cart, allowing her unfettered access. "Leave the money. Or don't leave the money. Just take the damn coconuts and be gone. I don't care, I really don't! Just don't kill me."

Baroness Zamora picked up the machete and a coconut. She held the coconut from the stem side and began slicing layers off the top, hitting it at a shallow angle, the blade easily cutting the husk.

"Not very good customer service at this stand," she noted.

"Ya think?" the coconut seller said, careful to keep a tree now between himself and Baroness Zamora.

"You're in danger of losing your tip."

"Which tip are we talking about, lass? I only ask because I'm rather fond of some of the wee tips you might be referring to."

Baroness Zamora laughed. The machete sunk into the coconut with a wooden thunk, exposing the water inside. Not a drop spilled.

"Come here, please," she said. "Hold this while I cut another."

The coconut seller didn't move, just stood gripping the tree trunk and shaking his head so violently his hair expanded out like a puffball. Baroness Zamora tapped her foot resolutely, the sole of her espadrille boots clicking sharply against the gravel. Obediently, the coconut seller slunk forward like an abashed child. He took the coconut and held it while Baroness Zamora grabbed another and repeated the machete-cutting process.

"What's your name?"

"Ned."

"You're from Glasgow."

"Aye."

"You're a long way from Glasgow."

"Look, are if you're going to chib me, do it. Get it over."

"What makes you think I'd want to kill you?"

"You're driving around on one of the most dangerous highways on the planet in that pink monstrosity, flashing cash like some stupid toff, which you're obviously not, which means it's a ruse, which means you're a trap."

"What're you doing here, Ned?"

"Oh, ya know, finding myself like some hipster-wanker?"

"Don't lie to me, Ned."

"It's a joke. I joke when I'm nervous. Which is pretty much non-stop right now."

"If you say. What're you doing here, Ned?"

"Body snatching."

"Frank and honest. I like that. Business must be good with the cartels fighting each other."

"Been slow lately. It'll pick up closer to Christmas."

"So why the coconuts?"

"Look, I'm just doing a job, right? I've got a quota to meet."

"A dead body quota?"

Ned nodded. "I wait 'til a pure wido rolls up, pulls out a gun or a knife, and then I know they're a right bastard. I'm discriminating, ya see? Got standards who I chib."

"You've seen the cash I'm carrying, the humvee open and running. On the backseat there's a suitcase stuffed with bank notes -- several different currencies of course -- and the digital codes for a dozen Swiss bank accounts. Let's make a little wager. We'll pretend I've pulled a knife on you, that I'm 'a right bastard'. You try and kill me. If you succeed, you take it all and go back to Scotland, or wherever you like. If you don't succeed, I get...oh, let's see...a straw for my coconut water. Deal?"

Ned shook his head.

"Why not?"

"Because you scare my intestines clean."

"Flattery will get you everywhere." Baroness Zamora finished opening the second coconut, flourishing the machete in triumph. "Now, about those straws?"

Ned pulled out straws from under the cart, coming uncomfortably close to the baroness. The baroness offered him one of the coconuts.

"That's for me?" Ned asked.

"*Para ti.*"

"What's that now?"

"Yes."

"Thanks to ya."

They both sipped from their respective coconuts.

"O, to go back to selling ganj from a chip van," Ned said wistfully. "Those were the days: my costumers were happy, I was happy, there was less danger of having my innards emptied out in front of me by some insanely dangerous woman."

"Ned from Glasgow, how would you like to be my back up?"

"Euh?"

"Of course, you would. You're hired. Now, where is your boss?"

Ned's frizzy hair deflated somewhat, falling in front of his face so he looked like an aging hippy who had just sprinted a quarter mile away from the cops. "She'll kill me for this, you know that."

"I doubt it. She'll want to see me. You see, I'm *her* boss."

# CHAPTER ELEVEN

-- CHATTAHOOCHEE HILLS, FULTON COUNTY, GEORGIA. SOON --

The blind electrician grabbed the worn-out spacer with his bare hands.
"Earl, don't!"
Electrical spacers do just as their name implies; they created space, they kept things apart that need to be kept apart. In the case of this old spacer, the things it kept apart were high-voltage cables powering 20,000 households in a subdivision of Atlanta, Georgia.
"The wand, Earl! Use the wand!"
The blind electrician was not wearing a hot suit, or holding a conductor wand, nor did he employ any of the special protections normally used when dealing with titanic amounts of electricity. He simply grabbed the spacer with his hands.
His. Bare. Hands.
"Earl, what *are* you doing?"
This was against the advice of every professional in the power generation industry, and most especially against the shouted

warnings of his new supervisor, Preston, on the ground below.

"Please!" Preston screamed to no avail.

Anyone else grabbing the spacer in the same manner would have been electrocuted instantly.

The blind electrician chuckled, enjoying the young supervisor's angst. Preston was fresh out of some university, with some fancy electrical engineering degree. He had been on the job less than a week. This was the first time he'd seen Earl work.

The other members of the line crew stood around the arial lift truck, smoking and laughing to themselves as the supervisor pleaded with the blind electrician. They'd worked with Earl for a long time. They'd seen it all before.

"There's enough voltage coming out of that sub-station to vaporize you! Put on the gloves at least! Earl, are you listening to me? Earl!"

Earl's smile broadened. "This'll get his coveralls in an wad," he said to Herb.

Herb, in his disincorporated form, hovered in the air next to Earl, his figure hazy like heat steaming off a summer highway. Being beyond the perception horizon of the corporeal universe rendered Herb invisible to the people below.

Earl reached down and picked up a hacksaw. He began cutting the wire clamps holding the spacer in place.

Preston shrieked.

Earl giggled like a little kid. Herb joined him.

In an open field next to the power lines, the choir from a nearby Episcopalian church launched into a rousing rendition of "I Shall Be Released". They had followed the blind electrician for years, believing his ability to work in highly dangerous electrical environments without the benefit of safety equipment was a gift from God. They swayed and raised their hands toward the wires, their white and gold choir robes shining in the sunlight. Earl, the blind electrician, waved in the general direction of the choir.

"That's cool," Herb said, indicating the choir. "You've got backup singers."

"Gotta have a little fun or life ain't worth living."

"Great view, too." Herb surveyed the suburban landscape. "You can see three different golf courses from up here."

"Wouldn't know," the blind electrician said.

"Trippy, all that electricity flowing through those wires," Herb remarked.

Earl nodded. "It don't care if you're good or careful; slip up once and it'll crisp you like a baked ham on Thanksgiving."

"I like cranberry sauce," Herb said, looking down. The ground was at least a hundred feet below.

"Me too." Earl finished hack-sawing through the clamps. He pulled the old spacer free from the line. The voltage potential should have jumped to the wedding ring around his finger, travelling in a flashing arc up his arm. But it didn't. Instead, the arc twisted and forked over his bare skin. The voltage flowed around him, over him, but never through him.

"Wow, man!" Herb exclaimed. "Dude, you got serious cojones. Electricity scares the crap out of me."

"You just gotta understand it, is all." Earl answered. "You notice it, it notices you, you nod hello, it sizzles, you keep going, and it keeps going."

"Earl!" Preston yelled. "Who the hell are you talking to up there?"

"Don't mind him," Earl said, unpacking a new spacer. "Preston's young and eager. That'll make you stupid every time."

Herb crossed his legs and hung in the air. He frowned quizzically. "Strange stuff is happening, Earl. I need help."

Earl snorted. "Strange stuff is always happening. What's going down?"

Herb described the tarot card summoning in Mark's basement in detail, making sure to highlight his feet leaving the floor at the same instant Beth-Ann broke the chalk line. Earl listened intently, tightening the clamps on the new spacer with a pneumatic wrench. He sucked his teeth when Herb finished.

"That's some slippage." Earl said. A note of worry entered his voice.

"Didn't have enough perspective to put it back."

"This 'guy' who slipped through, what's he like?"

"Oldish, I guess. Looks like a bird. Bald on top. Small eyes."

"Human?" Earl asked.

"Don't know. When I looked at him he seemed to lose all his

hard edges. Kinda hard to tell what the guy is if light bends off him in weird ways."

"You talk with Noodles yet? He might be able to get around that. That nose of his, man. Better than mine."

"Well, he is a dog. He's got that going for him."

"I'll do a scan of the whole electro-paradisiacal spectrum, all wavefronts and frequencies, see if there is any residual to track...soon as I get my lunch break. Where did you say this summoning took place?"

"Michigan."

"Michigan is a big place, boy. Can you be more specific?"

Herb thought for a moment. "I'll have to get back to you on that. Geography can get fluid on me sometimes, you know?"

"Yeah, I get it."

Earl finished installing the spacer and signalled for the ground crew to lower the bucket. The nearby Episcopalian choir broke into the "Hallelujah Chorus", holding hands and swaying in time with the music. The bucket slowly came away from the power lines, the tiny lighting arcs wound down as the voltage potential diminished.

"Take it easy, Earl," Herb said.

"Only way I do take it," said the blind electrician, smiling broadly.

Being blind, Earl did not see Herb smooth away into nothing, but he could feel the sudden absence of his fellow perceptor.

He shook his head. "Boy smokes too much weed."

## CHAPTER TWELVE

*-- MICHOACÁN DESSERT, MEXICO. THEN, BUT A LITTLE LATER THAN THE LAST THEN --*

"How is it you're the doc's boss and ya never been here before?"

Baroness Zamora regarded Ned as if he'd just asked the most obvious question in the world, so obvious the question itself was its own answer. "It's because I'm her boss that I've never been here. She does her job well, so I don't have to be here. Understand?"

Ned nodded and said, "Completely baffled, to be honest. This way."

Baroness Zamora followed Ned, sipping from her coconut.

They hiked up the hillside away from the coconut stand, dense scrub and sunbaked rocks bordering the trail on either side. The scotsman sweat in the heat of the Mexican noon, frequently wiping his brow. He shot a look over his shoulder at Baroness Zamora who seemed unaffected by the heat.

"How ya do that, then?"

"Do what?"

"Not sweat. At all. And your hair is perfect. The heat don't touch ya?"

"Heat, cold, pain -- all of these sensations are just information relayed to the brain. Treat them like information and ignore what doesn't benefit you."

"Oh, aye. Brilliant. Ignore what doesn't benefit me...like global warming...or taxes...or the fact I've a wee lass strong-arming me up this here shite of a mountain." Ned shook his head causing his hair to frizz outwards aggressively. He mumbled to himself, "Ignore you and I'll be dead inside of a Glasgow minute."

"Problem?"

"Naw. Everything's peachy as shite."

They stopped where the path curved around a granite outcropping. Ned placed his fingers against a knob of rock. The rock fractured. A jagged section folded outwards with a hissing sigh, revealing a smooth stairway leading downwards. Quartz-like crystals bathed the stairs in cool light.

"After you," Baroness Zamora said, tossing away her coconut.

"Right. Balls."

They descended several hundred feet into the hillside. At the bottom of the stairway a corridor curved off to the left and right, its walls lined with plates of stainless steel, the floor tiled and spotless. The air was much cooler and drier.

"Impressive," the baroness remarked.

"The architect who did this is the same wanker who designs sets for James Bond films," Ned said. "One of those minimalist wankers, in love with 19th century Japanese prints and Bauhaus knockoffs. Bloody toff."

"Ned, you surprise me. A bit of an art aficionado, are you?"

"I'd a life once."

They walked along the curving corridor. Several ancillary passages branched off, each twisting away with wild abandon, the steel-plated ceilings holding back tonnes of earth and rock. Some corridors bore signs with directions to strange sounding departments within the secret lair, like 'Quantum Robotics', 'Nanotech Intelligence and Surveillance', and 'Psionic Defences'. Walking past one marked 'Self-Torture and Interrogation', the baroness heard several matronly voices discussing the virtues of pliers. She decided not to ask.

Ned led them down another flight of stairs to a hermetically sealed door. To one side stood a set of lockers, a small bench placed before them.

"Suit up," Ned said, opening a locker and taking out a white disposable hazmat coverall, complete with boots and gloves. "Take off anything metal."

"Why?"

"Because we don't want it flying about our heads, do we? You don't have any metal implants, by any chance?"

"None."

"No piercings? Tattoos with metallic ink?"

"Banish the thought."

"Ever worked with metal?"

"Not that I recall."

It took several minutes to put on the hazmat gear. Baroness Zamora grimaced as she slipped her feet into chemical-spill boots, but otherwise showed no emotion.

"Ya alright?" Ned asked.

"Quite," Baroness Zamora said.

"Let's get this over."

Ned punched a code into a keypad. Hydraulics rolled the door aside. They entered the airlock and the door rolled back, sealing them in. They waited as the air was filtered, then the interior hatch rolled open.

Beyond was the most comprehensive genetics lab in the world: a rabbit warren of cryogenic chambers, operating theatres, refrigeration units, a self-contained medical waste incinerator, banks of autoclaves, cryostat closets, all separated by steel-and-glass bulkheads giving a panoramic view of the entire facility. Fan-shaped titanium plates covered the exterior walls and ceiling, curving and swooping for no good reason other than pure aesthetics. The damn thing was beautiful, Hollywood beautiful.

"Impressive," Baroness Zamora said.

"Yeah, I'd vacation here if it were up to me." Ned waited for the sarcasm to land. It didn't. Ned sighed.

Table-bots wheeled past, their laser-guidance systems illuminating the floor with ruby spiderwebs. One carried a tray loaded with pill bottles, a jug of orange juice, and buffalo chicken wings. Ned fell in behind it. "Come on, then."

They followed the table-bot past several glass chambers where robots sorted and drilled and spun and generally made the loud whirring noises that robots like to make. Baroness Zamora paid them not the slightest bit of attention. Anything that wasn't relative to her immediate purpose was a distraction.

The table-bot came to an abrupt halt in front of a set of double doors. This chamber was different. It was completely sealed off by titanium plating. Several other robots stood about, humming and shaking. The table-bot trembled, rattling the vitamin bottles on its stainless-steel top.

"It's shivering," Baroness Zamora said.

"It's the magnets. Soulless bastards can no' go any further, so they wait here for her." Ned picked up the tray and opened the doors.

Inside, a fully functioning MRI spun and jackhammered around a corpse, the tag still dangling from the lifeless toe, the rings of superconducting magnets humming away contentedly like ferric kittens. Opposite it lay a control booth with banks of screens enclosed by titanium shielding.

A woman dressed in a hazmat coverall studied the monitors. She appeared of Middle Eastern descent with smooth caramel skin and piercing green eyes behind thick glasses. Her movements were small, economical, surgical. Her short stature and smooth skin made her appear much younger than she was.

"All right, doc, where do you want me to put your nosh?"

Without looking up the doctor said in a soft, almost shy voice, "Just over on the prep table will be fine, Ned."

"Right, there's your wings." He hitched a thumb toward the baroness. "This rich nutter says she's your boss."

Baroness Zamora cleared her throat. "Good day, Dr. Noor."

The doctor looked up and blinked rapidly. "Baroness. I did not know you were coming. Care for some wings and orange juice?"

"An odd pairing, don't you think?"

"Not at all," Dr. Noor said. "Sharp taste sensations stimulate the brain. Picks you up after a morning analyzing data."

"I'm sure it does."

Ned backed toward the door. "Well, I'll just leave, shall I? Corpses don't fall into secret labs by themselves, right."

"Stay, Ned," Dr. Noor said.

"I'd rather not. Nothing personal, but you two nut-jobs scare the shite out of me."

The baroness turned and said simply, "I, your boss, insist."

Ned's shoulders sagged. "My life," he said to himself. "One moment it's swinging in a hammock, next it's finger foods with vivisectionists and manics."

Dr. Noor tucked into her chicken wings, pulling the skin off the bone with her teeth. She chewed vigorously, then wiped sauce from the corners of her mouth. "Now baroness, I must ask why have you come to me?"

"This Scottish coconut seller, what level of clearance does he qualify for?" Baroness Zamora asked.

"Absolute disclosure. No need to worry. He's been secretly augmented."

Ned's eyebrows shot up. "Eh? Who did what to Ned now?"

"Where did you find him?" Baroness Zamora asked.

"On a road outside Inverness, by a truck full of chickens which exploded," Dr. Noor said. "The truck exploded, not the chickens. But the chickens were in the truck at the time."

Baroness Zamora turned to Ned, the questioning look on her face gentle but resolute.

Ned shrugged and explained, "Right. I was driving the truck for some shite I met down the pub. This shite wanted me to drive to the army base at Fort George, supposed to deliver chickens to the soldiers stationed there. Unbeknownst to me, this shite planted a bomb on the truck. He was nouveau Marxist dobber or Alt Eejit or *Biba Dushi* some such shite. Thought he was sticking it to the army. Anyway, we was driving and this shite had the trigger in his back pocket. I hit a bump in the road, the shite lands on the button, and next thing I know I'm laying in gravel on the side of the road, my clothes smoking, the truck on fire."

"The 'shite' was a test subject of mine," Dr. Noor interrupted.

"Remotely controlled, by me of course, using implants and brainwashing -- an early field of study, since abandoned for our genetic mutations. I was following the truck at a distance. After it exploded, I came across Ned. He was covered in chicken feathers. The quills had lodged in his skin, due to the force of the blast."

"I was bleeding all over!"

"You were throttling the test subject with your feathered hands."

"Shite was gibbering on about not being in the arms of God or some such shite. I just helped him along."

Baroness Zamora smoothed back her hair curtly, a sign she was becoming bored. "Dr. Noor, I need something from you."

Dr. Noor put down her food. "You have my complete attention, baroness."

"I wish you to shorten the timeline. Move up the shipping dates to next week."

Dr. Noor did not wrinkle a brow nor flutter an eyelash. She knew the baroness was capable of anything, with near unlimited resources and a will steelier than Pittsburgh. It had been Baroness Zamora, after all, who had built the ultra-secret genetics lab in one of the most desolate and dangerous environments on the planet. The baroness could literally move mountains, if she wished. Altering human genetics on a global scale was a logistical impossibility to anyone else, but for the baroness it was a Q4 target.

"The next phase of the 'Beyond Truth' directive?" Dr. Noor stared levelly at the baroness, and asked, "What part of human D.N.A. do you wish to change?"

"Obedience. I wish to hardwire unquestioning obedience into the human race."

## CHAPTER THIRTEEN

-- LEASUIREX SHADY LANE RETIREMENT HOME, SCARBOROUGH, ONTARIO. NOW --

"Quickly donkey!"
Lovenight assisted Lady Montique as they dashed across the hallway into the staff change room.
"What the hell was that?" Lovenight demanded.
They stood next to a rack of coats. Lady Montique searched for outerwear to cover her nightclothes, rubbing the fabrics between her fingers, examining the stitching and cut of each garment. She tossed coat after coat onto the ground, making sure to trod on them as she went down the rack.
She sniffed haughtily. "Don't take that tone with me, Eddie. I'll box your ears if you use it again. And be more specific. What the 'hell' was 'what'?"
"You turned us into cockroaches!"
"Don't be silly. I didn't 'turn' you into anything. I merely flash-evolved us into a sentient life form which will rule this

planet in its dying days under a red sun. Cockroaches! Eradicate the thought!"

"A sentient life form descended from cockroaches?" Lovenight asked pointedly.

"Alright, yes, I'll give you that," Lady Montique said. "Ah, at last!"

She pulled a gabardine trench coat off the rack, then went back for the matching cashmere scarf. After fighting to get her twig-like arms into the sleeves without breaking any bones, she then threw the scarf around her neck with a jaunty flourish. A wet, crunching sound emanated from her spine as she did so. Her face stiffened. Her eyes crossed and she appeared to be seeing something very far away that no one else could see.

"Everything alright, ma'am?" Reg asked.

Cords of sinewy tendon bulged on her neck as her eyes watered. There was a further grinding noise and then a crack. Relief washed over her face. She rotated her head gently, first to the right, then to the left.

"There. Does that occasionally, I'm afraid. The vertebra degenerate and cause obstructions. One of the pitfalls of aging. Can't be helped."

"You sure you're all right, ma'am?"

"Tickety-boo, Reg. Thank you for your concern." She reached out a boney fist and whacked Lovenight on his ear. He yelped and grabbed the side of his face.

"Eweoow! Why did you do that?"

"Because you're behaving beastly. Imagine, not even inquiring into my well-being after a trauma."

"With such a gentle disposition, one wonders why? Eweoow!"

"Donkey! Keep quiet! See if the way is clear."

Lovenight eased the door open and peeped out. At the far end of the corridor wheelchairs clustered around a TV, the seniors sitting in them staring at the flickering screen while sipping soup from mugs. Other than the electronic hum coming from the television, the scene was eerily quiet. The support workers went about their jobs in a listless, rote manner. Everyone seemed resigned their 'ends-were-nigh', and there was nothing to be done about it except watch TV and sip soup.

"Well?" Lady Montique asked.

"It's a chamber of horrors out there," Lovenight replied.

"Except for the soup," Lady Montique said flatly. "It's quite lovely."

"Nothing like soup," Reg agreed. "From what I remember."

"Rest of the hallway is clear." Lovenight's nostrils flared. "Let's make a break for it."

They slipped into the hallway and headed toward the elevators.

"Act natural," Lovenight whispered. "We're just two visitors taking our elderly relative for a walk."

"Donkey! Don't call me elderly."

"Well, if the shoe-leather complexion fits -- eeeoww! Stop hitting me!"

As they passed a fish tank Lovenight noticed two of the goldfish stopped swimming to watch him with bulbous eyes. As a matter of principle, he flipped them a rude finger gesture.

"That's creepy."

"What is, sir?" Reg asked.

"Those fish. They're staring at me."

"Oh yes, sir. Never trust fish, sir. I had an uncle, used to keep koi."

Reg fell silent. After several seconds Lovenight felt compelled to ask. "And? Your uncle? The koi?"

"Yes?"

"Never trust fish?"

"Absolutely, sir."

"Reg?"

"Sir?"

"Don't talk to me."

"Shut up both of you! We're not out of this yet. Keep your wits up."

They reached the elevators and Lovenight stabbed at the call button with his index finger. No one seemed to be paying any attention to them.

"I think my luck is holding," Lovenight said.

The elevator doors opened revealing a squad of security guards, each holding a taser wand which glowed hot and ready.

They didn't resemble your average security detail. These men were burly land-sharks with not an ounce of body fat, complete with shaved heads, rippling muscles, and alert eyes. Their movements were quick, balanced, economical. These were killers. Even their nametags seemed overtly aggressive with names like: Butch, Olaf, The Crippler, Ivan, Wankface, Stump-or-Dump, and Derek.

For half a moment Lovenight wondered who would give their child a name like 'Derek', then the guards surged forward. His training took over.

Time accelerated. Lovenight slipstreamed into a secondary time current. Everything around him slowed.

His clothes flashed briefly as they were incinerated by the time-friction differential. The rushing guards became shimmering, slow-motion forms, surrounded by blueish luminescence. Lovenight dashed through them like they were statues, stopping to reverse each taser-wand so the weapons were held by the contacts. As he moved, the luminescent halos alternated between blue and red depending if he was moving towards or away from them. The shifting blue-red light tinted the air, completely infusing the secondary time current. In under a nanosecond, he finished the temporal sabotage.

The job done, Lovenight slipstreamed back into primary time.

Each guard stiffened as the taser wands sent streams of electrons scrambling through their nervous systems. They fell forward, stiff as pins, faces stretched tight with shock and surprise.

Lovenight reappeared in a blinding white flash, completely naked, causing Lady Montique to blink rapidly.

"Bloody hell!" Lovenight exclaimed. "That was a ludicrously expensive suit."

"Stairs might be a better idea, ma'am" Reg suggested, looking at the scattered twitching bodies occupying the lift.

"Sensible as always, Reginald." Lady Montique said, turning to the stairwell. "Let's hurry. They'll be more, I'm sure."

"What about my clothes?" Lovenight said, doing his best to cover himself.

"Your clothes are your own affair, Eddie. You're one of the

only individuals on this Earth who has mastered chromatic manipulation. One would think you'd be resourceful enough to clothe yourself. Go on, find something! Reginald can assist me until you catch up."

"A naked man!" yelled one of the seniors clustered around the TV at the far end of the corridor. "There's a naked man by the elevators!"

All heads turned to stare at Lovenight. The attendants froze in shock, holding trays of pills while the residents openly gawked. Several seniors waved a friendly hello. One hooted boisterously and had to be restrained by a support worker.

"Hurry!" Lady Montique commanded. "And for god's sake, don't draw any more attention to yourself."

Lovenight caught up with Reg and Lady Montique outside the front doors of the retirement home. Upon seeing him, Lady Montique cleared her throat disapprovingly -- the worst censure she could have given short of shooting him in the leg. Reg's cookie-duster moustache bristled.

"Couldn't find something meant for a gent, sir?" Reg asked.

The lady's overcoat Lovenight had stolen looked like it had been last used in the 60s. Whether it was the 1860s or 1960s, he could not say. He pulled self-consciously at the mohair lapels. "I didn't have much to work with," he said defensively. "Can't expect much from the lost-in-found in a retirement home."

Without another word they headed toward Lovenight's rental car.

However, before they had taken two steps, the receptionist with a slightly goat-like appearance stepped out from behind one of the Japanese maples and levelled a semi-automatic rifle straight at their hearts. She released the safety, her index finger on the trigger. Looking directly at Lovenight, she said, "Make sure you check in with reception before removing any resident!"

With that she sprayed them with bullets.

Lovenight reappeared in another flash of light, followed a

nanosecond later by the sound of bullets striking glass, steel, asphalt, concrete, and more steel. Holes riddled the rental car, leaving it a smoking, slumping hulk, the front tires flat as crepes. The air smelled of cordite and lead. The bullets had struck the bricks, the bushes, the sidewalk, everywhere in fact other than Lady Montique and Reg.

The receptionist fell forward, dead.

"Bloody hell!" Lovenight said, covering his privates with both hands as the last of the blue-red luminescence left his skin. The stolen coat had not survived the time-friction differential.

"Eddie, enough of your tomfoolery! To the car!"

"What car?" he cried. "We have no car! The car we had is spewing oil and gasoline!"

"Not your car, Eddie. Mine!"

"Watch your step, ma'am," Reg said as he guided her over the prone body of the receptionist. "Try not to step in the blood."

"But...I'm naked...again!" Lovenight protested.

"Donkey! We can't afford to waste any more time on your fashion deficit! I have an afghan throw in the back of my car you can cover yourself with. Afghan throws are terribly useful, in all sorts of emergencies. Now move!"

Lovenight and Reg followed Lady Montique into the resident's parking. She stopped in front of a vintage automobile.

"What, in holy-hell, is that?" Lovenight asked, not at all trying to mask his incredulity.

"That," Lady Montique replied haughtily. "Is a 1936 Stout Scarab, with leather, wicker, and wood interior. Highly exclusive and very rare."

Bulbous headlights fronted the snub-nosed hood. The sleek side panels and tapering body gave it a vaguely insect-like shape. Grilles seemed to be everywhere, on the lights, across the rear window, over the rear-mounted flathead V8. All the handles and wheels had been recessed into the aluminum body. The interior was more like a vintage aeroplane than an automobile; three chairs (one for the driver), a fold-out table, and a full-sized bench-seat, all under a woven wicker roof.

"It looks as if a giant dung beetle grew tired of the life-insectile and suddenly decided it wanted to be a car."

"Donkey! They are a treasure! You required an invitation simply to purchase one."

"And if someone invited you to ingest cyanide...?"

"Don't be a philistine, Eddie. It's unbecoming. Reginald, if you would?" She held out the keys and Lovenight snatched them quickly.

"Oh no," he said. "If anyone is driving that earthbound Hindenburg, it's me."

"Fine. Reginald, toss Eddie the afghan throw on the seat, would you?"

Lovenight caught the crocheted blanket and wrapped it around himself like a loin cloth before getting in the driver's seat. The wool itched in all the wrong places, which, after a glass of wine and tray full of oysters, Lovenight might have appreciated.

"How do you see out of the back of this automotive monstrosity with all that chrome?" he asked while flicking the ignition switch. "And there's no side mirrors."

"Hindsight is overrated. Look to the future, Eddie! Or at least what is in front of you."

"What's in front of me is..." Lovenight struggled to find a word to encapsulate his disgust at the suburban mess sprawling before him. He settled on, "...Canada."

"Never been to Canada," Reg said from the back seat. "What's it like here?"

Lady Montique tilted her nose up. "It's like a painting by René Magritte -- everything looks normal, yet one is never quite sure exactly what is going on."

The Scarab rumbled off into the night, the eight-cylinder thundering like an unchained biker gang.

"You sure you're all right to drive, sir?" Reg asked. "Two slipstreams in one night, that takes it out of a bloke."

"Nonsense, I'm perfectly able," Lovenight replied narrowly missing a bus stop and a tomcat.

"You don't even know where you're going!" Lady Montique scowled.

"No, but that doesn't mean I'm not going in the right direction," Lovenight retorted.

"Luckily one of us has a modicum of intelligence. Turn right here."

The Scarab banked wide around the corner, passing two raccoons eating out of a trash can. Their eyes shone like silver marbles in the Scarab's headlights.

"Did you see those rodents watching me!" Lovenight exclaimed. "They're trifling with me!"

"Stop talking nonsense. We've vital work to do!"

"What work? It's only the three of us left. I thought we were escaping, or, you know, hiding, or something sensible like that."

"We must find out what the Governance is up to. They've eradicated our network, decimated our operatives, and sent a parlour assassin after me! Before we lost contact with our ether ninjas, they informed me the head of the Governance was implementing a new initiative. After the next intersection, keep left."

"Look, I realize this is above my security clearance, but since it's only you, me, and bone-boy, don't you think I should know who the head of the Governance is?"

Lady Montique's expression could have soured milk. "I suppose you have a point. Her name is Baroness Zamora."

"And who is she when she's at home?"

"The only person living who is telekinetic *and* can hyper-evolve, not to mention her limited slipway capabilities. She has extensive psionic defences, unlimited wealth, is an expert marksman, holds a dozen PhDs, is well versed in Krav Maga, and has the ability to create incorporeal appendages -- her 'trans-kinetic hands' as she calls them. Her whereabouts at any time are a well-guarded secret."

"Okay, so not a cock-up. How did you get so much information on her?"

Lady Montique went very still. "I too, Eddie, have my dark secrets."

"Fair enough. So how do we find her?"

"We must consult one of the Paragons of Reality."

There was a long pause. Lovenight looked at Reg who shrugged his bony shoulders. He looked back at Lady Montique. His eyebrows shot up questioningly. His hands fanned the air, trying to draw in some context. When she offered none, he eventually asked, "Paragons of Reality?"

Lady Montique glared at him. "Don't you ever do the required reading which goes with your job?"

"I studiously avoid it."

"That will get you killed one of these days, Eddie. The Paragons of Reality are the foundations of the universe."

"I thought it was based on necro-quantum mechanics or general incorporeal-relativity or something."

"Donkey! Do your homework! Necro-quantum mechanics and general incorporeal-relativity are merely models for perception. Perception is anchored to the Paragons. They are the lenses to this reality. They are not however, the reality. Do you understand?"

"No. But keep going. This is bound to get interesting."

"Heisenberg," Reg said suddenly from the back seat.

Lady Montique swivelled towards the dead cabbie. "Werner Heisenberg, Reginald? The renowned German theoretical physicist?"

"Met him while I was driving for Niels Bohr. He said electrons don't exist, only when someone was watching them, or if they were interacting with something else."

"See Eddie? Reginald understands." Lady Montique reached out and smacked Lovenight on his bicep with her sinewy fist.

"Awweew! Don't hit the driver!"

"Heisenberg's uncertainty principle: the very effect of observing reality changes it, Eddie. It's necro-quantum theory: 101. Try not to be such an undergrad for once."

"Pardon my French, but up Heisenberg's stiff bottom!" Reg grumbled. "I would've loved to have taken the boots to that one, bloody *bosche*! He wanted Bohr to work on the bomb for the Nazis. Bohr was having none of it! Quite right, too!"

"Reginald!"

"Begging pardon, ma'am. Some things still stick in the old craw."

"What're you two talking about?"

Lady Montique sighed. "Read a book occasionally, Eddie."

"Can you simplify it for me?"

"I just did."

"Can you simplify the simplification?"

"Fine. Perception is a shorthand for belief. Belief in God, science, nihilism, pop culture, greed, power, corruption -- whatever an individual's belief system is based on, perception provides support for it. It's the code for reality."

In some remote part of his brain an alarm sounded. Lovenight didn't like alarms. Alarms generally meant imminent danger. Alarms meant becoming a cockroach and tasting the floor with your hands, or slipstreaming and losing all your clothes. Alarms were bad. Alarms were to be avoided at all costs.

"Do you understand, Eddie?"

"Not at all," Lovenight said.

"Donkey. Turn here."

The Scarab swerved suddenly, tires screeching as they fishtailed into a parking lot. Lovenight shifted into neutral and turned off the engine.

"We're here," Lady Montique announced.

The unremarkable office building before them could have been located anywhere. It was a pinnacle of un-remarkableness. Four floors of glass and steel set in concrete. It entirely failed to stick out like a sore thumb, and that was the point. It was the architectural equivalent of white bread. Its mantra might have been something along the lines of *nothing to see here, keep moving along, nothing suspicious or sinister at all about this office tower.*

But for Lovenight, an elite chrono-operative and professional rogue, there were several details which screamed *hang on one minute!*

One was the parking lot. It was full of Honda Civics. Nothing but Honda Civics. Row after row of well-crafted yet affordable Japanese compacts, all the same model, all the same year, all the same colour -- a distinctly inoffensive shade aptly named 'Mellow Puce'. Just looking at the sedans made Lovenight sleepy.

Another suspicious detail was the businesses listed on the illuminated sign as tenants of the building: Xavier's Inline Dentures, Xenophobic Driving School, Xenomorph's Duct Cleaning, X-Ray's by Ray, the Xylophone Emporium, Xerxes' Frozen Meats, Xanadu Imports (Honeydew a Specialty!), XXX Ribs and Wings...and one more. The last business snagged Lovenight's eye and would not let go.

"Lots of 'X's there," Reg chuckled. "What're the chances?"

"None, Reginald. The whole building is a front. All the businesses are mere shells."

"Except the last one," Lovenight corrected. "My incredible powers of observation and deduction tell me we're looking for the offices of the 'Paragons of Realty'."

"No one likes a showoff, Eddie."

## CHAPTER FOURTEEN

### -- GRAND RAPIDS, MICHIGAN. NOW --

"Mark! Beth-Ann! I'm home!"

Mark's mom stomped down the basement stairs. Not that she intended to stomp. It was just how she always walked. Mrs. Henrietta Büdenbender, a solidly built woman of Germanic heritage who favoured blouses and putting her hair up in braids, wore a silk scarf tied around her neck which flounced atop her prodigious bosom. Her apple cheeks blushed red. Her tiny eyes beamed. She appeared glad to be home after her shift at the Waffle Shack.

"I brought waffles in case you're...oh."

For a moment she wasn't sure she was in her basement, due to the strange man dressed in a baggy black suit sitting cross-legged inside a purple chalk triangle. But it definitely was her basement. There was her son Mark and his friend Simon. So it must have been her basement. And something was definitely wrong. She'd never seen the boys looking so pasty and white.

"Please," the man in the black suit said. "Join us."

"Sweetie?" She walked slowly towards the card table where Mark and Simon sat. She looked quizzically at the zucchini muffins with the half-burnt birthday candles. She would have to ask them about those later. Right now, both boys looked like they had spent the last hour in a dryer tumbling with their fears.

"Who's this?"

Mark did not answer. Instead, the man in the black suit said, "Who I am is of little importance. What I do, on the other hand, is of exceeding importance. It would not be hyperbole to say of the utmost importance."

Mrs. Büdenbender squinted. "What's going on?"

"Finally a worthwhile question," said the man in the black suit. He tossed the *Pax Arcana* to Simon who instinctively caught it. "Your son and his friend summoned me by means of a merchant's substitution, binding me within this triangle. Bit of a lark for them, I believe. Nonetheless, they succeeded, much to their chagrin." While he spoke, he kept his gaze levelled at Mark who continued to wheeze and periodically suck on his inhaler.

"Why don't you just step out?" Mrs. Büdenbender asked, not quite yet understanding what was going on but willing to play along for the moment just in case the strange man started making sense.

"Would that I could! But since they used an evocation rather than an invocation, they have bound me within this triangle. I could no more leave than you could spontaneously fly about this room."

"All right, then," Mrs. Büdenbender said. She had a lot of practice with people making outrageous claims. She had been a primary school teacher for twenty-two years and had weathered many arguments not at all based in fact. It was the reason she didn't immediately phone the police. She was adept at defusing heated situations, especially where zucchini muffins and chalk were involved.

She placed the Waffle Shack take-out down on the table and clasped her hands together. "How can we help?"

"What I require, and what your son and his friend are going to provide, is release." He fixed a stern eye on them. "They will send me back, now, or I will have your guts for afters."

"Honey," she said turning to Mark and ignoring the very strange threat. "Why don't we help this man? Hmm? He seems upset."

Mark nodded robotically. Simon opened the *Pax Arcana* to the page the man in the black suit had dog-eared. He skimmed over the esoteric symbols, trying to understand the complex set of instructions. His brow furrowed with the effort.

"It's a nullification incantation," the man in the black suit said. "It will eradicate...the summoning."

"Will it bring...?" Mark stopped himself asking the question. He cast a sidelong glance at his mom who failed to see it.

"As I said, it will eradicate all effects of the summoning and release me," the man in the black suit said, winking at Mark.

"All right, let's do this."

Mrs. Büdenbender sat at the card table. Simon shuffled, then laid out the tarot cards according to the diagram in the *Pax Arcana*. The spread was entirely new to Simon, not the traditional Celtic cross he was used to. This spread resembled the letter X wrestling with a fish. Simon scanned the spread, trying to grasp the subtle meanings the cards were trying relay to him.

"It's too complicated," he said. "I can't figure it out."

"You can and you are," the man in the black suit insisted. "It's already started. Can't you feel it?"

Simon did feel it, as did Mark and Mrs. Büdenbender. It was like the squeeze you feel in your ears when you dive too deep. A slow, vast force, pressing in. And with every tarot card Simon turned over, the pressure grew.

A chill twisted around Mrs. Büdenbender's spine.

"What is this?" she asked. "My God, what's happening?"

Images on the cards bled together, all those archetypes and symbols mingling like they were at a cocktail party. The Knave of Wands threw sticks for pale white dogs to fetch, while a hermit consoled several maidens in flowing gowns. A lobster bathed in the light of the moon beside the corpse of a man stabbed with nine swords. Each time Simon tried to make sense out of the spread, the scene would shift, the archetypes forming new synergies and interpretations.

The walls began to moan. The card table shook. The candles

flickered.

"It's unraveling, the binding," the man in the black suit said, his eyes keen and sharp. "It's working."

"I can't hold it," Simon said, his head trembling with effort. "I can't."

"Don't look away!" the man in the black suit shouted. "Soon you'll have Beth-Ann back. Just don't look away!"

Mrs. Büdenbender stiffened, her eyes darting from the man in the black suit to Mark. Mark tried avoid her stare.

"Mark, what is he talking about?" she said very quietly.

In lieu of an answer, Mark sucked on his inhaler.

The lights dimmed. From nowhere a wind blew through the basement, a hot dry scirocco racing toward the triangle-of-conjuration.

"Mark?" Her tone was steely and insistent.

"Yes, yes," said the man in the black suit, oblivious to the concern growing within Mrs. Büdenbender. "The spell is loosening. I can feel the pull back."

Simon's pupils vibrated, trying to take in the shifting panorama before him. It was like seeing the whole of creation, all of man's emotions and hopes and failures and shortcomings laid bare before you, one vast hodgepodge encompassing the entirety of human experience. Way too much for an undergrad.

"Mark! Where is Beth-Ann?"

Mark finally met his mother's eyes and said with a nod to the strange man, "The spell switched him for her."

"It's working!" yelled the man in the black suit. He was fading, became incorporeal, while a glowing nimbus of cyan light grew around him.

Mrs. Büdenbender surged from her chair, her prodigious bosom bouncing with the effort. She yelled, "Where's my Beth-Ann?"

"Mom! No!"

There was no way she could have stopped, even if she wanted to. Mrs. Büdenbender vaulted into the triangle and slammed into the semi-translucent man, his cyan nimbus engulfing her as well. They tumbled out of the triangle in a twisted heap.

Simon looked away from the tarot cards, covering his eyes.

Instantly the cacophony faded, the lights brightened, the wind fell away. For a solitary second, there was silence. Mrs. Büdenbender and black suit man lay in a tangled mess on the floor, her plump torso almost completely obscuring him.

"Mom!"

Mark got up and raced over, stopping a few feet from her. Something was wrong with the way her body lay across the man in the black suit and the way his feet extended. The angles seemed impossible.

"Mom?"

"I'm okay," Mrs. Büdenbender said softly.

"Let me help you."

"Just a moment, dear. I seem to be tangled."

"Get off of me," the man in the black suit said.

Mrs. Büdenbender tried to get up, but lost balance and fell sideways, revealing the man in the black suit protruding from her stomach just below her prodigious bosom. His legs dangled out her back. Their bodies had fused together, forming a human X. Mark gawped, trying to get enough air into his lungs to speak.

"What the hell?"

The man in the black suit looked down, saw what had happened, and sighed. "Damnation. You've conjoined us."

# CHAPTER FIFTEEN

## -- CHICAGO, ILLINOIS. SOON --

"Jesus-suffering-Christ!" Noodles the pug yelped, as he defecated a small yet odiferous pile of scat inside the council chambers for the City of Chicago. "This is the worst news I've gotten since my bloodsucking, whore-of-a-therapist got off with time-served."

Herb's disincorporated body hovered nearby. He was thankful it was after-hours, for he knew if the council had been in session Noodles would have defecated on the mayor's shoulder.

"Definitely," the film student agreed. "It's harshing my buzz."

"Major slippage into the incorporeal, with a residual summoning? What the hell were you dough-heads thinking?"

"Wasn't really thinking. I was dealing with a tricky floor at that point."

"Hey, don't clean that up!" Noodles barked at his assistant, Randolph "Fat Cheeks" Jones.

"But, you've left it under the major's seat," Fat Cheeks protested.

"Leave it, you cud-muncher! That jackass knows what I think of him."

Fat Cheeks backed away from the scat, returning the poop-and-scoop baggy to the satchel he carried. Inside the satchel were all manner of items Noodles might demand on a moment's notice: chew toys, dictionaries, skin lotions, a particularly pungent paté, all manner of items really.

Herb nodded toward the poop. "That's a political statement."

"Damn right it's a statement. Maybe that rancid pig-man of a major will think twice about rezoning off-leash parks." For good measure, Noodles scooted across the carpet, wiggling his bum side to side the whole way. "Herb, if you're going to ask for my help, have the freaking decency to do it in person."

Herb shimmered as he coalesced beside Noodles. He sat down on the chamber floor and crossed his legs. The pug sniffed at his shoes.

"You sure the floor didn't turn into a cabbage?"

"Absolutely sure. Stomped on it."

"You gotta be tough on floors. Sneaky bastards."

"That's what I say."

"Okay. More details. What was this being like?"

Herb described the man in the black suit, the way light slunk off him, the disappearance of Beth-Ann, the *Pax Arcana*, the triangle-of-conjuration, everything. Noodles listened intently, occasionally licking his genitals but mostly listening intently. When Herb finished Noodles sat for a moment, lost in thought. His bulbous eyes took on a far-away look as he cocked his head to the side. Finally he rose up and sniffed the air. Using his olfactory nerves as cosmogonic receptors for both the corporeal and incorporeal, he probed several planes of existence. His eyes jiggled as he inhaled.

"Something stinks," he said finally.

Fat Cheeks smiled and joked, "Your poop?"

Despite his nickname, Fat Cheeks wasn't fat. He was a slender man of thirty-six with a wife and two boys under five. As an aspiring blues guitarist, he looked more like a boy-scout than a bluesman, with his cherubic face and smooth skin. In an effort to makeover his image he adopted the nickname 'Fat Cheeks'. It was meant to sound like 'Redbone' or 'Howling dog', and give him some gravitas as a blues performer. It didn't. Audiences couldn't get past his boy-scout looks. So he had taken a regular job as Noodles' assistant; a job that would have tried the patience of a Buddhist monk at the best of times.

"Shut up! It's not my poop, you fawning milk dud!" Noodles scratched his ear and turned back to Herb. "You talked to Earl?"

Herb nodded again. "Nothing on the electromagnetic. Said I should check with you."

"Damn straight you should talk to me. This is somewhere on the incorporeal-quantum. Any fool can see that."

"Yeah," Herb agreed, then checked himself. "What?"

Noodles ignored the question and chased his tail. Fat Cheeks knew his employer was considering the problem and wished not to be disturbed. He caught Herb's eye and put his finger to his lips. Herb nodded. They waited patiently.

The pug finished and stood for a moment, his tongue lolling out, before saying, "Look, Herb. You're a stand-up guy and all."

"Yeah, I am, when I stand up. I'm sitting now, ain't I?" Herb checked the location of the floor to make sure this was the case.

Noodles yipped, drawing Herb's attention back to the matter at hand. "What I mean is, I don't hate you as much as I hate most people. But this here situation you've brought me, it stinks. I mean it really stinks! There's a vileness to it, a quality to the stank smelling like abomination and horror. I'm taking a hard pass. My advice to you is to stay well clear of this one."

Herb looked lost. He rested his chin on his fist. "Yeah, I understand. It's a total mess. Beth-Ann is missing and it's all my fault. If I just had kept my feet on the ground...none of this would have happened."

"It's not your fault," Noodles said.

Trying to cheer up anyone was a stretch for Noodles. Berating, castigating, excoriating, those were things he excelled at. Someone needed to be railed against? Perfect! Noodles was your dog. But trying to cheer someone up was, well, not exactly in his wheelhouse. He did his best by not urinating on Herb and saying, "You were dealing with a treacherous floor, man! We're talking about a complex interaction between the electromagnetic, incorporeal, and transcendental-quantum. The vectors of the quirks, quarks, fiberons, and flabberons involved, well it just makes my tail twist! If anything, you stopped a total meltdown."

"Wow," Herb said. "Thanks. You sure know a lot for a--"

"A what?" Noodles barked at Herb. "A what? Say it! A 'dog'? Were you going to say 'dog'? Well, that's right ape-boy, I'm a dog and damn proud of it! So you can take your human-centric racism, complete with your primate privilege and your homo sapiens entitlement and shove it up your hairy sphincter!"

Herb looked around, puzzled as to what was suddenly happening. "I was going to say you sure know a lot for someone who didn't go to university."

Noodles cocked his head to one side, his pug eyes jiggling. In that instant he realized Herb didn't see him as a dog. He never had. Herb only saw him as a person.

"All right," Noodles said. "Damn you."

"All right, what?"

"All right, I'll help. Let's go find this Beth-Ann."

# CHAPTER SIXTEEN

-- GRAND RAPIDS, MICHIGAN. NOW --

"Stop screaming!" the man in the black suit shouted in exasperation. "It's not helping at all."

Mark paused his screams long enough to take a breath. He'd been screaming pretty well non-stop for the last five minutes, while his mother and the man in the black suit tried to co-ordinate movements. So far, they had only managed to rise up onto Mrs. Büdenbender's knees.

"No one has died," the man in the black suit continued, straining to look up at Mark from under his mother's ample breasts. "We've just been fused together."

Upon hearing the words 'fused together', Mark shrieked again. He continued to shriek as he watched his mother struggle to stand. Mrs. Büdenbender heaved her bifurcated body up onto one of the folding chairs and sat.

"Beth-Ann," she said, half in a daze.

"It's all right, really!" Simon yelled, snatching up the *Pax Arcana*. "We can fix this."

He opened the paperback and found the pages blackened; not burnt, but glossy, as if they had been dipped in bitumen and hung to dry. The book slipped from his quivering fingers. His eyes fell to the tarot cards on the card table, also blackened and shrivelled.

"The feedback from the interrupted transference overloaded the errata," the man in the black suit explained. "The book and cards are useless. That key is lost forever."

"Why is there no blood?" Mrs. Büdenbender asked no one in particular. Her voice sounded frail and far-away.

"Because we've been fused together," the man in the black suit repeated wearily.

Mark struggled with his inhaler. After several puffs he managed to ask, "What does that mean? You keep saying 'fused together', but what does it actually mean?"

The man in the black suit indicated Simon with a nod. "Your friend opened a inflation-slipway, which was about to return me to...where I came from." His gaze turned to Mrs. Büdenbender. "In the very instant I was being transferred, this abundance-of-flesh, your mother, stampeded over, and knocked me out of the slipway. Corporeality reasserted itself and fused us together. Our bodies are now one. We share several major organs and a circulatory system, although we still maintain separate hearts and minds. That's what it 'actually means'. Now, let me ask you, can you fathom any of that? Can you? Of course you can't, because your mind is a feeble, tiny box with closed pathways, only capable of secreting endorphins when you eat or fornicate!"

"That's so rude," Mark said.

"Beth-Ann!" Mrs. Büdenbender said, suddenly. "Where's Beth-Ann?"

After a long and deliberate pause, the man in the black suit said, "Perhaps we should all get comfortable. This will take some time to explain."

It was difficult finding a position Mrs. Büdenbender and the man in the black suit could sit in comfortably. His torso emerged from hers where her floating ribs should be, while his pelvis and legs exited her back near her kidneys, which created geometries ordinary furniture just could not accommodate.

"It's like trying to prop up a starfish on a sofa," Simon commented, only to be silenced by Mark with a hard stare.

In the end, Mrs. Büdenbender sat forward, allowing the man in the black suit to rest his shoulder on the armrest while a stack of pillows propped up his legs. It was the best they could come up with. Both Mark and Simon pulled up chairs quite close, waiting like ballboys on a tennis court, ready to assist if Mrs. Büdenbender listed over.

"Think of me as a curator," the man in the black suit began.

"You work for a museum?" Mark asked, inhaler at the ready in case the forthcoming answer made him hyperventilate.

"Not exactly," the man in the black suit explained. "What I curate is like a museum, not an actual museum. It has various galleries, each connected to others via a series of corridors. I call it my museum, but in reality, it does not belong to me. If anything, I belong to it."

"What's in these galleries?" Simon asked.

"It depends on what you're looking for."

Mark's face twisted with exasperation. "What kind of answer is that? It makes no sense."

The man in the black suit shook his head. "From your stunted perspective it makes no sense. But just for an instant I want you to focus your pea-brain and try to imagine a place where nothing exists until you look for it, then it does! Think of particles -- minuscule, granular bits tinier than quarks -- then, by your effort to observe them, they appear, like condensation on a cold glass. Speaking of which, I would like some water."

"I'm still confused," Mark said, taking a puff from his inhaler for good measure.

"I'm sure you are. Let us call the contents of my galleries 'grains of potential'. These grains of potential, once coalesced, interact with one another, perpetuating their existence. Some will find themselves alone and isolated from the others; they will slow, losing energy and heat and potential. Those cease to exist. But the others keep going, feeding off interaction. Eventually they begin to congregate, forming vast networks, creating matter, space, time, energy, everything. Then, after a critical amount of time has gathered, the grains of potential find a slipway out of my museum. All at once they exit, leaving nothing but void."

"Like a body and a soul!" Simon exclaimed. "The museum you're describing is like the body, and the grains are like bits of the soul, or cells or something. Sorry, that analogy kinda fell apart on me."

"Similar, yes," the man in the black suit said. "A gallery...a body...both are vessels. What's important is what they are filled with."

"These, 'grains of potential', are they still in your museum?" Mark asked.

"Yes, for now. But when they leave, they will flood this universe, obliterating it and all that is here. It will be the End of Motion, the End of Heat."

"And Beth-Ann?" Mrs. Büdenbender asked.

"She is in a gallery in my museum."

"And how do we get to her?"

"May I have water? I find my throat parching."

"Mark, would you get a pitcher from the kitchen and some glasses?" Mrs. Büdenbender asked. "I suddenly could use a glass myself. Or two."

Mark hurried up the stairs.

"How can we get to Beth-Ann?" Simon asked. "And how can we get the two of you un-fused?"

"We need to reopen the inflation slipway into my gallery. Once there, I have certain tools which will allow me to separate from this woman."

"And how would we reopen the slipway?"

The man in the black suit shrugged. "You're the potter and I'm the clay, remember? You created the slipway. It's still here, in this room, ready to be utilized. You need to find another key to open it. Maybe if you had any other pieces of universal errata, like the book?"

A dark shadow crossed over Simon's face as words caught in his throat. He was about to say something when Mark returned.

"Thank you, dear," Mrs. Büdenbender said. "I don't remember

when I've been this thirsty."

Mark filled a could couple of glasses.

Simon said, "Don't Mark." He didn't know why they should refuse the man in the black suit the water he asked for. His gut just told him it was a very, very, bad idea.

"Pass it to me, Mark," his mother said, but for some reason Mark passed the glass to the man in the black suit.

"Be sure you don't spill it," the man in the black suit said. It was an odd thing to say because Mark had already handed him the glass.

The man in the black suit held the glass with both hands, closed his eyes, tipped the tumbler to his lips, and drank. When the tumbler was finished, he stopped moving. For several seconds he remained motionless, just holding the glass with his eyes closed.

"Hey, curator or whatever," Simon said, trying to get a response from the man in the black suit. "Hey."

Finally, Mark reached over and took the empty glass, placing it on the card table. The man in the black suit's head slumped forward.

"Oh dear," Mrs. Büdenbender said. She held his wrist, feeling for a pulse. After a moment she pulled her hand away and looked straight into her son's eyes and said, "Well, he's dead."

# CHAPTER SEVENTEEN

### -- UNKNOWN LOCATION. UNKNOWN TIME --

Beth-Ann wasn't scared of being alone.

What with mom working late most nights at the Waffle Shack, and Mark, her dork-of-an-older brother off with his doofus friends all the time, she was used to being on her own. She liked it. It had taught her she could fend for herself if she needed to.

But this place wasn't normal. It was about as far from normal as you could get.

She stared up at the red and purple night sky, a band of asteroids cutting across it. She had never seen a night sky that seemed bruised and on fire and so full of stars. The dusty ground sloped upwards to an escarpment topped with jagged rocks. Harsh weeds dotted the landscape, the only living things on the wind-blasted terrain. A dry riverbed cut through the barren valley floor, disappearing behind rocky screes in the distance.

What was this place?

Wherever she was, it wasn't Earth. Earth didn't have four

other planets hanging about in the night sky. They were so close she could make out craters and continents. One was dusty and red, another had rings and was shrouded in swirling purple and yellow clouds. The biggest was silvery white, half of it below the horizon. The smallest one looked like a glossy, blue-green marble hanging directly overhead.

One thing for sure, she had to figure this out for herself, because there was no way Mark and his geekoid friends were going to be any help. If there was a way to get here, wherever here was, there was a way to get back. She would figure it out, by herself, and then rub Mark's ugly face in it.

A hot breeze blew down the slope, picking up grit and sand. She turned downwind and considered what to do.

None of this made much sense. One second she was in the basement trying to get back the sidewalk chalk her dork brother had taken from her, then there was a push and a sense of extreme pressure making her ears pop, then she was here. Being on a different planet didn't scare her. Standing up for a clarinet solo in front of Mrs. Morton and the rest of the band with Lizzy Renfield and the pretty girls snickering at her, that was scary. This was just, different, and weird.

If there was a way to get here, there was a way to get back. That was for sure. All she had to do was figure out how.

Then the music started.

The sound crept down from the escarpment ridge, like a reluctant fog smoothing over a valley at dawn. If she had to guess what kind of instrument made that droning, eerie hum, she would have guessed some kind of brass horn played with a mute. A brass horn the size of a bus, that is. It was low, humming, and haunting. Haunting not in a scary way, more like it made the whole landscape desolate and otherworldly.

"Okay, well, there's something," she said to herself.

She picked herself up, dusted the dirt from her track pants, and started up the hill, heading towards the droning music rolling down from above.

## CHAPTER EIGHTEEN

-- GRAND RAPIDS, MICHIGAN. SOON --

"The dude was right over there," Herb said, pointing to the chalk triangle in Mark's basement. There was no sign of Mark, or Simon, or the man in the black suit. Other than that, everything was just how he left it, more or less.
"When?" Noodles asked.
"When what?"
"When did you leave them, stoner-boy?"
"Last night. No, wait, I think I fell asleep at some point. Two nights ago, maybe? Time can get slippery on me."
"Focus Herb!" Noodles took a few tentative sniffs and snorted. "Jesus Christ, there's so much cosmogonic warping here it's making my skin itch."
Herb walked over to the card table. The tarot cards lay curled up, their faces blackened and glossy. He picked up the *Pax Arcana* and flipped through its black pages.
"We were just goofing around," he said. "No one deserves to have their little sister taken from them. Bergman was right, 'Life is an outrageous horror.' We live. We die. That's all...Hey, waffles!"
Herb grabbed the Waffle Shack take-out off the table and

opened the Styrofoam container. The smell of maple syrup and butter wafted up. "Nothing like waffles."

"Stop snacking!" Noodles snapped. "And quit your existential whining! No one likes a film snob." Noodles squinted as he scanned the basement with his bulbous eyes. "Alright, let's find out where this poop-muncher has taken the little girl." He padded over to the chalk triangle and sniffed. "Definitely slippage residue," he said finally. "The incorporeal-quantum field is stretched out right to hell. Man. The whole basement is a time-space sinkhole waiting to happen."

Fat Cheeks froze, his head swivelling around. "Are you sure it's okay to be here? Time-space sinkholes sound like mandatory overtime, to me."

"Sit down and shut your pie-hole while I'm diagnosing! Change your diapers, while you're at it."

"So hurtful," Fat Cheeks sighed and sat at the table, patiently waiting for Noodles. He was used to his boss's abrasive manner, knowing sooner or later it would subside to a merely irritating level. So he sat, and waited, humming a Muddy Waters tune, tapping out the rhythm with his fingers. His hand inadvertently brushed against the water glass. He took up the glass, filled it with water from the pitcher, and drained it. An instant later his face went blank.

"Why'd you do that?" Herb asked, after Fat Cheeks finished.

Fat Cheeks sneered at him. "I was thirsty," he said, his voice low and oddly hollow.

"Weird," Herb said to himself.

"What the hell are you two talking about?" Noodles yelled.

"Nothing," Herb answered, "What you got?"

"Lots. Too many masking smells, and the stretched reality of this location is mixing everything up. I need a scent article. Find something of the kid's, something I could get a good sniff on."

Herb waded upstairs, returning a few minutes later with a play-worn teddy. Noodles took several quick sniffs off the raggedy bear, then criss-crossed the floor inhaling and exhaling.

"Anything?" Herb asked.

"Got her coming down the stairs, mulling around, then dashing to the conjuration point," Noodle said. He paced around the chalk, smelling every inch. When finished he plopped down and licked his nose with several purposeful licks. "This is where she crossed over."

"Over? Over to where?"

"How the hell should I know? It was your freaky friends doing the summoning."

"What about the man in the black suit?"

"There's nothing."

"Nothing?"

"Stop repeating everything I say, stoner-boy!"

"How can there be nothing?"

"Again, how the hell should I know? I smell you, your two college buddies and their body-spray cologne, a warm doughy smell I take to be the mom, and the acrid pong of a preteen brewing hormones. That's it. There's no scent from any other being, human or otherwise. There is, thanks to you nub-heads, a tremendous, spiralling, whirlpool of incorporeal, cosmogonic, and quantum energies emanating from that reality-pimple of a triangle you dip-wads conjured into existence. Other than that, nothing! No black suit man."

"Huh."

"Huh? That's your only comment? Huh? Pathetic." The pug continued to sniff around the basement.

Herb focused on the facts he knew: there was no scent residue of the man in the black suit according to Noodles, but Herb had seen the man with his own eyes -- granted, they were incredibly stoned, drug-addled eyes at the time, but still his own eyes.

Something was amiss.

Mark and Simon were missing. Mrs. Büdenbender had been here, the Waffle Shack take-out attested to that, but now only her cold waffles remained. If there was one truth Herb knew, it was people don't just disappear and leave behind perfectly good waffles.

Something was definitely amiss.

The tarot cards and the *Pax Arcana* were ruined, and in a very peculiar way, yet everything else was the same as when he'd gone for help. What had they been doing while he was away?

"I told them to hang out," Herb muttered. "This is not hanging out."

"Got something," Noodles said from behind the couch. "Smells like European cheese combined with stale gym socks."

"Simon's backpack," Herb said, picking it up. "He wouldn't have left without it." He sifted through the stuffed bag, searching for some clue as to where Mark, Simon, the man in the black suit, and Mrs. Büdenbender had gone.

"If you find whatever is making the cheese smell, save it for me," Noodles said.

Herb dug down, flipped over latest issue of *Shamanism Today* and a glint caught his eye. He plucked it out, holding it between thumb and forefinger. It was a seal, about the size of a half-dollar, made of shimmering onyx with the bas-relief of a ziggurat carved on one side and palm fronds on the other. Whoever the ancient artificer was who carved it was a bonafide master. There was depth to the image, such precision, it oozed with life.

"Smells ancient," Noodles said, his nose wriggling as he sniffed the coin. "Third millennia I would say. Definitely pre-Homeric. With an incredibly dense cosmogonic gravitational field encircling it. What's this friend of yours do?"

"He's a sociology major."

Noodles snorted derisively. "Waste of a perfectly good life."

"Simon's a good guy. A little intense at times when he's...you know..."

"Messing with the esoteric?"

"Yeah."

Noodles scratched behind his ear. "A bit of a hothead when he's summoning malignant forces from the incorporeal, but otherwise, a drip. Got it. Not the kind of guy who's a tomb robber in his spare time."

"Yeah."

"So how'd he get this shiny little artifact, the one that's got several micro-dimensions encrusted around it? And the summoning book? What else does sociology-drip have in his magic bag?"

Herb shrugged. "Yeah. Don't have a clue."

The pug's forehead wrinkled. "Wait a minute." He trotted over to the censer beside the couch and flipped open the latch. The brass interior held the remains of several bundles of burnt sage. A woodsy, smoky smell wafted out.

"Here's what I don't get," Noodles said as he rooted around the ashes at the bottom, moving the cold embers aside. "This guy, Simon, is obviously a novice. You don't use sage for a cleansing. That's strictly reserved for the indigenous peoples of North America. Frankincense, sure. But not sage. So this runt is obviously a poser, and yet is able to pull off a major summoning most grand magnus warlocks couldn't handle on their best days. How is that possible?"

He stopped abruptly, his piggish tail freezing in mid-wag.

"Got something. Come here. Blow gently on the bottom. Careful, don't touch it."

Herb shrugged and did as Noodles instructed, gently blowing into the censer, his breath sweeping away the burnt remains. From the ashes a golden amulet emerged, which Herb thought was odd because amulets didn't usually lie at the bottom of censers, especially amulets made of pure gold.

"Wow, would you look at that!" Herb said.

The amulet was about the size of Herb's palm. Its shiny surface appeared untouched by age. Stylized waves adorned the edges, while parallel lines spiralled away to a vanishing point at the centre. M.C. Escher would have been impressed by the way the art tossed the observer's focus about like a beach ball at Coachella.

"Trippy," Herb said.

"Trippy on steroids," Noodles agreed. "Jesus-suffering-Christ, what's it doing now?"

As Herb and Noodles watched the parallel spirals began to rotate, moving across the metal, slow and easy. There was a hollow, whistling-wind sound. A breeze blew the hairs on Herb's forehead. As they stared the lines fuzed, becoming indistinct as they grew together, then reversed and opened, allowing depth and space to enter.

A tunnel formed. Its walls scintillated with lights, some hot-button red, some electric blue, others aquarium green. The lights pulsed, sending undulations down the length of the tunnel, disappearing into a vanishing point of pure golden illumination in the distance.

For a moment they were silent, then Noodles turned to Herb and said, "Just what the hell kinda friends do you have anyway?"

In that instant, Fat Cheeks rushed up from behind and shoved them both. Herb and Noodles buckled, then fell forward, the amulet blazing with intense light. Space became wrong. It shrank away, the deflation sucking Herb and Noodles and Fat Cheeks into the tunnel.

The amulet swallowed them whole.

# CHAPTER NINETEEN

-- SCARBOROUGH, ONTARIO. NOW --

The lights were still on in the Paragon of Realty offices. In fact, the lights were never off. Someone was always there.

Lovenight kicked open the door. He charged into the unremarkable reception area wearing nothing but his afghan loin cloth; his index finger pointed like a child playing cops-and-robbers with only a finger for a gun. He scanned the reception desk for potential hostile threats and was slightly disappointed when he entirely failed to find any.

"Stop trifling with me!" he hissed.

Reg helped Lady Montique through the still-swinging door.

"Edmund, stop it at once!" Lady Montique said firmly. "You're wasting precious time."

"Wasting precious time is one of my most endearing qualities," Lovenight retorted.

"Why are you holding your hand like that?"

"Best defence is to make people think you have a weapon, even when you don't."

Lady Montique scoffed. "No one is going to believe your finger is a gun."

"It's not much, I'll admit." Lovenight lowered his hand.

The unremarkable reception area consisted of a desk, phone, a chair, and an utterly unthreatening seating area. Smooth jazz played from speakers recessed in the ceiling. A small aquarium gurgled away in the corner, next to a potted philodendron.

Lovenight stared at the aquarium. "Those goldfish are eye-balling me!"

"Never trust fish, sir," Reg said. "I had an uncle, used to keep koi."

"Edmund! Reginald! Focus on the mission!" Lady Montique chided. "We must find the Paragon of Reality."

"Do you hear that, ma'am?" asked Reg.

They went still. Beyond the reception area, a row of perfectly ordinary cubicles stretched to the back wall of the office. A door in the back wall was open. Through it came the faint sound of a photocopier spitting out paper.

"There," Lovenight said, pointing. "The copy room."

"Well done, sir," Reg said. "Proceed with utmost caution, I should think?"

"Always Reg. You first."

"Can't, sir."

"Why?"

"It would be presumptuous, sir. Above my station. The glory must go to you."

Lovenight glared at the dead cabbie for a moment, a lone muscle on his jaw twitching. Then, without a word, he slid away towards the doorway, moving like a deadly shadow. Reg and Lady Montique followed at a distance. When he reached the doorway Lovenight leapt inside, his finger-gun out and ready.

A man of average height stood next to the copier as it spit out pages. He wore a wool cardigan and leather loafers. His hair was short, neat, and combed. A plain set of glasses sat on his unremarkable nose, just above his thin-and-forgettable lips. The man was the living embodiment of everything mind-numbingly average; a flesh-and-blood conglomeration of microwaved meals, khaki pants made from stretchy cotton, network sitcoms, overly complicated expense reports, baloney sandwiches, ho-hum sex, and lite beer.

The oh-so-bland man turned slowly, looking enquiringly at the trio.

"Can I interest you in a reasonably priced back-split close to good schools and transit?"

His voice was the human equivalent of vanilla pudding.

Lovenight had been played many times, by the best mental tacticians and manipulators on the planet. He prided himself in being able to out-crazy anything anyone threw at him. But this, this was an original tactic, an unknown gambit. It completely flummoxed him.

The only response he could muster was to say, "Pardon?"

"Can I interest you in a reasonably priced back-split close to good schools and transit?"

Lovenight shook his head as if trying to dislodge a piece of wax stuck in his ear. "I heard what you said. The question I mean to ask is why say it?"

The man shrugged. "Isn't it a perfectly normal thing to say? This is a realty office. You've come into the realty office, so I assume you must be looking for some realty. Therefore, a reasonably priced back-split close to good schools and transit is a perfectly normal thing to say. Perfectly normal."

Lovenight stood still for a moment, parsing every phrase the man had said, looking for any hidden traps and/or meanings.

"No, it's not."

"Yes it is," insisted the man. "I have the statistics. Would you like to see them?"

Cautiously, Lovenight said, "It might be a perfectly normal thing to say in an average realty office, but this realty office isn't normal or average, is it? I mean, every car in the parking lot is the same model! The exact same! Even the colour is the same. That's statistically impossible!"

"Statistically, it's the most normal parking lot in North America. All other parking lots have it wrong."

"Hah! I can prove this isn't normal."

The man pushed his glasses up to the bridge of his nose with his index finger. "Give it a go."

Lovenight began to roll up his sleeves then realized he didn't have any. He considered rolling up his afghan-turned-loincloth, but decided against it. "You don't respond to a maniac dressed in an improvised loin cloth -- accompanied by a crabapple-of-human-being and a zombie with an excessive moustache -- by offering to sell them real estate!"

"You don't?"

"No, you don't! You scream, you beg for your life, or you flee! Those are the only acceptable responses of any individual, sane or otherwise."

"Oh." The man thought for a moment, crossing his arms over his cardigan. "Can I have a do-over?"

Lady Montique cleared her throat. Her throat-clearing would have stopped an ocean liner. She pulled herself as erect as she could, the effort causing her spine to crackle like rice crisps in milk.

"Enough, you're one of the Paragons of Reality, aren't you? Your job is to keep the 'real' in 'reality', is it not?"

The paragon nodded and said in a meek voice, "It is and I am."

"What is your Realm of Influence? Over what part of reality do you preside?"

"*Vis insita.*"

Lovenight's eyebrows arched upwards in an attempt to hold back the stack of confused wrinkles threatening to spill down from his forehead and infest the rest of his face. "Visa is a-sitting, what? Speak English!"

"Inertia, and the Principle of Inertia, The One who Keeps, the Force in all matter which resists change. I enforce the Rule Sedentary. I counterbalance. I make sure everything stays perfectly normal. You're sure I can't interest you in a reasonably priced back-split?"

"Absolutely not, unless it comes with a fourteenth century manor house complete with full wait staff and the best wine cellar this side of Bordeaux."

"Well then, perhaps you better step into my office."

The paragon's office was perfectly normal. It contained one

of those desks built to go into a corner, a swivel chair, a computer, a wastepaper basket, a wall clock, a bookshelf ladened with reference books, a family photo with one of the three children only partly in frame, a single under-watered *ficus benjamina*, an inspirational poster of a grizzly bear holding up a paw captioned with the phrase 'Don't gimme no sass!', and not much else.

Lovenight picked up a package of labels off the desk and examined it with a sneer. The word 'LABELS' had been handwritten in capital letters on a label stuck to the package.

"My god man, you've labeled the labels!"

The paragon's eyes flickered. He cleared his throat before asking calmly, "Exactly who are you?"

"My name is Edmund Lovenight, esquire. This is the Lady Eleanor Anastasia Firth Montique. Behind me is Reg, a dead cab driver. We're not to be trifled with."

"So noted. My name is John H. Smith." He adjusted his tie and squirted hand sanitizer onto his palms, rubbing them vigourously. "My wife likes me to add my middle initial, she thinks it makes me more 'edgy'. Have to keep the spice in the marriage, or so I'm told."

"Someone...married you?"

"Donkey! You're wasting time!" Lady Montique exclaimed. She turned to the paragon and straightened. "Mr. Smith, I'm the Principle Operative and Spymaster General of the Outliers. Perhaps you've heard of us?"

John H. Smith shook his head.

"We're a sixth column agency, working to undermine and sabotage nihilistic, fascist threats from both the corporeal and incorporeal realities. However, recently, we encountered a substantial onslaught which has wiped out the entirety of our organization, save those you see before you. To speak plainly, Mr. Smith, we're in need of your help."

The paragon jittered slightly before saying, "I'm afraid I can't be of much help. Things have been fairly normal around the office, which is the point of this office when you think about it."

"Normal? You call dozens of puce coloured imports normal?" Lovenight interjected.

"Edmund, shut up. Mr. Smith, can you give us any indication

what has happened? What hyper-natural hostiles were active in the last few days?"

The paragon pushed his glasses farther back his nose. "Sorry. That's not how I work, you see. I only balance reality when it goes askew. What force puts it out of skew in the first place is beyond my job purview. My job, basically, is to never leave this office."

Lovenight's eyebrows shot up. "Are you sure you have all your brain-ducks in a row?"

"A Paragon always has to be here, you see, maintaining reality. If I leave, all sorts of shenanigans and goings-on might occur which were not perfectly normal."

"But you said you were married."

"I am. She drops by every day. Brings me lunch, tells me what's going on with the kids. All perfectly normal."

"Kids?"

"2.4 to be precise. Perfectly normal."

"That's not normal, that's average! And what's a .4 child look like anyway?"

"I have a school photo in my phone, I think. Let me have a look-see." John H. Smith reached for his desk drawer.

Lovenight raised both hands. "No electronics! Parasites all up and down the electromagnetic spectrum! Put it away! Away, I say!"

John H. Smith shrugged. "Perhaps later."

Lady Montique snapped her fingers an inch under Lovenight's nose, causing him to recoil in confusion. She then, very ladylike, extended an open palm to the paragon, inviting him to continue speaking. "You were saying, Mr. Smith?"

"Oh yes, well, there's not much I can tell you about the 'hostiles' or 'onslaughts' or anything like that. Not my job. But I can tell you how things are going around the office."

John H. Smith paused. The silence lengthened, became awkward, then moved on to intolerable.

"Well?" Lovenight prompted, his hands shaking as if he was holding the paragon's shoulders and trying to jiggle the information out of him. "How have things been around the office?"

"Thanks for asking! Oh, you know, fairly normal...except

things are shifting away from inertia. The balance is sliding towards chaos and entropy. Normally, reality runs like a fine-tuned machine, purring away, the Earth revolving around the Sun and all of that. Perfectly normal. Bliss, I call it. But every now and then there's this abnormal trend throwing the whole machine off."

"And what can be done about that?" Lady Montique asked.

"Oh, well, what I do is counterbalance, trying to achieve a state of equilibrium and make a new normal."

"How, exactly, do you counterbalance reality?"

"Well, for instance, if there is a trend towards unrest I try to soothe things out. I cause populations to be more inclined to drink chamomile tea, develop baking competitions for television, change radio station formats to adult contemporary and yacht rock, things of that nature. If there is a trend towards stagnation, I create aerobic dance fads, promote football rivalries, stoke minor revolutions, the list goes on. My motto is 'Too sedate? How's an earthquake? Too agitated? Why not relax?'" The paragon looked away sheepishly for a moment, then added, "I'm still working on my motto."

"Work harder," Lovenight suggested.

"Mr. Smith," Lady Montique said briskly, steering the conversation back to the dire matter at hand. "By what means do you counterbalance reality?"

"Oh, it's easy really. This office changes by itself most of the time."

Lovenight's eyelids narrowed suspiciously. "What do you mean 'this office changes'?"

"This office building is a fulcrum which seeks balance. If there is a shift in universal reality, the office changes to compensate. Thus, the fulcrum moves and the balance is restored. I make adjustments and suggestions. For instance, if there is a surge of chaos, the paint on the wall becomes a more neutral shade of beige, like 'bored mushroom' or 'flaccid wheat'."

"None of that vibrant and excitable, 'mouse brown' for you, eh, John?" Lovenight snipped.

The sarcasm flew right past the paragon.

"Exactly," he said dryly.

Lovenight yipped, feeling the pinch of Lady Montique's boney fingers as they squeezed the fleshy part of his forearm. He fell silent under her withering glare. She turned to the paragon and smiled firmly. "If I may ask, Mr. Smith, what has changed in your office recently? Perhaps it will give us a clue as to what the Governance and Baroness Zamora are up to."

The paragon reached into a desk drawer and pulled out a squishy stress-relief toy molded to resemble a pineapple. He placed it on the desk. "Two days ago, this abomination appeared."

Lovenight took the squishy pineapple and examined it, flipping it over in his hands, tentatively giving it a squeeze. The foam felt oddly satisfying once compressed. He pumped his hand several times, squeezing the pineapple which always returned to its original shape.

"Typical trade show swag," Lovenight said. "Promotional merchandise handed out at conventions, team-building exercises, and similar complete wastes-of-time." He read the business slogan off the bottom of the squishy pineapple, "Pineapple Head Shops: 'Feed your head only the best -- Feed it Pineapple'." Lovenight took a moment to wince before carrying on with his examination. "There is no incorporeal or temporal signature about it, as far as I can tell. Mundane, it is. Seems like it belongs in an office."

"Other than the boorish display of wit and the remarkable ineptitude in terms of advertising acumen, what's so abominable about this foam pineapple, Mr. Smith?" Lady Montique asked.

The paragon took a moment to wipe his glasses with a lint-free cloth before saying in a perfectly normal, reasonable tone, "It's the first indication of the end of existence."

# CHAPTER TWENTY

-- SAME PLACE. SECONDS LATER, AFTER A SUITABLY STUNNED SILENCE --

"When placed on pizza, I agree with you," Lovenight said. "Pineapple is an abomination. But isn't it a bit much to say this foam pineapple is the first indication of the end of existence?"

John H. Smith pushed his glasses up to the bridge of his nose. "Do you know what the French word for pineapple is?"

Lovenight shrugged. "I've never needed a pineapple to go with my quiche."

"*Ananas.*"

"*Ananas?*"

"*Ananas.*"

"Okay. And this is relevant...how?"

"Do you know what pineapple is in German?"

"Again, not much call for pineapples in a Munich beer hall."

"*Ananas.* How about Danish or Dutch?"

"I'm going to guess *ananas* only because I sense how this is going."

"*Ananas* and...*ananas.*"

"Not really very imaginative, don't you think?

"In Italian, Hungarian, Icelandic, Swedish, Armenian, Greek, Hebrew, Macedonian, Russian, Persian, Latin, Finnish --"

"Not Finnish!" Lovenight gasped, but immediately regretted it because the sarcasm was bound to sail past the paragon once again.

Sure enough, the paragon replied, "Oh, yes, Finnish for pineapple is *ananas*, as well as Hindi, Polish, Portuguese, Chez, Georgian, and Arabic."

Lovenight fluttered his hands impatiently. "So?"

"Don't you see? The English word 'pineapple' is the anomaly, a deviation from the norm. Usually something completely normal should have spawned to balance the equation, like another Don't-give-me-no-sass Bear poster, or a practically arid *ficus benjamina*. Something has upset normalcy in favour of entropy."

"*Piña!*" Reg exclaimed loudly, startling everyone. The cabbie's moustache bristled.

"What?" Lovenight asked.

"Spanish," Reg explained. "For pineapple. Also an exception to the linguistic ubiquity of *ananas*."

"Reg?" Lovenight said softly.

"Yes, sir?"

"You're a Dadaist, whether you like it or not."

"Thank you, sir," Reg said smiling.

Lovenight returned his attention to the stress-relief pineapple. "Let me get this straight," You're afraid of a foam rubber pineapple, just because it's a pineapple?"

"There's more. Watch this." The paragon took the pineapple and held it above the desk, pausing momentarily for an intense dramatic effect, then slammed it down as hard as he could.

Several unexpected things happened.

The pineapple bounced back and forth between the exact same points on the desk following the same arc each time. Its pace was languid, but relentless. Back and forth and back and forth, never ceasing. The arc did not deteriorate. The pineapple did not slow. As it neared the zenith of the trajectory it expanded, then as it started its descent it would shrink in size, until it hit the table, rebounded, and grew larger again.

"Strange and strangely-er," Lovenight said, watching the

pineapple with utter fascination for several bounces. Eventually the paragon plucked it out of the air.

"As I said, an abomination."

Lovenight rose out of his chair, his head tilted slightly to the side as if trying to shake a pinball-thought into the double-score bumper located at the back of his brain. "You said this office is a fulcrum. It adjusts to reality, counterbalancing the weird by making mundane objects."

"You're paraphrasing, but that is the gist of it."

"And this pineapple, shouldn't be here, because it's hearsay rendered in a novelty item?"

The paragon's forehead wrinkled. In a completely guileless manner he asked, "Do you have to repeat everything someone tells you in order to understand it?"

"It's my way, ya dig? I'm on to something, let me tell you. Now, back down John H. Smith and let me do my voodoo!"

Lovenight crept around the desk, examining the seemingly innocuous stress relief pineapple sitting forlornly in the middle of the faux mahogany veneer. It appeared completely normal now, no hopping about endlessly, no self-compression or expansion. Harmless. A simple, yellow, brown, and green coloured piece of foam which was incredibly satisfying when squished between the palm and the fingers.

Lovenight glared at it like it was a ticking plutonium bomb about to detonate.

"Let's assume this office was doing its job, counterbalancing this crazy, lopsided universe. This squishy pineapple then, is a bit of hyper-normal, so normal it's out there! This thing is the counterbalance!"

In response, Reg wiggled his moustache.

The paragon smoothed his cardigan incessantly, discomforted by Lovenight's logic. "So normal, it bounces back and forth like an inverted metronome? So normal, it remains in motion until acted upon by an external force? Dear me. That would mean some kind of outré-universal errata had somehow crossed over into our reality."

"You said this appeared on your desk two days ago?" Lovenight asked.

The paragon nodded.

"Did your wife come by that day?"

"She brought me a tuna salad sandwich. We sat and ate in the lunchroom. Then she left. Perfectly normal."

"And when you came back to your office?"

"The pineapple was sitting on the desk."

"Could someone have snuck into your office when you were eating lunch with your wife?"

The paragon shoved his glasses back up his nose and thought for a moment. "I suppose, but no one ever comes in here. It's very quiet."

Lovenight snapped his fingers and yelled, "Eureka!" He leapt up on top of the desk and straddled the pineapple, careful to keep his otherwise naked body covered with the knitted afghan.

Lady Montique shielded her eyes. "Donkey! Come down from there at once! I have no wish to see what I am currently seeing!"

Lovenight ignored her, focusing on the surrounding walls. He proclaimed to the room, for no apparent reason, "I found a first edition of *Dark Carnival,* Ray Bradbury's first published book, one of only three thousand copies, before it was mistakenly burned by a gang of illiterate neo-Nazis who were under the false impression it was *Fahrenheit 451.* Inside was Bradbury's expired library card.

"I found the exact spot where the Magna Carta was signed in 1215 by King John, three kilometres away from where it had originally been thought to have taken place, in the kitchen of an Indian take-a-way which made a spectacular chicken vindaloo."

The paragon stared at him with a mixture of fear and fascination. The higher functioning parts of his brain which usually allowed him to form words entirely failed him. He looked to Lady Montique for some explanation, his eyes as wide as Coke bottle bottoms.

"I found a three-leaf clover in a field of four-leaf clovers," Lovenight continued. "I found an extinct species of crayfish alive and thriving in the waters off Grand Cayman; they bribed me with pearls not to tell anyone. In Tanzania, I found a mouse graveyard beside an elephant graveyard."

Reg leaned close to Lady Montique, and asked, "Begging your pardon, ma'am, but I believe his brain's gone potty. Should I pull out the old ball-peen hammer and put the blighter out of his misery with a little knock-knock?"

Lady Montique teetered a moment, considering, then shrugged and said nonchalantly, "Let him work."

"What's he doing?" John H. Smith asked.

"This is only a guess, mind you, but I believe Edmund's trying to convince this office it's normal for him to find improbably lost items."

"I found the Holy Grail being used as a candy dish in a French bordello."

The office shook slightly.

"I found a pair of John Lennon's glasses in a pawn shop mistakenly labeled as Vladimir Ilyisch Lenin's. I bought them for a song."

Tremors rattled the filing cabinets and windows. The paragon looked around, wide-eyed and amazed.

"It's getting ready for a big one," he said.

"I found Hammurabi's signature on a postcard from the Tower of Babel. I found Jesse James' pressed flower collection."

The walls creaked. The floor heaved.

"I found the primordial soup wherein all life on earth began, frozen under several kilometres of Antarctica ice. It tasted salty."

A tumultuous sound, like several bulldozers driven by concrete giants, resounded throughout the building, rocking its foundations and shaking the dust off the *ficus benjamina*. Lady Montique shook gently in her chair. The paragon cast fevered glances behind and beside him. Reg moved close to Lady Montique, ready to spirit her away in the event of a building collapse.

Then, something fundamental shifted. It felt like the moment when knuckles crack and all tension flows away from the bones; only this shift was all-encompassing, ubiquitous, and far-reaching.

Lovenight scanned the room. His eyes fixated on the bookshelf. He leapt down and raced to it.

There was a faint glow coming from an empty space between two reference books. As Lady Montique, Reg, and the paragon crowded closer, the glow shimmered slightly, like a reflection on rippling water, then was gone.

"What was here?" he asked the paragon, waggling his fingers in the empty space.

The paragon peered at it with a mixture of amazement and disgust, like a groundskeeper would glare at a rare and ugly weed in the middle of a pristine golf green. "Just a moment," he said, reaching into his jacket pocket and pulling out his smart phone.

Lovenight leapt back and away. If there was an Olympic medal for the standing back-jump, he would have secured a bronze. He stuck the landing and went into a fighting stance, hands raised and fingers splayed. "No electronics!"

"Won't take a second," the paragon said, swiping and tapping away. "Please don't be alarmed. This is my work phone, it's never been linked to any network. I keep all my inventory spreadsheets on it. One for everything in this office. Some would call me obsessive, but when it comes to my periodicals, pamphlets, books, sticky notes, paper clips, staples, folders, and binders, I like to know exactly what's what."

"You keep an inventory of your paper clips?" Lovenight asked.

"Indexed by size, style, coated, non-coated, torsion, and friction-potential."

"What century are you from?"

Reg scanned the spines of the neatly arranged books on the bookshelf. "*One Hundred and One Things To Do With A Squeezed Lemon*," he read. "*A Beekeeper's Guide to Herding Cats, The Ethical Banker's Handbook, Everything You Need To Know About Unsustainable Ranching, Activities Your Mongoose Will Enjoy.*" Reg shook his head. "Rather eclectic selection of books you have here, Mr. Smith."

The paragon nodded. "They're just normal errata."

Reg's moustache twitched slightly. "Come again?"

"Normal errata. Perfectly normal. Wouldn't be normal if we didn't have errata. That would be abnormal."

"Still haven't the foggiest notion what you're on about."

"Oh dear, let me explain. Everything, including reality, contains mistakes: a misplaced comma for example, or the human appendix, male nipples, bakeries for dogs, things that need to be left out."

"Oh, I take your meaning. Like platypuses and bolo ties."

"Exactly. Now, when publishers discover mistakes in their printed matter, they issue a list of corrections called errata, correcting the original mistakes, you see? With reality, once the correction has been 'published' -- so to speak -- the errata end up here. Things that NEVER SHOULD HAVE BEEN."

A puzzle expression furrowed Reg's leathery forehead. "How did you do that?"

"Do what?"

"Make your voice all echoey when you said 'never should have been'."

"Oh, you mean like NEVER SHOULD HAVE BEEN, like that?"

"Yes, how do you do that?"

"No idea, really." The paragon tapped his smartphone. "Ahh, here it is, third shelf, fourth book in...ah, that was... *Pax Arcana: The Handbook to Arcane Tarot Card Readings and Incorporeal Summonings.*" The paragon's face became pinched and concerned. He whispered softly, "Oh dear."

Lady Montique stepped forward and slapped the paragon squarely across the cheek. She waited a moment for the look of shock to fade from his face, then slapped him again.

"I've had quite enough of your bureaucratic dawdling. You're wasting my time, and believe you me, there isn't a great deal of it left." She grabbed him by his lapels. "Quickly now! What is it about this book that's startled you, you annoyingly boring man?"

"My fifteen-year-old nephew came in a few days ago, asking for it."

"Your nephew?"

The paragon nodded. "His name is Cody."

Something crashed outside the office, sounding like a dozen sheets of glass shattering, one after another in quick succession. Mere seconds later a large metal fist, the size of a basketball, punched through the door with enough force to rip the metal hinges in half.

In strode an armoured robot shaped to resemble a sumo wrestler. Its gunmetal plates rumbled as nano-motors and servos chugged away. The automaton juggernaut smelt of ozone and engine grease and heat.

Lovenight tried to slipstream out of primary time but discovered much to his dismay he couldn't. Something blocked his way. Again and again he tried, to no avail. The effort caused his afghan loincloth to slip off, leaving him naked, staring at the metal monstrosity.

"Bugger," he cursed.

"Well, all the cockroaches gathered together," a voice purred from outside the door.

In stepped Baroness Zamora, her trans-kinetic hands now visible as they wrapped Lovenight in shimmering, heat-haze bands. Her eyes, bright and electric, immediately snapped to Lady Montique.

"Lydia," Lady Montique said curtly.

Baroness Zamora smiled. "Hello mother," she said.

# CHAPTER TWENTY-ONE

-- MICHOACÁN DESSERT, MEXICO. A SHORT TIME LATER --

Lovenight lay restrained on a metal table. No light penetrated the surrounding darkness, not a sliver anywhere. Judging by acoustics, the space was approximately the size of a bachelor apartment, about 400 square feet. The metal beneath his naked body remained cold despite the hours he had been strapped to it.

They had confiscated his afghan loincloth. He sorely missed it.

Strange the things you miss once they're gone, he thought.

Each time he attempted to slipstream out of primary time he came up against a psionic wall, some sort of incorporeal distortion, intense and encompassing, a pan-dimensional prison created by Baroness Zamora's potent ego. During one attempt he came within centiseconds of creating a temporal slipway, only to read these words written in dark matter: WELCOME TO THE EGO CITADEL OF THE BARONESS ZAMORA, PLEASE ENJOY YOUR STAY AND AVOID LEAVING ANY PSYCIC BAGGAGE

UNATTENDED.

"Bloody fascist," he cursed. "Don't tell me what to leave unattended."

But that wasn't the only wall surrounding him.

In the darkness the nano-drones whirled and whined, creating a high-pitched tone Lovenight instantly recognized. Electronic micro-reapers, thousands of them, hovered nearby, encasing him like a guppy in a fish tank -- a fish tank studded with death-dealing explosive drones thinner than a wasp's stinger, but a fish tank, nonetheless.

"Electronics," he lamented. "Harbingers of Man's Desperate Final Gasp!"

In times of dire crises, when his inner alarms were ringing off the hook and there was no hope of rescue, Lovenight took to castigating electronics.

"What bloody good are they?" he railed to himself in the darkness. "I mean, what's the point? Watches counting your every step? Telephones you can never get away from? Constant scrutiny by complete strangers on social media? Videos of cats! Memes of failure revered as art? My dear god, the banality of it all."

A heavy door cracked opened. The room filled with light, searing his eyes. Something went 'flick,' and the lights came on.

The interrogation room resembled the inside of a German-engineered dishwasher. Every surface was plated with stainless steel. Arrays of LED lights suspended by armatures hung from the ceiling, blanketing the room in crisp, white light. Sluiceways covered the floor in a grid leading to a central drain covered by a fine mesh. Micro-reapers hovered near the walls, scanning for the merest hint of movement. Instrument carts packed with tools of torture gleamed with minty, just-washed freshness.

Through the glare of the open doorway Lovenight saw human shapes walking toward him.

"Hello!" a cheerful sounding voice said.

Lovenight groaned and wondered, "Dear god, what fresh hell is this?"

"Oh, he's awake!" said another voice.

"Awake already!" exclaimed a third voice. "My, a fine

constitution, this one."

The forms crowded over him. His vision adjusted to the light, allowing Lovenight to focus on their faces: three women, all in their thirties, with short bobbed hair and full, plump cheeks. Each smiled a smile warm and sinister, a combination Lovenight would not have thought possible beforehand. The women looked like the welcoming committee from some local community association, except they wore full-body rubber aprons and hazmat gloves.

"Hi, my name is Jenn," said one with blonde highlights, whose upper front incisors overlapped giving her a slightly rabbit-like appearance. "Welcome! How're you today?"

"I'm strapped to this table. How are you?"

"Just fine, thanks for asking."

"If there is anything we can do, just let us know," said another with straight hair the colour of winter tires. "I'm Sophie."

"And I'm Rachel," said the last who had a receding hairline and a forehead the size of an iceberg. "We're here to help."

Lovenight took a moment to consider how he was feeling at that exact moment. As usual, his linguistic acumen served him well.

"Sod off."

All three ladies looked at one another and laughed heartily. It was the kind of communal female laugh which made men everywhere check their zippers. After several peals, the ladies stopped and regarded Lovenight with a sympathetic eye. "Oh, you're cute!" Rachel said. "We're going to get along famously!"

The three ladies busied themselves with objects outside of Lovenight's field of vision.

"Forgive me for being obtuse, but what exactly are you ladies here to help me with?"

"With your self-interrogation, silly!"

"Self...interrogation?"

"Yes," said Jenn, walking over with a stainless-steel utensil that resembled a speculum, except with more spikes and serrated edges. "Self-interrogation. We're like the staff overseeing the self-checkout aisle at the grocery store. If you need any assistance, we're here! Why don't you start with this and work your way up." She handed him the speculum-shaped utensil.

Since his hands were still strapped to the table, he waggled it about slightly, saying, "What am I supposed to do with this?"

"You see!" said Rachel with that warm-and-sinister smile on her face. "You need our help already."

Ten minutes later Jenn removed the speculum and placed it in a steel bedpan. Sophie wiped Lovenight's sweating brow with a washcloth.

After he stopped screaming, he managed to say, "Well, I've self-interrogated myself and found several disturbing revelations, which I will bring up with my therapist in our next session. Thank you all for your assistance. I'm sure this will make me a better person in the long run. To wit, I declare this self-interrogation over. Now then, moving on. Where's Lady Montique? Where's Reg?"

Sophie shrugged, the effort dislodging her hair. She tucked it back over her ear with a gloved hand. "Sorry, I can't you help with that. Is there anything else I can do?"

"You can untie me, get me a bathrobe and a martini, then drop me off at the nearest luxury spa, preferably one with a bevy of masseuses and lots of bandages."

Sophie giggled.

Lovenight cocked his eyebrow. "I can't help but notice you're steadfastly ignoring any request I make. I thought you were here to help?"

"With your self-interrogation only."

"How's that work, exactly?"

"Well, we provide 'opportunities of unpleasantness', or OOUs, until you confess."

"Confess? To what? You haven't asked me anything."

"That's the beauty of self-interrogation. You have to guess at what we want to know. We don't direct or influence your confessions in anyway, therefore the confessions are pure and untainted."

"Easy enough. I confess to everything. There? Happy?"

She looked at him trenchantly. "We need details of course. Hidden, secret details, that only you would know. We need specifics."

"Can you give me a hint?"

"If I did, that would influence your answer. It would point to something we expect to hear, and might allow you to leave out other details we don't know about yet. With self-interrogation, we find subjects are more forthcoming with information. All in all, it's quicker, thorough, and less costly than traditional torture."

"So, you're the good cop and I'm my own bad cop?"

She giggled. "Me? Good? How so?"

"Well, you're giving me succour and comfort during this ordeal, wiping my brow and all. You see?"

"What, this?" she asked, holding up the washcloth in her gloved hand. "This is soaked with a mixture of hand lotion and a particularly nasty nerve agent. Right now it's working its way into your skin."

As if on cue, blinding pain sizzled across his forehead.

Lovenight screamed, loud and long, until his lungs ached from the effort. It felt like his subcutaneous fat had spontaneously combusted. He was in danger of blacking out when Sophie pulled out a second washcloth and smeared some greasy unguent over his brow. It smelled harsh and astringent, but it instantly put out the fire raging beneath his skin.

"There, beautifully done!" Sophie said as if commenting on a rack of freshly baked sticky buns pulled from the oven. "I think he's ready to start confessing."

"Oh, I'm ready. Let's go!"

Lovenight began confessing and didn't stop. He confessed to every sordid thing he had ever done, or thought of doing, or wanted to do. Each confession came complete with vivid details, and when appropriate, schematic diagrams.

After several hours of listening, Rachel twisted his nipple to get him to stop.

"Okay, maybe a little direction is needed here," Sophie admitted.

"To speed things up," Rachel added.

Lovenight nodded enthusiastically. "Sure, whatever you

want."

"Let's start with how you joined the Outliers. Recruitment, training, everything."

"Well, really, I was lucky-- eeowww!"

Jenn produced a pair of needle-nose pliers seemingly from thin air and twisted the soft flesh between Lovenight's thumb and forefinger. She released the pressure and allowed him to draw breath.

"Don't be cheeky," she admonished.

"I wasn't. I was being serious. It was luck -- eeowww!"

"If you keep giving me answers like that, what comes next will be excruciating for you, Mr. Lovenight."

"It's the way I work!" he insisted, speaking as rapidly as he could in an effort to stave off another twist from the pliers. "I've always trusted my luck! Luck is my friend. It's gotten me into fabulous parties! It's granted me a lifestyle filled with leisure and indulgence. It's kept me alive through impossible situations with no hope of escape! My luck never lets me down."

Rachel and Sophie looked at each other, grimacing.

"I'm afraid that doesn't quite hold true," Sophie said. "After all, you're here with us."

To punctuate the point, Jenn waggled the pliers in front of Lovenight.

"That doesn't prove anything, I'm afraid," Lovenight said. "I mean, my luck might be saving me now from a far more heinous and permanent fate."

Dumbfounded, Jenn said, "I need a coffee," then gave Lovenight one last twist with the pliers, just because.

"Good idea," Rachel agreed. "I bought some lovely crullers and left them in the lunchroom."

"You're a gem, always thinking of others."

"Oh, but before we do, I have something for our guest." Sophie retrieved a yellow bio-hazard bag from the corner, stepped forward, reached in, and pulled out a severed head.

It was a jolt to see Reg without his ever-present cap on top of his head, not to mention his legs, torso, arms and hands. His lifeless eyes were still lifeless, only now in an unmoving and never-likely-to-move again sort of way. His mouth hung agape. His

Teddy Roosevelt moustache was untouched, however. Small mercies, Lovenight thought.

"I'll kill you for this," Lovenight said.

"I'll leave you two to get reacquainted," Sophie said, placing the severed head on the stainless-steel slab just beside Lovenight, the unfocused eye sockets gazing at him.

The self-interrogators left, flicking off the lights and shutting the heavy door, once again sealing Lovenight into total darkness. Immediately the micro-reapers buzzed to life, this time coming close and surrounding the slab in a bubble, almost daring Lovenight to try to escape. The whirling of their micron aerofoils created a thin breeze which cooled Lovenight's cheeks.

"Stop trifling with me!"

On a hopeless whim Lovenight tried to slipstream, once again seeing a sign in dark matter, which now read, THE BARONESS ZAMORA HOPES YOU ARE FINDING YOUR STAY IN HER EGO CITADEL DEMORALIZING AND SOUL-LEECHING. PLEASE TELL US HOW WE ARE DOING BY FILLING OUT THE INFORMATION CARD LOCATED IN YOUR LOWER SUBCONSCIOUS.

Something moved beside him in the dark.

Lovenight stiffened. He could hear a sort of sloppy, rolly noise, accompanied by tiny crunches and crackles. The something tugged at his wrist, or more precisely, the something tugged at the restraint around his wrist.

"Reg?" he whispered. "Is that you?"

The something made an echoey lapping sound, followed by a gruff wheeze, then the tugging continued.

"Reg? If that is you and you can't speak because you no longer have lungs or vocal cords or a voice box, tug the restraint once."

The tug came, strong and undeniable.

"Reg! How wonderful you're alive...I mean not dead...or I mean...! Anyway, its wonderful!"

Another strong tug came on the restraint.

"Are you trying, as I suspect, to chew through the restraint with your teeth?"

Another strong tug.

"Perfect. Do you have a plan to get past the swarm of angry

killer micro-reapers?"

Two tugs this time.

"Okay, two tugs means 'no', I'm assuming. Fine, Reg, you set your chompers to work and I'll find a way past the killer electronics."

The gentle gnawing sounds resumed. Lovenight relaxed back onto the cold steel slab, confident his luck was working, even though he was still naked, in the dark, with only a disembodied head for companionship, surrounded by micro-reapers.

Yes, things could only get better.

# CHAPTER TWENTY-TWO

-- SAME SECRET LAB IN MEXICO. STILL NOW --

    The robotic-incarceration transport trotted into the warehouse, articulated hooves clopping on the tiles. It resembled a mechanical deer; its legs spindly and fragile, its torso boxlike and long. In place of a head stood laser scanners mounted on stalks, sweeping the ground with ruby spiderwebs of light. On its back it carried a prisoner-restraint compartment which resembled a chrome sarcophagus -- fully customizable and air conditioned, of course. Four actuated tentacles controlled the position of the sarcophagus, allowing it to be carried horizontally or vertically. The sarcophagus stood upright, its face plate hinged open, allowing Lady Montique to see where the robot was taking her.
    She sucked her teeth at the ostentatious display before her.
    The warehouse was vast, easily as big as several airplane hangars stuck together, with rows of shipping containers and enough robots to start a revolution. Part of the secret lab, it functioned

as a supply and storage facility, keeping the lab fully stocked and providing a distribution terminal for whatever in God's name the Governance was producing here. Waiting for Lady Montique at the end of an automated assembly line was the baroness. Dr. Noor sat close by at a command console, enraptured by an inventory display as it updated.

Thousands of pharmaceutical glass vials containing a blue liquid rolled off the assembly line. Robots packed the blue vials in cryocoolers, then transferred the cryocoolers to self-driving skids, which whirred away only to be immediately replaced by more skids. The robots had their work cut out for them.

Baroness Zamora stabbed at the remote she held in her hand. The mechanical deer stopped before her.

"You always told me the most important part of any bedroom was its closet space," Baroness Zamora said, spreading her arms wide. "Well mother, what do you think of my closet?"

After taking it all in, Lady Montique sighed heavily. "Dear me, you've become a caricature."

"What was that, mother?"

"Look around, Lydia. You're standing in a secret genetics lab built into the side of the mountain: a more common trope of spy novels and comic books you'll not find! Next, you'll tell me all about your nefarious plans because your ego demands it."

"I will not!"

"You will."

"Will Not!"

"Will."

Baroness Zamora balled up her fists and squeezed her eyes shut. She hopped slightly. Her face tensed as if she were stifling a scream. After a moment, she opened her eyes.

"Stop psychoanalyzing everything I do, mother."

"I can't help it, Lydia. You're predictable."

"I hate you!"

"And now we arrive at the petulant explosion. Whatever it is you're doing, Lydia, stop."

A cruel grin snaked across the baroness's lips. "Why, mother, I'm simply finishing the work we started together. Isn't that what you want?"

"Lydia, this is not what I taught you!"

"The only lesson you ever taught me was selfishness. It was a good lesson, mother. And I learned it well." She walked over to a workbench and picked up one of the vials with a pair of tongs, holding it up for her mother to see. The vial glowed sapphire blue. "Do you know what this is, mother?"

"One can only hope it's your sanity and you will drink it immediately."

"Precisely what it is -- sanity! Sanity for the human race!" Baroness Zamora replaced the test tube in its rack. "Sanity, in the form of human DNA. An entirely rewritten string of genetic code, which when implanted into the humans will program them to obey our bloodline. Genetic obedience to us! Our descendants -- your descendants -- will rule humanity for all eternity. It will literally be in their DNA! Complete, unfailing, permanent obedience."

"Genetic obedience?" Lady Montique's eyes narrowed. "Unimaginable!"

"A new age of peace, order, and good government. If we say, 'This segment of the population will stop procreating', they will do just that. Unquestioningly. If we say, 'This segment of the population will cut their daily caloric intake by half', that is precisely what will happen. Think of it, mother! No more pandering and polling, no more politics behind a smokescreen of democracy or autocracy or what have you. No more wars to prop up public opinion. We rule, and they obey! Simple! It's what the vast majority of the populous want anyway, to serve their Governance, be fed, and entertained. It's peace, it's stability, all in one little DNA strand."

"Don't be absurd, Lydia. What you describe is stagnation. It's lobotomizing an entire species, everything that makes mankind great and prosperous."

"Wrong, mother! It's our only hope at surviving as a species. Humanity is the woolly mammoth in the room -- doomed to extinction because of our highly specialized evolution. You yourself told me our species would be short-lived. You were right, mother. At our current rate of consumption, we'll have depleted all natural resources the earth has to offer within a few hundred years. Air pollution will be toxic, pushing us to live underground. Tribalism will force us to wage war unending, until someone hits the nuclear buttons. Then, we're done." Baroness Zamora threw her arms back, indicating the warehouse behind her. "But this is our salvation! This is the end of our self-ruination. This is the start to a new epoch, when mankind will truly work together in harmony without the yoke of conflicting worldviews neutering us."

Lady Montique regarded her daughter with disbelief. "Even if your rewritten DNA code can do what you claim, you couldn't possibly go around splicing it into every individual's DNA. It's impractical."

"Wrong again, mother!" Baroness Zamora flounced across the lab, stopping before a shipping container.

"Stop being so lurid, Lydia," Lady Montique chastised. "You're like Bette Davis at a therapy session for the chronically melodramatic."

Ignoring her mother, Baroness Zamora opened the shipping container.

"Behold!"

"Behold what? I can't see a thing from this monstrosity you've caged me in."

Baroness Zamora grumbled, then fiddled with the remote for several seconds. The robot trotted over, allowing Lady Montique to peer in.

Hundreds of cryoboxes stacked on steel shelves stuffed the refrigerated container, each clearly labeled with shipping instructions printed in a dozen languages and alphabets. Baroness Zamora pointed to the first cryobox on the first shelf.

"This one is the first to be shipped, the very first, destined for the Weiner Fertility Clinic in Hamburg, Germany." She pointed to another. "That is heading to a sperm bank in Dublin, Ireland. We also have shipments heading to Dublin, California; Dublin, Australia; Dublin, Ohio. Who would have ever thought there were so many Dublins!" She traipsed down the aisle, calling out destinations as she went. "Over here we have shipments to Cape Town, Perth, Kalamazoo, Kuala Lumpur, Karachi, Harare, Bern. Hundreds of boxes, all destined to genetic labs, fertility clinics, sperm banks; any place man is using genetic science to aid with procreation or health. An existing distribution network ready and waiting to be hijacked! Don't you see the beauty of it, the simplicity? Of course you do, but you're too stubborn to admit it. My mutation will be sewn into every bit of human DNA which passes through those clinics, infecting patents across the globe. When those infected have children, it will be encoded into their genetic makeup. And by the time those children have grandchildren, humanity will have changed forever!"

"The Weiner Clinic in Hamburg," Lady Montique said in a chilled tone.

Baroness Zamora nodded, an odd mix of satisfaction and pain on her face. "Yes, mother. Oddly fitting, don't you think? The clinic where I was conceived will be ground zero for the mass alteration of human genetic code. My forced mutation will ensure we, as a species, survive long enough to solve the conundrums of space travel and colonization, thus ensuring our continued existence."

Lady Montique swallowed. "I had you because I wanted a child."

The baroness wheeled on her, spitting out words as fast as she could. "You wanted a bloodline! Having a child was the inconvenience which went along with it! You had me when you were seventy years old because you're a selfish, old harridan who couldn't face mortality and wanted to see herself carried on. Well, I've done it mother. I've given you exactly what you wanted!"

Something swirled in Lady Montique's face; resolve flashed in her eyes. "What have you done with my agents?" she asked.

"Your Outliers, as you call them? Gone. All of them. I swept them aside with a mere thought, as I could have done at any time in the past, had I wanted to. Yes, mother. I indulged your little band for years to keep you occupied. I've always found it's best to let you think you're running the show."

Before Lady Montique could say a word, Baroness Zamora tapped the remote and the face plate snapped shut, once again sealing her mother inside. The tentacles thrummed and shuddered, lowering the sarcophagus to a horizontal position.

Baroness Zamora loomed over the supine sarcophagus and said, "You go cool off for a while. We'll have another show-and-tell session soon."

A faint mumbling sound rumbled beneath the face plate. Baroness Zamora hit the remote and the face plate popped open.

"You wish to say something to me, mother?"

"Yes."

"Well," Baroness Zamora said smugly. "I'm waiting."

Staring straight into her daughter's eyes, Lady Montique said, "I told you you would reveal your nefarious plans because your ego demanded it."

# CHAPTER TWENTY-THREE

### -- A SLIPWAY, WHERE TIME IS IRRELEVANT --

Fat Cheeks was dead.

His lifeless body floated aimlessly in the tunnel-between-realities, like a soap bubble on a breezeless day. The face was slack, the eyes vacant, the cheeks sunken. Herb felt for a pulse and found none.

"I'm sorry, Noodles," Herb said, trying to comfort the pug. "I thought something was wrong back in the basement, the way he acted."

Noodles took a long moment before he shook his head and said, "Not your fault. It's all rotten, I tell ya. I'm going to find whatever did this and kill him, or her, or them, or it, or all of the above."

Noodles lingered by his assistant for several minutes, finally giving the dead musician a farewell lick on the cheek before joining Herb. Herb tried to comfort the pug by patting his head, but Noodles shied away.

"I don't need touching," Noodles growled. "Let's just go."

They drifted down the slipway in silence. The lights which

seemed to make up the slipway's walls pulsed and shifted, changing patterns and directions often; sometimes following them, sometimes streaking off further down the slipway. Sometimes the lights would form rings and revolve around them. Sometimes they expanded and stretched out into paisleys or stars or fish-shapes. It was like being inside a twisting kaleidoscope, Herb thought. He crossed his legs and folded his arms and let the current, or whatever it was, take him. Might as well enjoy the ride.

Eventually, Noodles shifted, turning to face Herb as they levitated along, sans gravity, sans up, sans down.

"Just how did your sociology major friend get this amulet, anyway?" Noodles asked. He indicated the slipway with a flick of his eyes. "This is some major occult squirrel-droppings, right here."

Herb shrugged. "Simon just kinda always showed up with cool junk. I thought his mom worked at a museum or something."

"And what? She brought home the leftovers?"

"Kinda."

"Herb, I love you; you know that. But you gotta ask more questions, especially when a friend has some major hyper-natural artifacts thousands of years old. You see what I'm saying?"

"Not really."

"Ya, I figured. Fuggetaboutit."

"Those balls of light, freaky man, the way they pulse. Any idea what they are?" Herb asked.

"You freaking think I know?" Noodles snapped. He took several sniffs, his nose twisting slightly. "Never been this far out before. I'm going to take a wild-and-slightly-educated guess and say we're somewhere between the corporeal and incorporeal, in the inflation field between universes. There's no smell, no temporal slipstreams, nothing on the electromagnetic spectrum. Those balls of light, they ain't light. I can sense the fiberons and flabberons in them, but they're like greased cats, impossible to get ahold of."

"Must be inflation field then," Herb said. "The more we go towards something, the farther away it gets! Noodles, we gotta get out of here."

"Might be kinda impossible."

"So we're stuck? Forever?"

"Well, kinda, but since there is no time here, or no 'here' for that matter, forever is a moot concept, get me?"

"No here and no forever," Herb said, trying to wrap his head around the concepts, trying to get some perspective, but nothing came. "It's too much, man."

"Keep it together, stoner-boy," Noodles said. "Find a goal, something to work towards. Focus on that and we'll get through this. I got mine, to kill whoever took over Fat Cheeks like that."

Herb nodded. There was something he needed to do. Something he was partially responsible for and it was up to him to fix it. "I gotta find Beth-Ann."

"There you go, trooper. Now let's go get it done."

With that, both the film student and the pug started dog-paddling through the inflation field, sans up, sans down, while the lights strobed on.

# CHAPTER TWENTY-FOUR

-- MICHOACÁN DESSERT, MEXICO. NOW --

Lovenight felt the blood rush back into his hand as the restraint around his wrist snapped with a final, mighty chomp from Reg.

"Exceptional, Reg," he whispered. Something cold and leathery bumped the back of Lovenight's hand in a rather modest, 'just doing my job', sort of way. "Now, to escape this peril!"

For several long moments he considered what to do next. Reg had done his part, freeing Lovenight's wrist from the restraint. Lovenight now had to formulate some plan to get them out of the torture room, reunite Reg's skull with his body, rescue Lady Montique, and get them all the hell out of there. Oh, but first he had to sneak past the swarm of micro-reapers ready to kill him if he twitched the wrong muscle.

The problem was he didn't have the faintest clue how to do any of that.

Even though his right hand was now free he dare not move it. Any unauthorized movement on his part would trigger heat/motion kill sensors inside the micro-reapers. They would immediately perforate him, burrow deep within his body, lodge themselves close to organs and arteries, and then self-detonate.

"This is a sticky peril, Reg."

Another bump on his hand. The droning hum of the micro-reapers squealed upwards in pitch as their micron aerofoils revved in anticipation.

"Don't move, Reg! You've picked up some residual body heat from me. You need to cool down, man!"

Several long, heart-thumping moments passed. The droning hum lowered in tone.

"That was close, too close. It's a pickle of a peril, let me tell you!"

Lovenight racked his brain for a plan. Nothing came. Which was a shame. But not unexpected.

He inhaled deeply and tried again, beginning with listing his assets, which turned out to be a rather short list consisting of having one free arm.

He then listed his liabilities; including being naked, restrained, without weapons of any kind, not being able to move his one free arm, surrounded by adversaries at every turn, and skipping lunch.

Best thing to do was trust his luck at this point. His luck always came through in the end. He relaxed, cleared his mind, and waited, giving his luck a chance to work.

The plan came to him in that instant. It landed fully formed and ready to execute. It was beautiful, it was simple, it was perfect, and it was unexpected. It was an epiphany of the highest magnitude, unmatched in the history of world, except for perhaps the invention of Velcro.

The torturers deactivated the micro-reapers when they entered, he had noticed. He would wait until one of them came within reach, then quickly overpower and subdue her with his one arm. Then, all he had to do was get clear of the room and the rest of the escape would be a stroll in the proverbial park.

"Start packing, Reg," he said cheerfully. "We won't be here for long." Then, because he felt compelled to clarify his statement, he added, "I mean that figuratively, Reg, of course. Don't move at all. You might still be packing residual body heat."

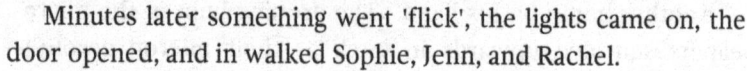

Minutes later something went 'flick', the lights came on, the door opened, and in walked Sophie, Jenn, and Rachel.

"Ready to continue your self-interrogation...oh dear," Jenn said. "You've tried to get free."

"No I haven't!" Lovenight said defensively.

"Yes, you have. Just look at that restraint! It's completely mangled."

"We'll have to replace that," Sophie said. "You've created a lot of extra work for us, Mr. Lovenight. Restraints like that don't grow on trees, you know."

A big black ball of dread welled up and surrounded Lovenight's heart. This peril was becoming imminent.

"Dear me, Mr. Lovenight," said Rachel coming closer but stopping well outside his limited range of motion. "We hoped you'd have reconciled yourself to the situation. Unfortunately, it's not to be. I'm afraid that means your self-interrogation is over and it's time for your self-termination."

"Look," Lovenight said, trying to sound reasonable and un-panicked when he was feeling anything but reasonable and un-panicked. "This wasn't my doing. It was Reg! You left the skull here and it just did what skulls want to do!"

Jenn glanced at Sophie, both of them looking utterly perplexed. Sophie pushed back her hair and said, "Skulls want to chew through restraints?"

"It's instinctual!" Lovenight insisted. "They need to chew on things; just like puppies, or nervous people, or beavers, or...or...Lithuanians. They can't help it!"

"That's the most imaginative excuse I've ever heard, Mr. Lovenight." Jenn said, pulling on a rather large set of rubber gloves up to her elbows. "Unfortunately, it's just that, an excuse. Rachel, if you would please."

"Think about this: I was restrained! How could I stop someone un-restraining me when I was restrained! I couldn't. I'm the restrained victim in all this."

"I'm so sorry, Mr. Lovenight," Rachel said, thumbing through apps on her mobile phone until she found the one controlling the micro-reapers. "I really had hoped we would get along."

"Look, perhaps we can discuss this first? Maybe get the speculum back and do some light interrogation at the same time?"

"Terribly sorry, but regulations are regulations. I'm sure you understand." With that, she swiped left.

The killer micro-reapers accelerated, rocketing through flesh at hundreds of points. In less than a tenth of a second they reached their targets and detonated explosive charges housed inside them.

All three interrogators dropped lifeless to the ground. It happened so quick they didn't even have time to look surprised.

Lovenight's eyes flicked back and forth several times trying to comprehend what had just happened. Slowly and carefully, he moved his arm. Nothing happened. Lovenight sighed with relief. He undid the remaining restraints and sat up on the table, searching for a reason behind this turn of events.

He didn't have to search for long.

Through the open doorway strode a robot resembling a deer carrying a chrome coffin on its back. Once inside, the coffin rose up like a metal spectre escaping the grave. The chrome visage hinged open revealing a scowling Lady Montique.

"Donkey!" she barked. "Don't just stand there with your mouth open. Pick up Reginald's head and let's be off!"

Lovenight padded down the cold, sterile hallway, Reg's head cradled in his arms. Despite his best efforts he was still naked as a newborn. In front of him the mechanical deer loped, leading the way. The articulated hooves clicked and hummed as it pranced along. It seemed joyful in a robotic sort of way, cavorting down the hallways of a secret laboratory, assisting in a clandestine escape. Yes indeed, the robotic deer was positively sunny when they stopped at the junction of two cross corridors.

"Which way, Reginald?" Lady Montique asked from her chrome coffin.

In response, Reg stuck out his blackened tongue, twisting it towards the left.

Lovenight shivered involuntarily. "This definitely wasn't in my job description."

"Thoughtless donkey!" Lady Montique chastised. "After the ordeal poor Reginald has undergone to save your worthless hide, you should be polite and humble, thanking him."

"It's like holding a fleshy football."

"Have some intestinal fortitude. Now, left you say, Reginald? Off we go."

The robot sidestepped merrily, then headed down the left branch of the corridor. Lovenight followed the machine, not so much because he wanted to, but because he had little choice in the matter. He quickened his pace and came up beside the robot.

"Look, if it's not too much trouble, do you think we could find some clothes for me along the way?"

"Always thinking of yourself! How selfish. Consider the good of the mission for a change, Eddie. Believe in something greater than yourself and then apply your efforts to it. It will make you a better person in the long run, let me assure you."

"I just want some pants!"

"Pants!" Lady Montique scoffed. "Such luxury."

"Look, by the way, let me ask you a question...not that I'm trying to segue out of this argument--"

"Which you are."

"Which I am," he conceded. "But regardless, how did you manage to redirect those micro-reapers? And come to think of it, how did you get away from the baroness after she encased you in this technological monstrosity?"

A thin smile twisted the corners of Lady Montique's wrinkled lips. "The poor dear, she thought she'd rendered me helpless having confiscated my truly universal remote. Disappointing, really. I expect better from my own flesh-and-blood. What she failed to realize is the truly universal remote wasn't the small decoy I carried around. The true T.U.R. is implanted inside me. It's imprinted on my spine. It's part of me, like my engaging personality. I can never be rid of it!"

Lovenight bit his tongue for a long moment before saying,

"Inside you there are bionics capable of hacking into any electronic device and controlling it? Bionic implants? Inside *you*? Any device! How?"

"Algorithms or A.Is or biotech hodge pokery, something along those lines. I didn't pay much attention to the hows and whyfors when the doctor-programmers explained it to me, I must confess."

"How does it work?"

"Simple. All I have to do is imagine a button for what I wish to happen, then I imagine pressing it. That's all. Of course, it takes time for these algorithm doodads to accomplish their hostile procurements, depending on the level of security trifles they must disable."

"Security trifles?"

"Oh, you know...fire curtains and re-bugging protocols and so forth. Technical jargon is beyond me."

"Obviously."

"So you see, when the baroness encased me in this robotic transport all I needed to do was wait until the T.U.R.'s offensive codes hacked and slashed their way passed enemy lines. Their mission accomplished, they flashed the 'all clear' in the corner of my mind's eye, *et voilà*, my very own automated palanquin!" Lady Montique paused, then said with a touch of whimsy, "I just might keep it. *Très élégant mais confortable.*"

Lovenight stopped. Reg's blackened tongue wiggled frantically, pointing to a set of double doors.

"I think this is us here."

"Splendid. Let's get Reginald's body back."

"And then?"

"Then, we must find this Mr. John H. Smith, and get him back to his office before the entire balance of the universe shifts and goes plunging into an oblivion, we'll never be able to escape from."

# CHAPTER TWENTY-FIVE

## -- REALLY, REALLY, REALLY UNKNOWN --

Eerie music spilled out from the cave at the top of the escarpment. The alien night sky above took no notice and continued in its unrelenting course. The rocky slope and ravaging wind also took no notice, none whatsoever.

The only one who did notice was Beth-Ann.

Beth-Ann peered into the cave, four moons wheeling across the night sky behind her. The cave was dark and only a few feet wide, more of a jagged fissure running back into the thickness of the ridge. She wondered why anyone would go into a cave with eerie music spilling out of it. That was just dumb. Teenagers-in-horror-movies dumb. Drivers-texting-while-driving dumb.

Still, there was something intriguing about this particular cave. It had a vibe. She was surprised that caves could even have a vibe. It gave off an "over-sized rabbit hole" vibe, rather than a "tiger's den with a glowing pair of eyes at the back" vibe.

A hot breeze blew sand into her face. What the heck, she thought. She stepped into the cave.

The air was damp and cooler than on the slope. In a way, it was refreshing. Beth-Ann carefully stepped deeper into the cave. The floor was flat and easy to walk on. After a dozen steps the fissure cut sharply to the right. A faint glow outlined the edges of the opening. Beth-Ann placed a hand on the slanted rock and peeked around the corner.

Bioluminescent rocks filled the cavernous space with greenish light. The rocks looked more like brain corals than limestone, with tight packed ridges and crinkles running over their domes. Above them, stalactites dripped condensation. How those brain-rocks had formed, Beth-Ann had no idea. Curious, she wandered deeper into the cavern, careful not to touch any of the delicate structures.

The floor sloped downwards, away from the desert night and the four moons. The air was fresh. The eerie music ebbed and flowed around the rocks, echoing loudly, then fading away. She felt a little afraid and a little brave at the same time. The greenish light threw her shadow up against the cavern wall, stretching it twice as high as she was. She pressed on, determined to find out where the music was coming from.

She emerged into a cavern the size of her classroom at school, a smokeless fire burning at the centre. Bright orange and yellow flames radiated a warm light. It warmed her heart to see it. At last, something normal, or close to normal that is.

Then she looked past the fire.

Near the rear of the cavern sat a girl with her back to Beth-Ann, staring at the stonewall. The rock was completely smooth, almost like a slate blackboard, creating a flatscreen for the fire-cast shadows to play over. The eerie music crescendoed, then receded to become a drone note, low but ever present. Even her band teacher, Mrs. Morton, would have been impressed with a controlled diminuendo like that. What made the music, Beth-Ann couldn't see.

"Hey," Beth-Ann said, by way of a greeting.

"Welcome to the Allegory of the Cave," the girl said, not turning around. Her voice echoed strangely, but not in a frightening way.

"What's that? Beth-Ann asked. "What's an allegory?"

"A thought experiment proposed by the philosopher Plato in his book *The Republic*, in which he compares humanity's perceived reality to shadows. I thought it might be appropriate for a meeting place."

Beth-Ann's face tightened with incredulity. "You're not a real girl, are you?"

The girl turned and Beth-Ann was surprised, but not shocked, to see her own face staring at her.

"No," the girl admitted. "I'm not."

"Thought so," Beth-Ann said smugly. "Nobody I know talks like that."

"Well then, perhaps you should meet more people."

At first, Beth-Ann suspected she was being ridiculed, but the girl's face remained impassive, completely lacking in guile. No, she wasn't being made fun of. It was an honest suggestion, and a good one the more she thought about it.

"What's your name?"

The girl thought for a moment, then said, "What would you like to call me?"

Since this was the most strange and bizarre encounter Beth-Ann had ever had in her twelve years of existence she said the most bizarre and strange name she could think of off the top of her head.

"Moist-Jujubes."

If the girl thought it was an odd name, she did not show it. She asked, "Is that one name, or two?"

"Make it hyphenated, like my name." Beth-Ann secretly hated her name. She thought it sounded stupid. Hillbillies on TV always had two names, like Billy-Bob, John-Boy, and Becky-Sue. She wished she had something cool and rich sounding for a name, like Téa or Gwyneth.

"All right," Moist-Jujubes said. "You may call me Moist-Jujubes."

Beth-Ann walked over to Moist-Jujubes and asked, "How come you look like me?"

"I have to look like somebody. Why not you?"

"It's creepy."

"Are you saying you find yourself creepy? An odd thing to

say, because something which is 'creepy' usually has an element of the unknown to it, a sliver of unfamiliarity. If you are saying you find my appearance creepy, then you are saying in effect parts of yourself are unknown to you and cause you to feel uncomfortable or mildly alarmed."

"That's not what I'm saying."

"But you just said you find my appearance creepy."

"Because you're exactly like me! Listen, forget it. I need to find a way home. Can you help me?"

Moist-Jujubes thought for a moment. "Difficult," she said finally.

"What's difficult?" asked Beth-Ann. "Either you know the way or you don't. Either you can help me find the way, or you can't."

"The question you pose is difficult because it is ambiguous. You say you 'need to find a way home' and can I 'help you'. What do you mean by 'home,' and 'help you'? And who will be the final judge to say if my intervention 'helped you' or not, or if you found 'home' or not? Do you really 'need to find a way', or not? The question you believe is simple is actually complex, with many facets and possible answers, depending on the meaning ascribed to the words."

This wasn't a dream, Beth-Ann was sure of that. No way she could dream up someone like Moist-Jujubes.

"Can you help me?" Beth-Ann asked.

"I can help you to find yourself, if that is what you want. And in finding yourself, you will find your way to what I believe you ascribe as your 'home'. But the question remains, will you like it?"

Beth-Ann stared at Moist-Jujubes, her lip trembling slightly.

Moist-Jujubes was not making fun of her or mocking her or teasing her. Moist-Jujubes was trying to help her. She truly believed that. Yeah, Moist-Jujubes was weird, but so what? Anyone who helped without asking for something in return, that was the true definition of what a friend was. Moist-Jujubes was her friend, a real friend, not like Lizzy Renfield and those popular girls letting her hang around just so they could make fun of her.

"I need help. I need to get home. I need to see mom and Mark again. Can you help?"

Moist-Jujubes nodded.

"Okay, then help. Please?"

Beth-Ann didn't have time to scream as Moist-Jujubes picked her up and tossed her into the fire.

# CHAPTER TWENTY-SIX

-- MICHOACÁN DESSERT, MEXICO. NOW --

Reg's body lay on an operating table, a Y-shaped incision running across his upper chest and down the centreline of his stomach, the resulting skin flaps pulled back and pinned open. It appeared the necro-autopsy was only half over, with several of his major organs in a neat line of jars on a shelf close-by. A bevy of fiberoptic cables, suction tubes, flexible magnetic endoscopes and startoscopes had been inserted into every orifice and incision.

Lovenight glanced sideways at Lady Montique. "That's a lot of work," he said drily. "Worse than Humpty Dumpty, if you ask me."

In protest, Reg's head -- still held by Lovenight -- thrashed its tongue about vigourously. It pointed in the direction of its body.

"Quite right, Reginald," Lady Montique said. "Now Eddie, enough of your griping. Fix Reginald immediately and let us be off."

"Prey tell, just how am I supposed to fix a headless corpse?"

"Oh, don't be so contrary, Eddie. Smartly now!"

Lovenight sighed and shuffled forward obediently. He placed Reg's head down next to its body and began searching for something that might help, opening drawers and cabinets, checking in closets, unlatching storage containers. He popped the top off one plastic bin and relief washed over his face.

"What have you found?"

"Something to restore my dignity! A set of surgical scrubs complete with smock! And plasticky sandals for my feet! Huzzah!"

Lady Montique scoffed. "It would take rescuing forty toddlers from a burning orphanage to restore your dignity, and then only if you had the decency to die of smoke inhalation immediately afterwards."

Lovenight pulled on the loose fitting scrubs and slipped into the foam resin sandals. He quickly tied the smock, then cooed appreciatively, wriggling his fingers with delight.

"Ooo, there's nothing like the feeling of over-washed cotton against the skin."

"Stop playing, donkey!"

Lovenight scrutinized every detail of the canopic jars and their corresponding organs. He checked each hose and tube entering Reg's corpse, tracing them back to the machines they originated from. He surveyed the damage done to the neck and open chest cavity. After several moments he realized he had no idea what he was doing. He decided to wing it, hoping luck would save him.

He began yanking cables out of Reg's open neck.

"Donkey! Don't bruise anything that shouldn't be bruised!"

"Just exploratory cameras and such. Nothing to worry about. Easily taken care of." The last cable came free with a wet, sucking sound. It fell to the floor, glistening with some bodily fluid or another. Lovenight said, "Bloody hell, what a mess."

"Fix him!"

"How? It's like trying to put paper towel back on the roll after the dog's eaten it."

"He saved you, now you save him. You owe Reginald that."

Lovenight hated to admit when someone had a fair and reasonable point. So he didn't. Instead, he grumbled. Reg's head stared at him expectantly.

"Oh, bloody hell. Don't blame me if this is one big cock-up."

He fitted Reg's head back on its body, gently pushing the ends of the spinal column back into place, inserting one end of the esophagus into the other, coaxing arteries, ganglion, tendons and muscle fibres together, making sure those pesky lymph nodes didn't fall out. Afterwards, he dumped the contents of the canopic jars back into the open torso, unpinned the skin flaps, and folded them back in place.

"There," he said, checking his work. "Now we wait."

The severed tissues struggled to reattach themselves, reaching out and making contact with their fellows, trying to find the position they occupied in life, all part of the Necronominal Probability Placement effect Niels Bohr had described to Reg.

"*Tempus fugit*, Edmund," Lady Montique said.

"Judging by the rate these tissues are knitting themselves back together, we'll be here all day."

Lady Montique frowned. "Do your best. Try to make Reginald look not so much like a..."

"A half-eaten shepherd's pie?"

"Exactly."

Desperate, Lovenight searched for something that might help. He rifled through a series of stainless-steel cabinets, pulling out drawers and opening cupboards.

"Brilliant! This should do the trick!"

"What have you found, Eddie?"

Lovenight held up a rectangular piece of greyish tissue pulled from a surgical tray. "Sterilized sheets of tilapia skin. Great for burn victims and..uhm...severed heads."

"Dear me. It puts me in mind of the slimy film which develops on top of tapioca pudding if you leave it out overnight. How do you know it's tilapia skin?"

"It's labeled, STERILIZED SHEETS OF TILAPIA SKIN."

He placed the sheets over every laceration on the corpse, tacking it down with adhesive. After a few minutes, layers of the fatty skin covered Reg's neck and chest like a gelatinous dicky.

"There," Lovenight said, standing up to survey his work. "That should hold, at least until the Necronominal Probability Placement thingy has had a chance to work." He picked up Reg, slung him over one shoulder, and carried him over to the robotic deer, laying him across its back. He then picked a storage bin containing the cabbie's clothes and cap and placed it beside the corpse.

"Fine work," Lady Montique said. "Now, let us find John H. Smith and be off!"

Lady Montique led the way through the endless steel and glass corridors, riding her robotic deer like Joan of Arc atop a white strider -- if, let's say, Joan had been over one hundred years old and her white strider wasn't in fact white but burnished chrome and not a horse but a robot, then Lady Montique would have looked *exactly* like Joan. Or Joan would have looked like her. Nevertheless, she, Lady Montique, led the way, confidently, boldly, without hesitation.

Lovenight was so bewildered by the constantly twisting and crossing passageways his head spun. Of course, that could have also been the lack of alcohol in his system.

"Keep up, Edmund."

"I'm trying. Do you even know where you're going?"

"Of course I know where I'm going. I know exactly where I'm going."

"Good. I'm glad you do, because I haven't been this lost since waking up in a Byzantine whorehouse."

The further they went, the more tangled Lovenight's sense-of-direction became. Each corridor serviced multiple floors. Depending on the corridor you turned down or the door you opened or the stairs you took, you were confronted with stairs or another door or another corridor or sometimes all three. Lovenight jogged along behind the robotic deer as it opened doors and traveled down stairs to find ramps leading to more doors which led to more corridors. Daedalus would have gotten a headache just looking at the architectural drawings.

"You're sure you know where you're going?" Lovenight asked, hoofing it through a tunnel which connected two hallways.

Lady Montique scowled at him. "Why do you think I hid in that retirement home? For the mushy peas and watery tea? Certainly not. I spent years leeching off their wifi network; monitoring the Governance's communications, reconnoitring electronically, finding as much information on the baroness as I could. This secret laboratory was one of the subjects of my attention. I know every security feature they've changed, and at least three ways to circumvent each one. That's how I found you, Eddie. And that's how I know there is only one room in this facility capable of holding a being as powerful as a Paragon of Reality."

A door in the curving wall ahead of them opened and out stepped an aging hippy wearing a Hawaiian shirt and shorts, with a mane of completely-white hair which frizzed out and surrounded his head in a rough halo. As soon as the hippy spotted the robotic deer he froze. His bushy white eyebrows shot upwards, completely submerging themselves under his frizzy bangs.

"Off with ya," he said in a heavy Glaswegian accent, shooing the robot away with small waves from both his hands. It didn't sound like a command, more like someone trying to avoid an unwanted friend they found particularly creepy.

"Apprehend him, Eddie! Before he raises the alarm!"

The aging hippy looked even more baffled and confused. "There's an alarm?" he asked, then ducked back through the door. Lovenight leapt and grabbed the handle, preventing the door from closing. Both men struggled and strained, pulling as hard as they could.

"Donkey!" Lady Montique yelled. "Must I do everything myself?"

The robotic deer trotted up and peeled the door backwards, warping the metal so badly it would never close again. The hippy stood exposed for a moment, dazed, his fizzed-out hair jiggling, then he bolted. Lovenight sprinted after him.

Instincts told Lovenight if something was running away from him, everything was right with the world. It meant whatever was running was scared. Lovenight liked things that were scared of him. Things that ran toward him were a lot more complicated.

Lovenight's rather simplistic notions of people running away from him were shattered when the hippy turned suddenly, a large machete in his hand.

"Right, you're asking for it, you are," the hippy said.

Unfortunately, Lovenight was unable to decelerate. He crashed into the hippy, knocking them both to the ground. For a moment Lovenight's vision was completely obscured by fizzy grey hair; then he was straddling the hippy's belly, one hand locked on the wrist holding the machete, his other forearm across the hippy's neck.

"Get off me, ya tosser."

"Drop the machete."

"Aye, sure. If that's what it takes."

The hippy dropped the machete, the blade clattering on the floor. Lovenight got to his feet, wrenching the hippy up with him.

"Don't trifle with me!" Lovenight said. "I'm not someone to be trifled with!"

"If you say."

"I do say. Now, here's what's going to happen--"

"Look, I'm going to stop you right there, big man," the hippy said. His accent was so thick and he spoke so rapidly Lovenight strained to understand what he was saying. "This will go much quicker if we just assume you'll threaten me with nasty things I don't want to happen, and I capitulate immediately. So, just tell me what you want and I'll do it. That way we can dispense with the nasty things, get out of each other's lives much quicker, and everyone's happy. Right?"

Lovenight paused for a moment, uncertain what to say to such an obliging captive. "So, right. Good then. No need for the standard turning-of-the-screws. Good. Okay. So, so, so..."

"Donkey!" Lady Montique trotted up. Several tonnes of heavy machinery balanced on four spindly legs was intimidating in itself, but when combined with the visage of Lady Montique, it was the equivalent to a very sharp hedge trimmer held over one's naughty bits.

"I think I've just wee'd me-self," the hippy squeaked.

"Take us to where they are holding John H. Smith," Lady Montique commanded.

# CHAPTER TWENTY-SEVEN

## -- THE REALLY, REALLY, REALLY UNKNOWN FROM BEFORE --

Both Mark and Simon assisted Mrs. Büdenbender as she struggled up the dusty red slope towards the cave. Above them, four moons loomed large in the purple-night sky. The fact there were four moons in the night sky would have amazed and alarmed each of them at any other time; however, seeing as Mrs. Büdenbender had recently fused with the man in the black suit creating an X-shaped human being, and seeing as the man in the black suit had then died mysteriously -- well, that was enough to numb anyone's holy-crap sensors.

A hot wind blew across the slope, belting them with grains of sand. Eerie music droned across the landscape, sounding like a thousand muted trumpets lamenting the loss of the woodwind section. With each step Mrs. Büdenbender winced, her features squeezed with pain. Simply walking was proving difficult, even with Mark and Simon assisting her. Her normally jovial face remained tensed and sweat-covered.

"You all right, mom?" Mark asked after one particularly sharp inhalation.

"I think his spine is resting on my sciatic nerve. I've got shooting pains all down my legs."

Simon hefted up the two legs he held, which protruded from Mrs. Büdenbender's hip at a downward angle, taking more of the weight, while Mark slightly lowered the limp torso he carried.

"That better?" Simon asked.

"Slightly, yes. Thank you." A giggle escaped her lips.

"What's funny, mom?" Mark asked.

"There was this cartoon you used to watch when you and Beth-Ann were kids, with dancing numbers and letters. It just struck me: I'm the human X." She laughed again. Mark and Simon laughed with her, a tinge of hysteria sharpening their shared mirth.

They laboured upwards towards the top of the escarpment.

Fragments of bizarre and alien memories flooded Mrs. Büdenbender's mind. The source was evident to her: they belonged to the man in the black suit. His body was dead, but his brain continued to hold the map of the man, all those worn synaptic grooves still trying to fire, bits of stray electrochemical energy drifting out hitting Mrs. Büdenbender with odd remembrances. The feeling was like deja vu combined with a dull headache.

There were memories of this slope, that cave, those moons, and ten thousand other fantastic landscapes: a giant monolith rising from a silvery pool surrounded by pink skies and lavender trees, man-sized crabs with exoskeletons of rock crawling along a passageway under the sea, tunnels of honeycombed lights stretching to infinity; and one specific memory which Mrs. Büdenbender found disturbing -- standing in front of a bonfire of bones, the radiant heat pressing against his/her skin, and the enormity of knowing you could be everywhere at once.

It was that memory which had brought Mrs. Büdenbender, her son Mark, and his friend Simon, here.

Back in her basement, after the man in the black suit died

drinking a glass of water, the memory of being everywhere at once leaked into her mind. Suddenly she understood his 'museum' with its interconnected galleries.

All those galleries, those universes, blinking and vibrating and bouncing off one another, or ignoring each other, or combining together. Those galleries were leaving, slipping outside the inflation field, slowly for now, but at some point in the future they would reach a critical state and leave en masse within a billionth of a second. That would be the end of everything, the universe popping like a cheap balloon.

But that wasn't all the man in the black suit's memory had to share. There were other things, two of which were of monumental importance to her.

The first was the man in the black suit hated his museum and wished for its destruction.

The second was where Beth-Ann had gone.

"Simon, I want you to understand I'm not mad."

"Okay, Mrs. B," Simon said, then paused, then warily asked, "Not mad about what?"

"That you brought an inflation-slipway into my house."

"A what?"

"The amulet you placed at the bottom of the censer."

Simon looked as if a trout had suddenly materialized in his underwear. "Oh, that."

Mrs. Büdenbender searched the foreign memories for a name. "It's called The Amulet of Amon'Zul, the Opener of Closed Ways."

"I...did not know that. The book said to put it in the censer so the smoke would be sanctified."

"What the smoke did was flood the immediate space-time with charged inflation-ions," Mrs. Büdenbender said, not really understanding the words which slipped into her mouth from the alien memories. "It allowed the locality to be universal."

"What does that mean, mom?" Mark asked.

"It's how we travelled here. The inflation-ions touched every point in the universe directly, not by proxy. It allowed us to follow Beth-Ann here, just by you touching me, and me taking a step."

"Great." Mark shifted his grip on the limp torso protruding from his mother as he stepped over a slate outcropping. "We find Beth-Ann and go back the same way."

"Where is Herb?" Mrs. Bündenbender asked as they crested the ridge of the escarpment.

"He left soon after Beth-Ann vanished," Mark answered. " He said he was going to get help."

"Dear me," Mrs. Bündenbender said. "I hope he's not gotten into more trouble."

"I wouldn't worry about it, Mrs. B.," Simon said. "He was pretty wasted at the time."

"That's not very comforting, Simon."

Mrs Bündenbender, Mark, and Simon paused for a moment at the cave mouth, listening to the direful music. Mark drew in ragged breaths that wheezed in the hollow of his chest.

"Mark, your asthma," Mrs. Büdenbender said.

"Yep, it's still there," Mark quipped.

"Very funny. Simon?"

"Still here."

Mrs. Büdenbender inhaled deeply. "All right, then. Let's go see what we shall see."

Together, they entered the cave.

The trio emerged into the small cavern about the size of a primary school classroom. There appeared to be the remains of a bonfire in the centre of the cavern's floor, with several benches encircling it ready for a sing-a-long if one happened to break out. Instead of a bonfire, a flame -- not much bigger than a candle's -- burned amoungst the charred embers. Its light glinted off the cavern's walls.

As they got closer, the flame began to sing. There were no words to the song, just a tuneless melody which meandered up and down. It was a tune sung by a little girl while playing alone. It was Beth-Ann.

"Beth-Ann!" Mrs. Büdenbender cried, addressing the tiny fire.

"Where are you? It's mommy! I'm here baby, I've come for you." The tuneless melody echoed throughout the cavern. Mrs. Büdenbender frantically looked around, trying to locate her daughter. "Beth-Ann, answer me!"

*She cannot hear you.*

Those words were spoken by a voice that wasn't a voice. It was a vibration, a feeling, a pressure close to the ear. The voice, which wasn't a voice, sounded like deep water whispering to them.

Mrs. Büdenbender turned about savagely. "Where is she?"

*She is beyond.*

"What do you mean, 'beyond'?"

*She is beyond heat; she is beyond motion. She is beyond this step.*

"What's she doing there?" Mrs. Büdenbender asked.

*She's trying to get back to you.*

"That doesn't make any sense! Make sense!"

*Because it doesn't make sense to your limited senses doesn't mean it doesn't make sense.*

Mrs. Büdenbender rested her hands across her prodigious bosom, and said quietly, "Who are you?"

Whoever it was fell silent for a moment.

*That is a complicated question.*

"Now you listen here. That's my daughter, singing. She does that when she feels alone or scared, which means she needs me. I need straight, simple answers, and I need them now!"

*I will attempt to give you what you ask for.*

"Good. Now, who are you?"

There followed another pause, and then, *I was, for a brief moment, Moist-Jujubes.*

Simon turned to Mark. By the thin light of the flickering flame Mark could just make out the incredulous look on Simon's face as he mouthed the question, *Moist-Jujubes?* Mark shrugged.

"All right, Mr. Jujubes," Mrs. Büdenbender said, her voice ringing with resolve. "Please tell me what you are."

*I am Everything. I am here at the beginning of heat and at the end. I am what is left over. I am what waits an infinity for infinity to end and begin again. I am the Cycle. I am what is beyond and what is near.*

"I didn't understand most of that, but thank you for trying. You're beyond, so you're where my daughter is?"

*Correct, in the most limited fashion.*

"Can you tell me what's happened to my daughter?"

*She was cast into the Universal Fire, the Navel of the Universe, and has been trapped by the Gambrel.*

"She was cast into a fire!" exclaimed Mrs. Büdenbender.

*It's not as you think.*

"Who is the Gambrel?"

*It is an entity born from the interplay of forces within me. One of the Seventy-and-Seven. It is their perspective of me, who is also me, myself to myself, which translates me into your illusion of me, your illusion of us. The Seventy-and-Seven are offshoots of myself, myself critiquing myself. Each is unique.*

"Nope," Simon said, throwing up his hands. "Completely lost now."

Mark smacked him hard on the shoulder. "Of course! From the book, *Pax Arcana*. 'And the number of Paragons of Reality shall be seven hundred and seven'. See? Seventy and seven - seven, zero, seven. Seven hundred and seven!"

*All you truly need to know about the entity who has trapped Beth-Ann is he took the name for himself: The Gambrel.*

Mark appeared puzzled. "Isn't that a kind of roof?"

"It's also the hook butchers hang meat on," Simon said. "My dad has one at his shop."

"So this guy is a meathook?"

Simon shook his head. "This guy hangs the meat he slaughters, and he's got Beth-Ann."

Mrs. Büdenbender's face blanched. "What does this Gambrel want? Why is it holding my Beth-Ann?"

*It wishes to be unopposed by the others of the Seventy-and-Seven. It yearns for autonomy. It can accomplish that by using your daughter as the link.*

"The link? The link to what?"

*To link itself to transformation, to become...me.*

"Somehow I can't help but feel that would be a bad thing," Mark said.

Mrs. Büdenbender waddled forward. "How can I get to her?"

*There is no way.*

"Horse hockey! If she got there, wherever she is, I can too."

*Any attempt to reach her now would allow the Gambrel to completely assimilate her. She would then be part of him, and he would usurp me, become me. All would be lost.*

"What can I do?"

*The question is wrong.*

Mrs. Büdenbender thought for a moment, then asked, "Is there anything anyone can do?"

*Yes. What is it you want?*

"I want my Beth-Ann back."

*Then you must wait, and be ready to act.*

Mark's arms shot outwards catching everyone's attention, which is why he shot them out in the first place. "Hey! You hear that?" he asked.

They listened intently for several seconds.

"Oh no," Mrs Büdenbender said when she realized what Mark had found.

The fire was silent. They could no longer hear Beth-Ann singing.

# CHAPTER TWENTY-EIGHT

## -- MICHOACÁN DESSERT, MEXICO. NOW --

The robotic deer coaxed the cell door open by wrenching it off its hinges. The sound of tearing metal echoed down the hallway as the door sundered and gave up hope of ever being a door again. The robotic deer tossed it aside.

John H. Smith looked mildly surprised as he stood up in the cell. Shackles around his wrists and ankles restrained the Paragon of Reality. He pushed his glasses farther back, magnifying his brown eyes to the size of a baby koala's. He blinked rapidly several times before saying, "Can I interest you in a reasonably priced back-split, close to good schools and transit?"

"Stop it!" Lovenight ordered, checking the corners of the cell. "Again, you're trying to be normal in an entirely abnormal situation. Which is weird. Not normal."

"Sorry," John H. Smith said meekly. "Force of habit."

Lady Montique trotted the robotic deer over to Mr. Smith who obligingly stood still as she clipped his chains in two. Mr. Smith rubbed his wrists.

"We should get back to the office as quickly as we can. No

telling what will happen to the counterbalance when I'm not there. Must make sure everything is perfectly normal. Dear me, I've lost all track of time. Any idea how long we've been in here?"

"Seventeen hours and thirteen minutes, or thereabouts," Lady Montique said.

"Dear me, we must get back. That's far too long." John H. Smith looked about nervously. "If I'm not there, problems start cropping up, and then problems compound problems, until whole systems begin to fail, star systems collapse, celebrities double-down on juice cleanses. And then, slippery times...oh my!"

Without any warning, he sprinted off down the corridor.

His mild manner and perfectly normal appearance belied the paragon's speed. John H. Smith ran like a squirrel, burning around corners, accelerating in the straights, every limb stretching and pushing in perfect balance, efficiently, effectively. Not a calorie of energy was wasted. Head up, chin down, arms pumping at his sides, the shackles around his wrists and ankles clattering as he sped along.

"Bugger!" Lovenight exclaimed. "I've never seen a man run so fast...in a cardigan!"

"Donkey! After him!"

Lovenight went flat out. His foam resin slippers squeaked as he banked a corner and sprinted after the paragon. Running was something he was unaccustomed to these days. Normally, he would slipstream up behind an adversary. He wasn't making any headway with this conventional running. He struggled just to keep the paragon in sight. His thighs burned. His lungs ached. In his mind he hurled a string of profanities at the paragon's back but didn't dare waste a drop of breath to spit one out.

John H. Smith dashed through a T-Junction, turned right, then stopped abruptly.

Which was lucky because at that moment Lovenight's exertion caused him to throw a sandal. He fell into a tumbling heap, rolling several times, flopping flat out on the floor before the realtor's loafers.

"You bloody bastard," he managed to say between heaving breaths.

John H. Smith said nothing, just continued to stare out a

window. Outside the late afternoon sun drew long, spiky shadows on the hills. Sun-scorched scrub and cacti cluttered the ground as far as the eye could see. The land itself looked bitter and twisted by the unrelenting heat.

The robotic deer trotted up, Reg still slung over its back, the metal sarcophagus upright.

"Where are we?" the realtor asked.

Lady Montique answered, "In a secret, underground genetic research facility in the Sierra Madres, close to the Pacific coast. Well, this part isn't so underground, obviously, but we had to let some natural light in somewhere."

An alarm went off deep in the recesses of Lovenight's brain; a wiggling, niggling alarm which refused to shut up even when he pretended not to notice it. Much to the chagrin of every sensible fibre of his being, he asked, "What do you mean, 'we had to let some natural light in'?"

For the briefest moment Lady Montique looked ashamed, then confessed, "I authorized the construction of this lab back when I founded the Governance." She shrugged, ever so slightly. "By taking the organization as far as I did, however noble my initial intentions, it became an amoral tool of absolute dominance, a fascist abomination of my own making. Then I had a revelation. A Saul-on-the-road-to-Damascus moment, and I founded the Outliers to oppose the Governance. I left, but my daughter stayed and took over my position. I pleaded with her to abandon the Governance. My deepest regret in life is I could not convince her. She vowed to soldier on, trying to corral humanity for the sake of its own existence, and I vowed to tear down all we had built together."

Lovenight's mouth hung open as if he was trying to stuff all the conflicting emotions in his brain into one bitesized mouthful and then spit it out, but the emotions were just too darn weighty and voluminous. So instead, he settled on a default response he often employed when flummoxed.

Lovenight blew a raspberry.

John H. Smith completely ignored Lady Montique's revelation and asked the rather odd question, "How did we get to Mexico so fast?"

"There's a private airstrip ten minutes north the Governance uses," Lady Montique answered. "It has several sub-orbital jets which reach into the stratosphere."

"How do we get back to my office, 4,000 kilometres away?"

"Tell me, Mr. Smith, have you ever been flash-evolved into a sentient insectiod, stowed away in the belly of a robotic deer, then hijacked an extremely sophisticated and experimental sub-orbital jet?"

"Not really, no."

"Well, there's a first time for everything, isn't there?"

As the illusionary monarch butterflies disappeared, the cockroaches scampered toward the darkness in a corner of the metal box. One cockroach, who was vastly more contrary than the rest, noted there was an additional member in their meagre swarm. This new member appeared ordinary in every way, looking like it would be completely at home foraging behind a water cooler or in a copier room dustbin. The contrary cockroach instantly distrusted him.

He is too stable, the contrary cockroach thought. He will trifle with me. I will not be trifled with!

"To the darkness!" the alpha commanded.

"The darkness! The blessed darkness!" the swarm echoed and followed her between a crack in the metal plates, squeezing down past hot electronic motherboards and coils of copper wire. Rods and gears whirled and spun, forcing the swarm to dodge and side-step around the dangerous metal. One swarm member rested on the back of the alpha. That one had a dead taste to him. The contrary one felt sorry for it, but still wanted to eat it.

"Nest here!" the alpha said, stopping in a chrome hollow formed at the intersection of a drive shaft and a micro-gear box. She let the dead tasting one rest against the metal cover and raised her wings, exposing her internal membranes in an attempt to cool herself.

Unfortunately, the contrary cockroach mistook her raised

wings as a signal to begin mating.

Something about mating with the alpha deeply disturbed the contrary cockroach, to the point where it wished to gnaw off its own genital pouch in a desperate attempt to avoid copulation. However, the biological drive to reproduce overrode its own base prejudices.

"Let mating commence!" it screeched as it backed into the alpha, attempting to initiate lovemaking. It was swiftly kicked away for its troubles.

"Donkey!"

The contrary cockroach felt great relief in having been rebuffed.

The swarm waited as the alpha poked imaginary buttons hanging in the air, performing a strange ritual. The metal hollow universe shook and rattled. Somehow the alpha controlled the metal universe, making it shudder and bellow. They waited patiently. Time dribbled past in big fat droplets. For the cockroaches it was mildly boring.

They sensed great momentum and pressure changing. They sensed coldness, then heat. They felt sustained acceleration and speed. For a long time, they did nothing but wait in the metal hollow as it flew. They waited so long the cockroach with the dead taste didn't taste as dead as it did before. It raised itself up on its own segmented legs and shook itself.

The contrary cockroach felt glad.

Finally, the metal hollow universe decelerated, shuddered violently, then stopped. Silence crept in. Pushing away from the corner, the alpha crawled upwards along a metal filament, yelling, "Escape the metal!"

"Escape the metal!" the swarm chorused.

Gears and actuators paused as the swarm passed by, one by one squeezing their way into the brightness atop the metal universe. Once outside their exoskeletons liquified. They transformed into hungry glowing balls of matter, sucking energy and mass from the immediate environs, growing in nanoseconds into their human forms.

Lovenight retained the distinct memory of trying to copulate with Lady Montique.

"Ewwww!" he howled.

"Disgusting, filthy donkey!" she cried.

They stood in the parking lot next to Lady Montique's 1936 Stout Scarab. Things had changed in the forty-one hours since they had been abducted from the Paragons of Realty offices.

Lovenight glanced around at the odd collection of vehicles in the parking lot, gawping at the rickshaws, golf carts, red rocket scooters, stagecoaches, Egyptian chariots, tricycles, double decker buses, and formula one race cars. There was even a panzer tank trying to blend in between two vintage Italian vespas.

"What the bloody hell is going on?" he asked.

"The balance," John H. Smith said, his voice breathy and strained. "It's completely off."

The office building they had been abducted from forty-one hours ago had undergone a sea-change. The building now resembled pulled taffy: a stretched, modernist, twisted-lollipop-of-a-building straight out of Frank Gehry's nightmares. It would have taken a drugged-out 60's love child versed in draughtsmanship and astral projection to draw its floor plan.

Gone were Xavier's Inline Dentures, the Xenophobic Driving School, Xenomorph's Duct Cleaning, X-Ray's by Ray, the Xylophone Emporium, Xerxes' Frozen Meats, Xanadu Imports (honeydew a specialty), and XXX Ribs and Wings. A whole new set of business had replaced them, their names both telling and disturbing: Alba Salix's Academy of Performance Art, Ambidextrous Anonymous, Abe's D.I.Y Calligraphy, the Aardvark Preservation Society, Á La Mode Commodes, Aerosols for All Occasions, Aerobic Auctions (Bid While You Work Out), Arks by Noah, and Adam's Rib Restaurant.

It gave Lovenight vertigo just looking at it.

"Bloody hell," he said. "That's marvellous."

# CHAPTER TWENTY-NINE

-- MICHOACÁN DESSERT, MEXICO. NOW-ISH --

Baroness Zamora and Dr. Noor stood in the doorway of the self-torture chamber, examining the scene before them.

The three dead bodies of the self-inquisitors lay close together. It appeared they had died at the same instant, falling lifeless to the ground. The interrogation table was empty, one of the restraints frayed and broken. The micro-reapers were spent.

"Interesting," Dr. Noor noted.

Baroness Zamora no longer felt the temporal slip-streamer butting up against her ego citadel. Her robotic incarceration transport no longer responded to her electronic summons. There was no psionic residue, no incorporeal exhaust, nothing.

Which meant the slip-streamer and her mother were no longer inside the complex.

The baroness seethed.

Somehow that vile, loathsome, fossilized human being, which due to an unfortunate accident of genetics happened to be her mother, that antediluvian shrew had managed to escape and rescue the others. It happened every time. Every time. It was infuriating. No matter, she would soon recapture her harpy-mother and then things would be different. No more trusting mere machines with her imprisonment. Next time she would be personally involved, every moment of the day.

"Come," she said to Dr. Noor, turning on her heel and hurrying off.

"Another problem?" Dr. Noor asked.

"They might have taken the realtor."

Robotic servers skimmed out of their way as the pair rushed past loading bays filled with refrigerated cargo containers. A small message-bot with a defective servo clipped the baroness's heels as it scrambled to get out of her way. The baroness shot it a look. There was a loud snapping sound as its motherboard cracked, crushed by the baroness's trans-kinetic fingers. The message-bot ground to a halt. A tendril of white smoke snaked up from its sparking ruin.

"Remind me to have Ned clean that up," the baroness said.

"Certainly," Dr. Noor replied.

Baroness Zamora strode around a corner, stopping abruptly, causing Dr. Noor to stiffen to avoid bumping into her. It took several moments and a dozen rapid eye blinks for her brain to comprehend what she was seeing.

Several strips of metal plating had been peeled away from the walls, balled up like layers of tissue paper, and left in the middle of the hallway. Ned's head poked out from the top of the metal pile. The scrunched and crimped-together plates formed a crude cocoon around the Glaswegian, immobilizing him. His face was a mixture of embarrassment, frustration, and resignation. Life was just not going to let up on him today.

"Hey ya," he said nonchalantly.

"What happened?" the baroness demanded.

"What happened? I'll tell ya what happened! Some scary-as-shite gorgon riding a metal hellhound trots up, corpse slung across the metallic demon, a rather cheeky bastard wearing scrubs as her point man. This gorgon threatens me with great physical violence then asks me to take her to the wanker with the wide glasses. Then she leaves me like this. That's what happened."

"And you took her to the Paragon of Reality?"

Ned's eyebrows furrowed together, creating more wrinkles than contained in a spinster's armpit. "You see what she did here, right? Made freaking origami out of half-inch stainless steel plate! Can you imagine what she'd have done to me bones? I would have taken her to Mother Teresa's tomb if she'd asked me."

Dr. Noor raised a hand and interjected, "So, for you, the threat of immediate physical violence, whether legitimate or not, outweighs the promise of delayed punitive action from your employer?"

"Aye, that's about right. For a coward like me, yeah."

"Interesting," she said. "I think we'll have to open up that brain of yours and examine the decision-making centres when exposed to various stimuli."

"Thanks for the offer, but my weekends are full-up."

Baroness Zamora held out a firm hand, silencing both of them. "Status report on genetics?"

Dr. Noor shrugged. "Complete, ready for shipping."

"Status report on shipping?"

Ned tried to shrug but the twisted metal stopped his shoulders. "Well, the work's been piling up since I've been tinned like a herring, if you get my meaning."

"I do, I do," the baroness said. "The message is very clear."

Dr. Noor's mouth stretched wide as her eyelids opened to their fullest. Her breathing accelerated, became almost a pant. Her face blanched. For a long moment she remained motionless, mouth gaping wide, then crumpled in a heap.

Baroness Zamora removed her trans-kinetic fingers from around Dr. Noor's carotid arteries.

"I'll send a robot to pry you out," the baroness said to Ned. "Clear the shipping backlog as quickly as possible and clean up this mess."

With that she whisked off down the corridor and was gone.

"Scary as shite," Ned whispered to himself.

It was then he felt the itch. An annoying, persistent, mind-engrossing itch; situated smack dab on the side of his right nostril. The itch grew, intensified. He tried blowing upwards at it. He tried not to think about it. He tried to move his neck to scratch it against a metal shard which remained maddeningly out of reach. Nothing worked. This itch revelled in his ineffective attempts to counter it, damn the thing. It pirouetted in celebration, burrowing deeper.

"Shite! Shite! Shite!"

He yelled down the corridor in the direction the baroness had gone. "Hey, could ya hurry up with those wankface robots? And send some face creme, or moisturizer, or some such shite, if it's not much trouble? I've an itch worse than being skewered by chicken feathers!"

# CHAPTER THIRTY

-- FARTHER ALONG THE INFLATION SLIPWAY --

Noodles the pug sniffed voraciously, his tiny nostrils flaring with each inhalation. "Wait just a goddamn minute, I've got something here. Smells like..."

"Like what?" Herb asked.

"Something rotten. Not like rotten-good. This is rotten bad."

"There's a rotten-good?"

"Yeah, rotten-good. You know, like a fish carcass on a sun-baked beach."

"Ah," Herb said, not knowing quite how to respond.

"This is definitely rotten-rotten," Noodles continued. "This is like patronage and mendacity and arrogance all rolled up in one lettuce-tasting sandwich."

"I like lettuce."

"Humans are weird."

Herb stopped and peered at the, for lack of a better term, walls. "You see that?" he asked.

"What?" Noodles responded, sounding not very interested at all.

"The lights. Something's happening."

The glowing spheres pulsed in rhythm, flowing in the same direction, picking up speed like chaser lights across a dance floor. It created an optical illusion, making it appear as if the tunnel flowed backward past Herb and Noodles.

"They're playing us," Noodles hissed, his gruff voice filled with anger.

"Yeah," Herb agreed. "Who's 'they'?"

"I dunno. But when I find them I'm going to kill them in style."

The slipway ahead rippled and widened, flaring outwards like an event horizon surrounding a black hole, the edges lost from sight. Beyond lay a whirling mass with a million shades of black -- an abyss. From within the abyss came a disturbance. Something grew. At first it was a mere shadow bouncing between sections of ultra-black, then it popped and widened, turning a vibrant shade of violet which somehow made it more immediate, more forward, more present than the rest of the void. Without warning, the event horizon collapsed, shrinking, returning to the tunnel of glowing red, blue, and green, the only remnant from the abyss a luminescent fog of purple roiling ahead -- directly in their path. The fog solidified, resolved itself into a human shape.

The shape stood up, took a few steps, then staggered and fell to its knees.

"You see that?" Herb asked Noodles.

"Yeah, I see it. And quit asking me that."

"Good. I thought I was tripping."

They floated forward cautiously. The figure moved slightly, raising itself up on its arms. It began to cry.

"Beth-Ann!" Herb shouted and rushed to her.

# CHAPTER THIRTY-ONE

### -- OLDE BASELINE ROAD, ONTARIO. NOW --

The Scarab skidded off the road onto the private drive. Reg gunned the accelerator over a small rise, causing the vintage automobile to vault into air. Lady Montique, Lovenight, and John H. Smith hung suspended for a moment before crashing into their seats. Reg didn't let up. He hit the gas. The Scarab clung to the road as it switchbacked through the pines and maples. After several kilometres it broke free from the trees, emerging before a secluded manor house in the drumlins north of Toronto. Reg twisted the wheel, fishtailing to a stop in front of the four-car garage.

"Rightee-o, here we are," Reg said cheerfully.

"Impressive reckless driving, Reg," Lovenight commented. "Remind me never to get into a car with you again."

"Certainly, sir," Reg replied. "And might I add, thank you, sir. I never got the chance to properly express my gratitude to you, for putting all my bits back in the places they belong. I'm feeling much better now, if you were wondering."

Reg was, of course, not entirely as he had been. His neck now protruded from his shoulders at a forward angle, making him appear as if he was constantly expecting an answer to an important question. In addition, his voice downshifted into a wheeze every so often as the air in his larynx stumbled across a newly formed alternate exit and on a whim decided to take it.

Lovenight nodded, accepting Reg's thanks. "Glad to hear it. Now, do us a favour?"

"Of course, sir."

"Shut up."

"Completely, sir."

John H. Smith searched the floor behind the driver's seat for his dislodged glasses, which had shaken off a few minutes ago and had flown by him several times as the Scarab sped through the country roads.

"Are you looking for these, Mr. Smith?" Lady Montique enquired.

"Oh, thank you."

"Think nothing of it. They became lodged against my spine a few, madding minutes ago. Eddie, escort Mr. Smith inside this gauche attempt at modern architecture. Reginald and I will remain behind in the car, in case we were pursued."

"Couldn't we just--"

"No, we couldn't! We need to know where that confounded book has gotten to and get it back to Mr. Smith's office if we're ever to have a hope of righting the balance."

"But if we--"

"Donkey! Don't be disagreeable. It's tiresome." Lady Montique raised her arm, displaying a small caliber pistol she held ready.

"Where do you keep those?" he asked in a shrill voice.

"A lady always must be prepared," she said in a smug tone. "You'd do well to follow my example."

"You really wouldn't shoot me, would you?"

"Don't be silly, Eddie."

Lovenight waited, but Lady Montique offered nothing further.

"That doesn't answer the question!"

"Eddie, we're in a bit of a rush, if you don't mind."

"Bloody hell, I'm going," Lovenight whined. He spilled out of the passenger door and looked up.

The manor house sat atop a drumlin. Most of the post-modern structure was glass framed by steel, as if some turtlenecked Scandinavian architect had vowed to punish the owners with sunlight. Topiaries cut into geometric shapes outlined a winding path up to the front door. Several large sculptures of concrete and scrap metal squatted uncomfortably on the manicured lawn while buried spotlights beamed upwards.

Lovenight whistled. "Somebody artsy-fartsy'ed this place to hell."

John H. Smith pushed his glasses back up to the bridge of his nose and nodded. "That's my sister. She's very...not me. Which is perfectly normal. Let's go. My nephew Cody should be inside."

They walked up to the front door, which was, at the insistence of the Scandinavian architect, a slab of basalt on rollers. The paragon pressed the intercom. They waited in silence a moment. Lovenight shifted his weight uneasily.

"Look, John, not that it's any of my business, but you're a paragon of reality, right? A construct the universe created to keep things keeping on?"

"Close enough."

"Okay then, and don't take this the wrong way, but how is it you have a family? Are they actors or something?"

"I monitor and maintain balance. I am, for all intensive purposes, the epitome of normal. Thus, I have a family because having a family is perfectly normal."

"Fine, I get that. Right. But I mean how? Were they grown in like seedcases or something?"

"They're not snap peas."

"I know, I know, but I mean did they spring fully formed from the side of your head? Did you grow them like triffids? Did they emerge from sea foam riding a giant clam shell? Was it a virgin birth? Did you pull them out of a cabbage patch? Did they arrive by mail?"

"By mail?"

"Like sea monkeys."

"Sea monkeys?"

Lovenight sighed. "Forget it. It's not worth it."

After a few seconds a voice came through the intercom speaker.

"Johannes, is that you?"

Lovenight turned to the realtor, his eyebrows arching into a question. "Johannes?"

"I told you, she likes to complicate things." Into the intercom, he said, "Yes, Sibyl."

"Come in, but don't interrupt. Frans and I are sparring."

"Frans?" Lovenight asked.

"His real name is Frank."

"Right, Sibyl equals complicated. Got it."

The front door rolled aside with an electric hum exposing the foyer. Instead of a closet or boot tray or umbrella stand or any of the normal items you would find in the entrance to a residence, this foyer featured a rock wall for climbing.

"Bloody over-the-top design concepts," Lovenight commented. "Interior designers will be the first against the wall when the revolution comes, mark my words."

They continued straight into the living room where a middle-aged woman in a karate gi shrieked out a battle cry. She squared off against a middle-aged man, also in a gi and wearing a traditional *hachimaki* headband. The mid-century teak furniture had been moved aside, allowing a clear, open space for their sparring. Suddenly both combatants launched themselves forward. The man opened with a predictable kick-punch combination, which the woman easily blocked and countered with a leg sweep.

"*Kiai!*"

Completely ignoring the couple, John H. Smith said, "This way", and walked towards a staircase near the back wall. Lovenight followed Smith up the stairs to a hallway on the second floor. They stopped in front of a door covered in posters for obscure heavy metal bands like the Insane Bees, Mooster, and Poison Jam Sandwich. Smith knocked on the door, calling softly, "Cody? Can we come in? It's Uncle John. I've brought a friend and we'd like to have a word with you. Cody?"

A loud, masculine scream echoed up from downstairs.

"Sounds like Frans forgot his jock strap," Lovenight remarked.

"Happens," John. H. Smith agreed. "Perfectly normal. Cody?

Are you in there?"

There was no answer. Smith turned the knob and the door opened.

"Cody?"

In an oversized leather chair, a youth sat gazing at a cell phone. With rhythmic precision his thumb swiped down the screen, a never-ending parade of images flickering passed his glossy, unblinking eyes. On a folding table beside the chair sat several empty cans of brown soda, the remains of an instant mac-and-cheese product, and balls of crumpled-up tissue. What was crumpled up in the tissue, Lovenight dared not think. The smell of the room could best be described as an acrid pong; something akin to a stale fart lingering in the discounted produce aisle at the supermarket. Discarded t-shirts, jeans, socks, and underwear covered the floor. In the corner stood a bed which appeared to have been dragged for several miles behind a speeding locomotive. Posters for more heavy metal bands -- Roadkill, Knutter's Ballsack, Smoo, etc. -- plastered every wall. The only things completely clear of clutter were a workout bench in the corner and the computer next to it.

"Cody? It's Uncle John H. Smith."

If any of Cody's neurons understood someone was talking to him his face declined to show it. The teenager continued to stare at his phone, lips parted, breathing through his mouth.

Smith stood before his nephew, his hand rubbing his chin as he assessed the situation. "Teenagers: tricky," he concluded.

Lovenight tapped his foot impatiently. The solution seemed obvious to him. Threaten and cajole the teenager by taking away his internet privileges, or saddling him with extra chores, or sitting him on the stairs for a time-out, or whatever parents do with unruly offspring. Brandish the nuclear option, so to speak, get the information, and get the hell out of there, that was his mindset.

*A little patience goes a long way*, a tiny voice inside his head warned. *And for god sakes, don't go off half-cocked like you usually do and mess things up.* The voice sounded very much like Lady Montique, which made it all the more annoying.

Fine. The proffered soft glove with kind words first, then, if that didn't work, the steel gauntlet, backhanded smartly across the face. A metaphorical steel gauntlet, of course. It was hard to find the bonafide item these days.

"Excuse me, Cody is it? My name is Edmund Lovenight. I'm an international spy and compatriot of your uncle. We need to talk with you concerning a massive, all-encompassing, existential threat."

Cody remained unresponsive.

"Look, Cody, this threat is turning out to be...very threatening, to all life, everywhere...is that a fair assessment?"

John H. Smith nodded. "Perfectly accurate."

"Okay, great. So, to sum up: all life, everywhere -- threatened. And we need your help to stop it. Now, put down the phone and talk to us."

Still nothing. Lovenight felt his patience sailing away, leaving a shiny bit of irritation in its wake.

"Look, Cody, we're in a bit of a rush, so if you don't mind...Cody? Cody? Cody, if you keep ignoring me, I'll be forced to do something I haven't thought of yet but believe me it won't be pleasant for either of us."

Cody continued to scroll down the feed on his phone, taking no notice whatsoever of Lovenight.

The last of Lovenight's patience slipped below the horizon. It was time to do the unthinkable. They needed to break the electronic enchantment bewitching this disagreeable adolescent. In order to do so, Lovenight would have to take one for the team. He wrapped his hand in several layers of fresh tissue to insulate himself, then reached over and yanked the phone away from the teenager.

The next several seconds were a blur to Lovenight.

Later, he vaguely remembered the teenager starting to move, then the boy became turbocharged, morphed into a gangly tempest, a gale-force whirlwind of sharp elbows and scraping fingernails. Surprised and confounded, Lovenight fell back from the sudden assault. The stolen hospital scrubs he wore were of no protective value. Dozens of scrapes appeared across his forearms as the teenager scratched and clawed after his confiscated phone. Instinctually, and without a single shred of reason, Lovenight held the phone behind his back. The raging tsunami of pimples and hormones screamed directly into Lovenight's ear: primal, feral shrieks which resonated through his sinuses. He dropped the phone, which was immediately scooped up by Cody.

"Zulch!" Lovenight cursed.

"What the hell?" Cody asked. "Taking a guy's phone? I'll mess you up, you see what I'm saying?" Cody glanced up and down, taking in the scrubs Lovenight wore. "You some kind of narc-doctor? Did mom send you? Get the hell out, you feel me? I'll mess you up, bad!"

Thankfully, John H. Smith imposed himself between his outraged nephew and Lovenight. "Cody, it's all right. Mr. Lovenight is here with me."

Recovering from the shock of the sudden attack, Lovenight dearly wished to wallop the unruly teenager. Embarrassment reddened his cheeks and his bruised ego yearned for comeuppance, but the sudden recollection of Lady Montique's disapproving stare stopped him.

"Uncle John? Fam, what up with this dude here?"

"We need to ask you something, Cody. Now, you're not in trouble, let me assure you of that. But you need to tell us the truth. Understand? You see, something of mine is missing. A book. It was in my office. Now, this is a rather special book, something of a one-of-a-kind--"

"I don't know nothing about no book. Does mom know you're up here, even? Did you just sneak up here while she and Frank were doing karate? You did, didn't you! Get out, Uncle John! Get out of my room!"

Now the tiny voice inside Lovenight's head said, *This is taking far too long, Eddie. Time to bring out the proverbial thumbscrews. But do it subtly, for god-sakes, and without too too much violence or you'll end up in the soup, understand?*

Lovenight silently thanked the tiny voice and set to work.

He did the unexpected: he began making the teenager's bed. Carefully he smoothed out the sheets, tucked in the sides, and fluffed the pillows. He hummed while he spread the duvet across the bed, making sure it was loud enough to be bothersome.

Cody's eyes widened with shock. "Dude! You can't do that!"

Lovenight stopped humming and sauntered over to the teenager, bringing his face within inches of Cody's. The boy smelled like a carton of expired milk.

Lovenight spoke in a low, measured tone, topped with a dollop of menace. "Seventy-two hours ago I was sipping Aperol Spritzers in Soho, trading dirty jokes with his Holiness the Dalai Lama. Since then, I've been kidnapped, tortured, shot at, turned into a cockroach, and tasted floor. Tasted...floor. Do you know what that means? It means I'm being trifled with. And when I'm trifled with, I become a purveyor of pain, a deliverer of discomfort."

"Eh?"

"I hurt people. Now, what'd you do with your uncle's book, you snot-nosed, pimply brat? Tell us, or so help me God, I'll rip through this room like a packet of electrons, find every embarrassing skid-mark and sticky patch and crusty bit, then get a certain antediluvian vixen I know to post video of them across the entire social media spectrum in High Definition. I've already located several questionable spots just by making the bed, so start talking!"

The sour smell coming off the teenager intensified. "Okay, jeez, relax fam. Just chill. There's this guy I know, into all that occult stuff, right? My older sister used to date him. He hooks me up with the dankest weed, you feel me?"

Lovenight dug his thumb and forefinger into nerve bundles located just below his jawline to keep from screaming. "No, I don't 'feel you'. I don't 'see what you're saying'. Nobody can! It's impossible to 'see' what someone is 'saying'. Also, stop telling me to 'chill' and 'relax'. I'm not your ham or fam or spam or whatever it is you're trying to say. Tell us where the book is."

"I took it, but I don't have it," Cody said in a rush. "Gave it to this guy, see what I'm saying? Okay, okay, you don't see what I'm saying. This dude, said if I ever found stuff on voodoo or tarot cards, you know, stuff like that, to like give it to him and he would hook me up. See?"

"So, this book wasn't the first thing you took from your Uncle John's office?"

Cody looked sheepish, glancing sideways at his uncle.

"What else did you take, Cody?" John H. Smith asked.

"This broach thing."

The paragon pressed his fingertips against his temples and rubbed. "So, that's what happened to the Amulet of Amon'Zul, the Opener of Closed Ways," he said in a pained voice. "I thought the dry cleaners had nicked it."

"Anything else?" Lovenight asked.

"And a coin."

John H. Smith looked close to tears. "The Seal of the Priesthood of Ur."

"Yeah, that."

"You sent ancient, powerful artifacts to your sister's ex-boyfriend?" Lovenight asked.

"Shipped it to him, overnight. Weed usually arrived the next day."

"This guy have a name?"

"Yeah, Simon. Simon the Pieman."

"Simon the Pieman?"

"Cause he gets me baked."

"What was his real last name?"

"Callaway, Simon Callaway. He moved to Michigan to go to some arts college."

"Give me his address."

"One sec." Cody scrolled through his phone. "You got a number I can text this to you?"

"I don't do any electronics."

Cody froze. For several seconds the teenager's brain struggled, trying to process that piece of information. "What, like, nothing?"

"No smart phones, no e-watches, no computers, no tablets. Anything with a chip is *verboten*. Matter of personal safety and philosophy. Hence, the tissues I wrapped around my hand to protect me from your twilight device."

"That's...weird. How do I give you this address then?"

"Read it to me. I'll store it in my memory condo."

"Huh?"

Lovenight sighed. "A memory condo is something your underdeveloped brain does not have the capacity to comprehend. Now, hand over the address of this Simon Callaway with alacrity."

"Huh?"

"Give me the thrice-damned address!"

Cody read out the address. Lovenight nodded, then turned to leave when a thought occurred to him.

"That man downstairs sparring with your mother...is he about a 44 Tall?"

Cody's stepfather Frank had immaculate taste in clothing. And since he was busy attempting to get out of the rear-naked chokehold, he didn't notice Lovenight stepping trippingly down the stairs wearing his midnight blue trench coat, black turtleneck, gaberdine trousers, and Chelsea boots (all taken from Frank's walk-in closet).

As they got back into the Stout Scarab, Lovenight asked in a bright and chipper tone, "How killer are these new threads?"

Lady Montique scoffed. "Outlandish. No one these days knows how to dress."

"If I'm being honest, I thought the sandals and hospital smock really brought out a roguish quality in you, sir," Reg confessed.

"You're a Philistine, Reg. No matter, things are looking up. We're leaving this poutine-loving nation and heading to Michigan."

"How's that looking up, sir?"

"Just drive, Reg."

"You said to remind you never to drive with me again. Impressively reckless, is how you described my efforts, sir."

"I know, Reg. However, these clothes are making me feel magnanimous. Now, onwards."

# CHAPTER THIRTY-TWO

-- GRAND RAPIDS, MICHIGAN. AFTER A SMALL PASSAGE OF TIME, NOW --

Strong smells of cooking and disinfectant leaked into the hallway. Lovenight breathed through his mouth to avoid the conflicting odours. Reg didn't seem to notice. They arrived at apartment 314, the address Cody had given them. Simon 'the Pieman' Callaway's apartment hid at the end of the corridor, next to a staircase at the back of the three-floor walk-up. The EXIT sign above the stairway flickered weakly as if on its last leg. It, and the entire building, had seen better days.

Reg looked sideways down the corridor and sniffed, causing his cookie-duster moustache to spasm. "Academics live here? Seems a trifle dodgy."

"Student ghettos usually are, Reg. Can't you smell the undergrad stench? Unwashed clothing mixed with energy drinks?"

"Reminds me of air raid shelters during the Blitz."

"Very similar, I would imagine."

Lovenight knocked on the door.

"Sir, do you think Lady Montique and Mr. Smith will be safe in the car? This whole neighbourhood seems not up to snuff, if you take my meaning."

Lovenight snorted. "I pity the foolish miscreant who attempts to carjack those two. Relax, Reg. Ah, it appears no one is home. Time to reconnoitre."

"Right you are, sir."

Lovenight reached deep into the folds of the trench coat and pulled out a set of lock picks he'd found in the Scarab. Why Lady Montique owned a set of lock picks was a mystery. When asked, she simply smiled and said, "A girl will have her secrets, Eddie."

Whistling, he inserted the tension bar into the cylinder, then picked at the tumblers.

"How could any self-respecting young scholar end up living in these dregs?" Reg asked.

"Are you suggesting I've led us to the wrong address? Are you questioning my memory condo? Are you implying my facilities are not performing at peak efficiency?"

"Don't you mean 'faculties', sir?"

"What did I say?"

"Facilities."

"Good catch. I take your point. New directive: from now on, question my facilities at every opportunity."

"Faculties, sir."

"I'm sure they'll have some inside. You'll just have to wait."

"Rats."

"Relax, Reg. This shouldn't take too long."

"No, sir. I mean, rats!"

"Rats? What're you talking about man? Make sense!"

Reg pointed. From a darkened corner by the rear staircase two sets of beady eyes glinted. If he squinted, Lovenight could just make out their hairy backs and fleshy tails hiding in the shadows. The rats watched him intently, remaining utterly still. Something about them made the skin at the back of Lovenight's neck itch.

"Zulch! They're big!"

"Biggest I've seen, sir."

"Reg, you ever know rats to be that bold?"

"Not that I can recall."

"Creepy," Lovenight said. Two more tumblers clicked into place and the cylinder rotated. Lovenight pushed open the door and rushed through. Reg followed. Once inside Lovenight shut the door quickly, making sure the rats remained in the hallway.

"That was close," he said. "Rats! Freaky things!"

"Wonderful companions, if you train'em. Me mum had a rat."

"I'm sure she did. Shut up."

"Righteeo."

Lovenight felt along the wall until he found a switch and flicked on the lights, then immediately regretted it.

The student apartment didn't amount to much more than a cramped living room with a galley kitchen, two bedrooms, and a bathroom at the back. The decor was a mixture of eclectic clutter: a coffee table which was once a construction skid, milk crates for end tables, sadistic looking chairs, and wall-to-wall shag carpeting.

"Careful, sir. The sofa appears to have mange."

"Ah youth," Lovenight said. "How tragically overrated. Start looking, Reg."

"What exactly are we looking for, sir?"

"The things Cody stole from his uncle. The...book...who's name I can't remember right now, the Amulet of somebody or something, whichever, and of course, the Seal of the ...just look around for any eldritch-seeming items. You know, ghastly or sinister or weird."

"Do we have a description of said items?"

"Well, I imagine they resemble a book, an amulet, and a seal," Lovenight replied dryly.

"Not very helpful in the least, sir."

"Look for something occultish! Something with a modicum of dread!"

They sifted through the living room. Nothing occultish stuck out. Nothing dreadful popped up.

"Let's check the bedrooms," Lovenight suggested.

"As you say."

The first bedroom was neat, tidy, clean; the desk clear of clutter, a garbage can shaped like R2D2 next to it. *Lord of The Rings* bedsheets covered the twin size bed, folded, tucked, and smoothed. Lovenight opened a tiny fridge in the corner to find it filled with cans of iced coffee.

"Disgusting what the kids drink, nowadays."

They checked the other bedroom.

Clothing lay strewn on the floor as if scattered by hurricane winds. Bedsheets were M.I.A. The futon sagged in all the wrong places. An erasable white board dominated one wall. Someone had circled in red marker the location and time of an upcoming lecture.

Lovenight read, "Professor Kilroy Johnson on The Underlying Metaphor of the Post-Excessivism Movement, Counterpointing the Re-Rococoists, Proving Non-Art, or No-Art, is in Itself, Art.'" Then, after a brief pause, he added, "Bloody art historians!"

Reg cleared his throat. "Begging pardon sir, but the rats are back."

Two rats lounged atop a small summit of mismatched socks in the corner of the bedroom. They regarded Lovenight with tiny black eyes.

"How'd they get in here? They're trifling with me!"

"If I might ask something of a personal question, sir?"

"No, you may not. What is it?"

"I couldn't help noticing -- you're constantly assuming people are trifling with you. Not only people, but animals, weather, events, and all manner of circumstances and situations."

"Your point?"

"Bit of an obsession, don't you think?"

"Certainly not."

"Come now, sir. Even the word 'trifle' suggests numerous phobias and paranoias."

"No it doesn't."

"Does."

"No, it doesn't. It's just a word. A harmless, innocuous word."

"Yes, it does. It suggests the one being trifled with, the 'trifle-ee' if you will, is seen as inferior to some degree by the 'trifler'.

From the fact that you, the 'trifle-ee', imagines most everything is a 'trifler', one may conclude you believe yourself inferior."

"Stuff and fluff."

"Sorry to say it, but there it is."

"Nonsense! I *am* being trifled with. Look at those rats! Just sitting there, all ratty! You see it, don't you?"

"No, sir. I just see two rats watching us. That in no way indicates some belligerent or salacious intent."

For some reason, he wasn't quite sure why, Lovenight's eyes welled with tears. He began to sob, putting his hands over his eyes so Reg couldn't see him. "Don't look at me," he pleaded. "Make them go away."

Reg ignored Lovenight's demand. Instead, he retrieved a box of tissues from the bedside table and passed them to Lovenight. His eyeless sockets somehow managed to appear warm and caring.

"You have to understand, people have trifled with me all my life," Lovenight said between sobs. "I was ridiculed as a teenager. Not bullied. Everybody says they were bullied. I was belittled, dehumanized, ignored. Ridiculed, dismissed, laughed at. I was--"

Without warning, Reg placed his index finger gently, yet firmly, on Lovenight's lips, shushing him.

"There there, sir. No need to tell me your backstory. It's the same as everyone's. Tragic. Emotional. It's left deep scars on your psyche. You're trying to overcome it, but you've reached this existential moment where's it's all become too, too much. You see? I know it already."

Lovenight tried to reply but could not with Reg's cold, dead finger pressed against his lips.

"Let me tell you a little something Niels Bohr told me. We were driving to his apartment at St. James Palace. Traffic was appalling. I says I was going Oxford Circus way, rather than driving through Leicester Square, when Professor Bohr says, 'We cannot think there is an Oxford Circus or Leicester Square.' Well, that floored me, it did. So, says I, 'You reckon Holborn down to the Strand, then?' Bohr replies, 'We must only consider the effect of going over to Holborn, and then down to the Strand.' Genius, right there! You see the point I'm trying to make, sir?"

Lovenight mumbled something.

"Oh, right you are sir." Reg removed his finger from Lovenight's lips.

"I think," Lovenight said softly. "You're trying to tell me what's passed is passed, and that only my life choices going forward matter. Nothing else, for all intents and purposes, exists."

Reg's moustache twitched. "Well, that's taking the plum out of the pudding, so to speak. But yes, basically."

"Thanks, Reg. Not for the incomprehensible advice, but for caring enough to give it."

Reg leaned forward. "And those rats?"

Lovenight looked over to the vermin. He stared at them for several long moments before saying, "They're just rats."

"Aye, sir. Just rats."

"Who just happened to follow us in from the corridor. Circumventing a door I shut for the express purpose of keeping them out."

"Persistent little blighters, I'll give them that." Reg snapped his fingers, the boney ends making a particularly crisp snap. "Sir, it occurs to me, this book we're searching for, along with those other things the boy took..."

"The Amulet of someone or something, and the Seal coin thing?"

"Yes, those. They're singularities, near infinite in their incorporeal power."

"Correct. And?"

"Shouldn't you be able to slipstream and see their Doppler shifts relative to normal spacetime? They'd be like, well, like neon tubes winding their merrily way through life! All you have to do is follow the shifts to wherever they end up. You bring them back, and Bob's your uncle, we're home in time for tea!"

"Brilliant idea, Reg!"

"Thank you, sir."

"I'll have to take credit for it."

"Expected, sir."

Lovenight stripped off the trench coat, turtleneck, gabardine trousers, and Chelsea boots. He entrusted them to Reg for safekeeping, who for the sake of modesty and not wanting to giggle, kept his gaze off the naked Lovenight.

"I'll find out where they went, then pop back to collect you. Won't be a moment."

"Righteeo, sir. Yes, give us a tap when you get back."

"Will do. And Reg?"

"Yes, sir?"

"Stay weird."

"Consider it done, sir."

Time accelerated. The student apartment filled with red and blue mists as Lovenight exited primary time and entered a slipway. Reg remained stiff as a statue from Lovenight's perspective.

Usually when he entered a faster time stream the red and blue mists remained relative to his movement, changing from one to another depending on whether he moved towards or away from an object. Move towards a zucchini muffin, the mist turns blue. Move away from a zucchini muffin, the mist turns red.

Three redshifts remained solidly redshifted no matter what direction he moved. Which meant those objects were constantly moving away from him in time.

"Freaky."

These were different from anything Lovenight had ever seen. The redshifts all originated in an open drawer of the desk. They remained solid with no object generating them. These were leftovers. These redshifts were where the objects *had* been.

If he squinted, turned his head just so, and slipstreamed down a notch, he could make out static forms in each of them. One resembled a book. Another an amulet. The last a coin.

He began oscillating back and forth between the slipway and primary time, accelerating and decelerating, flickering in and out.

The redshifts formed ribbons of crimson light, twisting out of the desk drawer and tunnelling through time and space leaving ruby trails suspended in midair. Their luminescence outshone everything around them.

Lovenight followed the redshifts out of the room, down the stairwell, and out of the building.

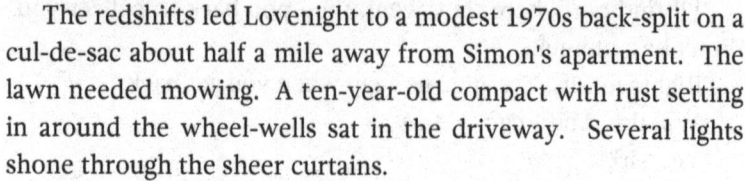

The redshifts led Lovenight to a modest 1970s back-split on a cul-de-sac about half a mile away from Simon's apartment. The lawn needed mowing. A ten-year-old compact with rust setting in around the wheel-wells sat in the driveway. Several lights shone through the sheer curtains.

The redshifts entered through the front door.

Lovenight walked in, following the streams as they passed through the kitchen, into the family room, through an open doorway and down to the basement.

"No whammies now," Lovenight whispered to the dark stairs.

In many ways it was like a hundred million similar basements all over North America. There was the obligatory Lay-Z-Boy recliner, old couch, velvet black light posters, a fold-out card table, a bar with a neon sign above it, vinyl laminate flooring, all very typical.

What was untypical about this basement was the triangle marked in purple chalk on the floor, the brass censer straight out of some Byzantine temple, the shrivelled tarot cards scattered across the fold-out table, the moldy remains of several zucchini muffins, and the Styrofoam container from Waffle Shack still full of delicious, but very cold and soggy, waffles.

"Who leaves waffles uneaten?" Lovenight wondered aloud.

And there, on the table, at the end of one of the redshifts, lay the *Pax Arcana*.

Whatever had been printed on its glossy black pages was now lost to oblivion. As he picked it up, the paperback crumbled into dust, the motes winking out of existence before reaching the floor. Nothing of the errata remained.

"Well, don't need to worry about that anymore," he said, dusting his hands off.

Lovenight turned his attention to the second redshift meandering around the basement, tracking it to a canvas backpack abandoned on the couch. Inside, the seal rested. A ziggurat covered one side, while on the other a rather odd assortment of fronds and leaves twisted together forming a dense mat.

"Zulch!"

Lovenight plucked the seal out of the backpack, keeping in his closed fist. Two down, one to go.

He turned and followed the last redshift over to the brass censer on the floor. He flipped the top open, and there at the bottom, amidst the ashes, was the amulet.

Parallel spirals on its face began to rotate, moving across the metal, slow and easy. A hollow-sounding wind blew through the basement. The spirals fuzed, then reversed and opened, allowing depth and space to enter.

For a moment, Lovenight couldn't understand what he was seeing. He squinted, trying to isolate the individual frames of the redshift. The amulet appeared to morph over a few milliseconds, widening and unfolding -- or maybe *opening* was a better way of think about it.

Lovenight decided immediately he did not want to think about it. Thinking about things like magical amulets shape-changing on their own accord was definitely not going to get him to any afterparty party anytime soon.

"Just leave it and hoof it back to Reg," he counselled himself. "It's not my problem. Let Lady Montique and the paragon figure out what to do with it."

He stood still, looking at the amulet, not taking his own advice.

Alarms went off in Lovenight's head. They blared loud and long, informing him under no circumstances should he even think of touching the magical amulet. No good could come of touching magical amulets. In fact, a lot of harm could come from touching magical amulets.

Lovenight usually listened to those alarms, following their advice with something approaching a religious fervour. But here was the problem; ever since he received Lady Montique's summons he had been treated like a surfboard in a tsunami: tossed about, pounded, and plowed under. Each new obstacle demanded he escape or help or liberate or discern or aid. Lady Montique telling him what to do and when to do it. None of it had been his choice. It all had been foisted upon him.

Now, he could go back and get Reg and the others and have Lady Montique continue to run the show. Or he could run away, forever hiding from those tsunamis which battered their way through his life and the lives of everyone he knew on a semi-regular basis. Or, he could try something different. Just this once, he could take matters in his own hands and become the master of his own fate.

Lovenight touched the amulet.

Lovenight instantly regretted touching the amulet.

The redshift deepened into a purplish hue, then brightened, transforming into a blueshift. The blueshift blasted Lovenight, completely enveloping him, obscuring and erasing the entire suburban basement until nothing was left except for Lovenight and the amulet before him and a vast, endless see of purple mist. The artifact widened, blooming into a tunnel of roiling ultra-violet, sucking and pulling at Lovenight.

"Bugger, bugger, bugger..."

He felt as if he was floating. Lovenight checked his feet. They didn't seem to be touching anything. He felt around with his toes in the purpleness, searching for something solid, something with purchase, something he could stand on or push off from. There was nothing.

"Something..." he said, gravely. "Something is trifling with me."

An easy current pulled him along through the deep deep purple. Lovenight drifted, and waited.

The tunnel swooped and banked and corkscrewed. The concept of 'up and 'down' became meaningless. Just as the dawn lightens the sky, tiny stars emerged along the tunnel. Only a few at first, then more until there were hundreds, thousands, all shining spheres, all chasing each other along, switching from rows to columns to spirals to waves to...

"All right, I get it!" Lovenight yelled. "Stop the light show and get on with it!"

Three figures came into view. One appeared to be a twenty-something hippy sporting an army-surplus backpack, another a girl just shy of her teenage years, the last a small dog.

"Freaking idiot, don't move!" the dog yelled.

There was a pop in his ears and pressure on his back. Some force propelled him forward so hard he almost lost his grip on the seal. Instinct took over and insisted he curl himself into a fetal position, arms covering head to protect his vital bits. He careened towards the trio, like a bowling ball hurtling toward shocked pins. He rolled to a stop just before them.

"You piss-poor excuse for an ape!" the dog lambasted him.

All three were looking in the direction he had come from. He looked back only to see the purpleness fading away.

"You asshat!" the dog snarled. "We've been looking for a way out for days."

# CHAPTER THIRTY-THREE

-- SLIPWAY IN THE INFLATION FIELD, WHERE TIME HAS NO MEANING --

"Jesus-suffering-Christ," said the pug. "I haven't been this pissed off since the vet squeezed my anal glands."

He snorted, then licked himself aggressively for several seconds. Lovenight had never seen such angry licking in all his life. Its tongue was a small, flashing, wet ribbon of, well, pugnaciousness. Lovenight's gaze flicked from the pug, to the girl, to the hippy. He blinked rapidly for several seconds as he searched his imagination for some plausible reason why these three should be together. Nothing came to mind.

The hippy covered the girl's eyes and said to Lovenight, "Dude, check your burrito."

"I'm not a little kid, Herb!" the girl protested and turned away on her own accord.

Lovenight realized he was slipstream-naked, again, and in the presence of sensitive eyes. He said to Herb, "You wouldn't happen to have some extra clothes I could use do you? A spare pair of Venetian leather trousers or a poet's shirt or something?"

"You're lucky," Herb said, rooting through his backpack. "I was planning on staying over at Mark's after the seance-summoning-thingy. I got an extra toothbrush too, if you need one." Herb pulled out a pair of cotton sweatpants and a t-shirt with a picture of Clint Eastwood wearing a poncho in *The Good, the Bad, and the Ugly*.

"You freaking hairless apes!" the pug exclaimed. "Humans and their clothes! You think any self-respecting dog would wear ripped jeans or crotchless culottes? It's not like we all don't know what's underneath them anyway. Stupid as hell."

Lovenight thanked the young man and slipped into the sweatpants and t-shirt. Both were oversized, fit rather loosely, and smelled vaguely of nachos. He pocketed the onyx seal still clutched in his hand.

"Now," he said, looking at the trio. "Who're you lot?"

"We could ask you the same question, cupcake," the pug retorted. "Oh, wait I don't have to! I already know who you are. You're the pervy idiot who let the portal outta here close behind him!"

"Pervy?"

"You were naked in someone else's basement. Sounds pervy to me."

"I was investigating a temporal anomaly, not that it's any of your concern."

"It is my concern, sunshine! Ya wanna know why? Cause I'm stuck here with Stoner Boy, Little Miss Catastrophe, and now you, the Pervy Cupcake."

"Why are you so angry?" Lovenight asked.

"Why are you so stupid?" the pug shot back.

"Just stop it!" the girl yelled.

"Guys, chill," Herb urged. "You gotta excuse Noodles. He just lost his best friend --"

Noodles the pug went rigid, the fur on his neck-folds bristling. "Don't! Understand? Just don't mention him! Jesus Christ!" Noodles trembled, his whole body vibrating with rage. His eyes looked ready to pop out of their sockets.

Without warning, Beth-Ann scooped him up and did the unthinkable: she petted him. For a tense moment Noodles struggled, his legs flailing in the air. He shivered violently once, then relaxed, falling into a rhythmic panting as Beth-Ann continued smoothing the hair on his back.

"It's okay, you're okay," Beth-Ann whispered. Noodles said nothing.

"My name's Herb," Herb said, raising his hand and giving Lovenight a peace-sign.

"Lovenight."

Herb appeared puzzled. "Is that an affirmation of some kind?"

"It's my name."

"Cool. No judgement."

"Look, why don't you explain to me who you are and how you got here, and then I'll tell you who I am and how I got here, and then maybe we can help each other get out of here, wherever here is. Alright?"

"You first, cupcake!"

"I'm not a...all right, fine. I'm a professional rogue and chrono-operative working for the Outliers, a sixth-column agency dedicated to stopping existential fascist threats, both corporeal and incorporeal...at least that's what is says on our calling cards. We operate across all dimensions. My modus operandi involves slip-streaming out of primary time into faster secondary currents and side-flows. Funny story, I was in a secondary slipway, investigating the whereabouts of several universal errata when I was pulled here."

Herb stared at Lovenight open-mouthed for several seconds before managing to say, "Fascism is such a drag."

"Truer words were never said, my spaced-out friend. Now, that's me in and out of a nutshell. What about you lot?"

"Pleased to meet you, Mr. Lovenight. My name's Herb and I'm a film major. This is my friend Noodles, he's a pug. And that's Beth-Ann. She's Mark's little sister."

"I can speak for myself, Herb!" Beth-Ann said.

"Okay, great, got it," Lovenight said. "No sense in going over that again. Any idea where we are?"

"Oh ya," Herb said. "I know where we are."

"Huzzah!" Lovenight exclaimed. "Well, my groovy friend, do tell."

"We're in the inflation field between universes. It's the space that keeps universes apart. The more you try to get somewhere, the further away that somewhere gets."

"Right. Okay. That's absolutely no help whatsoever."

"Something has changed," Beth-Ann said to Lovenight. "The lights, they're different now that you're here." Her hand swiped upwards in an arc, the lights responding, their brilliance responding to her touch.

"It's all flash," Lovenight said dismissively. "Someone is trifling with us, wants to put us off our guard."

"It's more." Beth-Ann insisted. "It's like you being here is breaking the lights up."

An idea crashed into Lovenight's mind. What had the realtor said? The book, the amulet, and the seal in his pocket were errata produced by the universe. Unwanted bits that just didn't fit. It was part of the balance of all things, a valve the universe used to blow off steam and keep on keeping on.

Lovenight pulled the seal from his pocket.

"Hey," Herb said, pointing to the seal. "Simon's coin-thingy."

"Indeed, Herb, a coin-thingy," Lovenight said, flipping the seal between his fingers. "A really average friend of mine called it, the 'Opener of Ways'. Let's see where this unwanted errata wishes to go, shall we?"

With that, Lovenight tossed the seal. It fixed itself in the space between the travellers, spinning continuously, just hanging there, never slowing, never speeding up. They watched it intently, waiting for something to occur. Time stretched on, which was difficult considering they were in a place where the concept of time did not apply.

"Exciting as a day-old turd," Noodles said.

"Well, let's see you think of something!" Lovenight shot back.

"Don't take that tone with me, mom-licker," Noodles growled.

"Uh-oh," Herb said softly.

"What?" Noodles asked.

"The slipway," Herb said, "It doesn't want to be a slipway anymore."

Light burst from the seal as the micro-dimensions inside it unraveled, flowing outwards in chaotic spirals, ripping the slipway apart.

Lovenight, Herb, Beth-Ann and Noodles found themselves falling, or at least experiencing the sensation of falling.

The four travellers tumbled through impossible geographies, twisting past spiralling tie-die fractals, triangle rainbows, clouds of vermillion haze, mountains made of eye-searing brilliance, into a sea of luminescent jellyfish the size of planets. Lovenight tried to scream, but the sound came out of his mouth as balls of fuzz that caught the wind shear and were ripped from time and space and thought.

A trumpet-shaped whirlpool made of quicksilver caught them, funnelled them up and around a star-laced firmament in a series of loops and banks. In a sliver of a second, the whole of creation was opened up to them. They saw everything, the cosmogonic, the entirety of spacetime. Think of a piece of paper -- only this paper is everything, an infinite plane that's been crumpled up, then smoothed out, then folded endlessly, becoming the most intricate of origamis.

It all collapsed in an instant. Vanished. Gone was the cosmogonic, as they entered the bulk beyond.

Reality changed as they continued to fall. In one instant Lovenight could see within himself; it was like looking at mirrors in a fun house, only one mirror was an x-ray and another was fiber-optic feed from inside his lower intestine and another was a living Kodachrome picture of him taken when he was a toddler and another was his DNA under an electron microscope and another was his reflection in Lady's Montique's eyes, and on and on, mirror after mirror, each one gifting him with another perspective of himself, and at the same time he still gazed out of his own eyes looking at his fellow falling travellers as they experienced themselves and each other.

And in one really disturbing moment Lovenight saw the film student Herb sitting cross-legged on a lotus flower, his six arms cutting celluloid film reels as he puffed away on a hookah, the smoke rising up forming clouds shaped like tacos, whilst nearby ten-times-ten thousand deities blew garlands to him. Herb, in that reality, was the newest bodhisattva, and he turned to Lovenight to pass on enlightenment, his perfect knowledge, his path to transcendence.

So spoke the bodhisattva: *Spoons make me laugh.*

Lovenight screamed. Fuzzy, fluffy balls tumbled from his mouth.

Some people just don't want enlightenment.

Reality wrung itself out, like a mom twisting a tea towel to get it dry, and everything changed again.

They stood on dusty ground under a purple sky with four planets bigger than Earth's moon hanging in the night. A cutting wind blew into their faces and up the slope where it whistled among jagged, red rocks at the crest of the hill.

"Oh, great," Beth-Ann sighed. "Back here again."

# CHAPTER THIRTY-FOUR

-- PREVIOUSLY UNKNOWN LOCATION, SOMEWHERE BETWEEN UNIVERSES --

 Herb dug perspective.
 There was nothing more satisfying than getting half-baked on a smooth hybrid, then opening his mind to the universe, which came flooding in, filling him, until he could go anywhere instantly or be everywhere at once or get lost in zero-mass quantum manifolds.  Traveling using perspective was a rush, a high, an experience, as poignant as any masterpiece by Hitchcock or Fellini.
 He equated gaining perspective with watching a good movie. As the lights of the movie theatre go down, the darkness wipes away the outside 'real' world and allows the mind to submerge in the celluloid images flashing on the screen.  The audience can

cheer for heroes, excoriate villains, see clues and connections characters themselves cannot see, all the while remaining above the narrative fray, having perspective on the whole.

Perspective gave Herb the entire space-time continuum as his own personal movie theatre.

His transport was cannabis, toking until he rode the thin line between buzzing and being blotto-whacked. After years of practice, he knew his limit. One toke over the line and perspective was gone.

It was the euphoric interplay between his stoned-conscious and inquisitive serenity that granted him detachment and insight. Like most things in his life, it was a difficult balance to maintain. And right now it was impossible. Being dumped unceremoniously onto an alien hillside will do that.

He waggled a finger at the offending landscape and said, "Don't harsh my buzz."

"This way," Beth-Ann said.

"You've been here before?" Lovenight asked.

"Yeah, the cave is up this way."

"Cave? We're not here to go spelunking. We need to get back to some place with not so many moons hanging about."

Beth-Ann shrugged. "Suit yourself."

Not seeing any alternative, Lovenight followed along. Slowly, the travellers trudged up the dry, rocky hillside. Beth-Ann carried Noodles, stroking his fur all the while.

Herb was agog. Noodles didn't seem to mind the pre-teen's attentions. Normally, if some unknowing pedestrian stopped and tried to pet Noodles, they would have received a blistering tongue-lashing for their troubles. If the unfortunate pedestrian actually made physical contact with the pug then ambulances were usually needed, or, if very unfortunate, lawyers. But Beth-Ann petted away with impunity.

This new guy, Lovenight, seemed okay to Herb. His soul fit him well, the silvery threads running over him in tightly wound lines. He had something to prove, Herb figured. Fair enough. We all have baggage.

Lovenight noticed the way Herb looked at him.

"You're a perceptor, yeah?"

Herb nodded.

"What do you make of this place?"

Herb cast his perceptive inner eye around, taking in the alien landscape, examining it with his oh-so-stoned perception. The red sands blackened, the purple sky flared. Bands of arcane energy streaked across the firmament in flashes like aquamarine lightening. Ghostly tumbleweeds rolled across the landscape, flowing up towards a cave near the top of the ridge where the wind whistled.

To his regular sight the cave looked like a crack in the rock face, just a bit of jagged blackness. But to his perceptive inner eye it was a volcanic eruption: pyrotechnic sparks burst from the cave in cascading fountains. The ground around the cave-mouth appeared blackened and charred. Just what he was seeing, Herb wasn't sure.

"Like something out of *Apocalypse Now*," he said, answering Lovenight's question.

"That bad, huh?"

"Oh yeah."

"Wait until you see inside," Beth-Ann said, still cradling Noodles in her arms.

She steered them into the cave, passing the bioluminescent brain-shaped rocks, their green shadows marching across the dark stones and fissures. Droning music echoed down the cave walls. At times, they could hear snippets of conversation, just a word or two at the edge of hearing, then nothing. The voices sounded filtered, as if they were coming through a pair of cheap speakers with balance off and reverb turned up full. The air became cooler the deeper they went.

They entered the cavern of the smokeless fire. It was empty. No bonfire. No shadows on the wall. No Moist-Jujubes.

Beth-Ann looked around, bewildered. "She was right here," she said emphatically. "I swear."

"It's okay, kid," Noodles said. "We believe you. Maybe this Moist-Jujubes just stepped out for a smoke. Let me see if I can sniff where she went."

"Where was the fire?" Herb asked.

Beth-Ann pointed to the centre of the room. "Over there."

Herb walked over to the where Beth-Ann had indicated. With every footfall the rock seemed to quiver. His soles tingled. The very stone appeared agitated, which was unusual for stones. Stones are usually pretty stoic. They're stones after all. To see them so emotionally charged was something.

"Floor is tricky, again."

Noodles sniffed the spot where the smokeless fire had burned. The fur between his eyes furrowed. "There's something freaking weird here. I can smell something similar to inflation ions, but it's flickering. It's like it's here and then not here."

"Like those whispering voices," Beth-Ann added. "You guys hear them?"

"Freaking A," Noodles said.

Puzzle pieces clicked together in Herb's brain. He backtracked all the way to the cavern's entrance, gazing at the floor. Just at the edge, he noticed the change. It was subtle, a slight shift in texture. Only if you knew what you were looking for would you find it.

"*Citizen Kane*," Herb said.

"Who?" Beth-Ann asked.

"It's a movie that rejected a linear plot structure, favouring overlapping narratives. That's what someone's done with this cavern. Covered over one time with another, so there's different layers of time in the same place. This place changes depending on who's here. And this is the seam."

They all peered at the spot Herb pointed to on the floor.

"I don't see anything different," Beth-Ann said.

Lovenight extended his leg and quickly stepped over the spot. He reversed and went back. Then over. And back. "Definitely something," he concluded. "It's like a breeze that suddenly blows the other way. Really nuanced, but yeah, time flows differently on either side of this spot."

"Way to catch up, cupcake. Herb just said the exact same thing."

"Look," Lovenight said in his attempting-to-sound-reasonable tone. "I'm trying to be a team player here and work with you, Skippy the Wonder Pug, but if you don't stop calling me Cupcake, I'm going to lose my cool super-quick. Yes?"

" Cupcake. Cupcake. Cupcake, Cupcake, Cupcake!"

"I'm warning you dog-breath, I'll Richard Gere you."

"Okay, I won't call you cupcake again....you sugar cookie."

Lovenight got down on all fours and locked eyes with Noodles. "Refer to me once more as any kind of bakery product and its gerbil time for you!"

"Stop it, you two!" Beth-Ann yelled, her hands balled into fists at her sides. "We need to figure a way to get out of here. Now, quit bullying each other so we can go home."

Both Lovenight and Noodles cringed and glanced at her sideways, avoiding direct eye contact. Lovenight stood up, his head hung low like an errant schoolboy who has set the gymnasium on fire. Noodles feigned interest in a loose rock by urinating on it.

Beth-Ann turned to Lovenight. "You said you can flippy-flip with time or something?"

Lovenight nodded. "Slipstream. Between time streams. But I can barely perceive this one; I have no idea where it flows. If I jump in and it's a slow stream, then you could all be waiting years for me to get back, or much worse, I could die."

"Downside to this is what?" Noodles asked. He stiffened when Beth-Ann glared at him.

"The floor," Herb said softly.

"Come again?" Lovenight said.

"It's tricky."

"Still not getting a clear picture, stoner boy."

"I'm getting a strange vibe off this floor."

"What vibe?"

"It doesn't want to be a floor."

"Cheque, please."

"No, listen." Herb shooed them back into onto the cavern away from the entrance. He arranged them in a circle. "It doesn't like having two time-streams on it, just like we don't enjoy wearing two pairs of pants. If we all stop being on it, it might be able to buck the annoying time-stream off. Now, everyone hold hands."

"Jesus Christ, Herb!" Noodles growled. "I don't have any hands to hold."

Beth-Ann picked up Noodles, then took Herb's hand.

Lovenight took hold of Herb's other hand and warned, "If anyone starts singing *Kumbaya*, I'll murder the lot of you."

Beth-Ann looked at Herb and asked, "Do you think this will work?"

He smiled mischievously. "You never know. And-a-one, and-a-two..."

They jumped on three.

The floor flipped, became a ceiling. Gravity reversed. They landed on their backs with a thud. There were several audible intakes of breath from the cavern's occupants.

Herb sat up to see Mark, Simon, and Mrs. Büdenbender sitting around what appeared to be the remains of a small bonfire. Only a single candle's worth of flame remained alive in the charred embers. From Herb's vantage, it appeared the man in the black suit was seated in Mrs. Büdenbender's lap, but his cannabis-fogged brain could not quite figure out why his complexion was so waxy and pale, nor why his eyes were clouded over.

"Herb!" Mark yelled. "How the hell did you get here? Oh my god, Beth-Ann!"

Beth-Ann sat up and locked eyes with her mother. Her eyes shone brightly for a moment, but the shine was quickly replaced by a perplexed look.

"Mommy?"

"Beth-Ann!" Mrs. Büdenbender said. "What have they done to you?" She struggled for a moment, and then, with Mark and Simon's help, stood up, the man in the black suit's lifeless body hanging from her.

Beth-Ann began to cry.

## CHAPTER THIRTY-FIVE

### -- THE ALLEGORY OF THE CAVE. --

Lovenight could not tear his eyes away from Mrs. Büdenbender.

She was bizarre, even by his standards. Truly, utterly, bizarre. The limp head, arms, and shoulders of a smallish man projected from her side just below her shoulders, while the corresponding legs dangled from her opposite hip like limp sausages. How the man had been fused to a middle-aged mother of Germanic descent, he hadn't the foggiest notion.

"Zulch!" he exclaimed, when his brain could not locate any other appropriate response.

Mark helped steady his mother on one side, while Simon assisted on the other. Across from them Beth-Ann cowered, hugging Noodles to her chest. The pug growled if any of the others locked eyes with him or stared too long at Beth-Ann. Mrs. Büdenbender's face wrinkled up and her eyes clouded over, her heartbreak evident.

"Sweetie, please don't. It's me, your mother."

"Mommy, what happened to you?"

"Well, it's quite a story. You see, when I got home from work I found your brother and Simon had summoned...this...this person," she indicated with a nod the lolling head just under her shoulder. "They were trying to return him to...where ever he came from, I suppose. He was very rude, and seemed most anxious to go. So I insisted they try, and they did, a very good try too. But just before this man went away he mentioned you, and well, I panicked. I didn't want him to leave before you came back. I tried to stop him leaving just as the magic spell was working--"

"It's not a magic spell," Simon said sullenly, eyes cast downward. "It was an evocation."

"Yes, sorry, not magic. Just as Mark and Simon were...evocating...I tried to stop him from leaving and this happened." She indicated the corpse half-submerged in her torso. "Then this person drank some water and died, which opened up his memories to me because they were still stuck in his brain which is now a part of me, I guess, which led us here by using the..." She checked the foreign memories. "Using the inflation-slipway your brother and Simon brought into the house in the...The Amulet of Amon'Zul, the Opener of Closed Ways. Dear me, that's a mouthful. And then we came here and heard this strange voice calling itself Moist-Jujubes, and this Moist-Jujubes said it met you."

"She's my friend."

"Yes. Moist-Jujubes told us you were thrown into some kind of navel fire--"

"The Navel of the Universe in the form of the Universal Fire," Mark interjected. "That's what it was called, but we don't really know what it was or where it was, so we couldn't find you."

Mrs. Büdenbender continued, her sole focus on her daughter. "We could hear you singing."

Beth-Ann nodded. "Singing keeps me calm when I'm feeling scared."

"And then this Moist-Jujubes told us this Gumbel was after you--"

"The Gambrel," Simon said. "It calls itself the Gambrel."

"Yes, anyway, this Gambrel person is after you so he can link with you, or something like that. But it doesn't matter now because we found you! And that's about us all caught up. What's been happening with you?"

Beth-Ann snapped her fingers and exclaimed, "The Gambrel must have been on this planet! He's the man in the black suit! That's why I ended up here. They swapped me for him."

"We didn't swap you for him!" Simon protested. "We were summoning a dark power and you got in the way."

Beth-Ann stabbed a finger at Mark. "Because he stole my sidewalk chalk without asking!"

"You don't ask someone if you can steal their sidewalk chalk, butthead!" Mark said. "And we just used some of it. I was going to give it back."

"Enough!" Mrs. Bündenbender commanded, using a tone her children referred to as her 'insanely scary mom voice'. "Look at me, all of you. Now, it doesn't matter who stole whose chalk, or who summoned the strange little man stuck to my belly. What's important is we work together to get back home. Can everyone agree on that? Good, now I don't want to hear any more fighting."

Mrs. Bündenbender turned to Lovenight. Under the influence of her motherly gaze, he had the irrepressible urge to stop slouching and check to see if his fingernails were clean.

"Thank you for helping my daughter," Mrs. Bündenbender said warmly.

Something fluttered in Lovenight's chest and he shifted his weight nervously. Not many people actually gave him heartfelt thanks. It was disconcerting.

"You're welcome," he said, hoping that would appease her.

Mrs. Bündenbender cleared her throat. "Who are you exactly?"

"Lovenight. Edmund Lovenight. Professional rogue and chrono-operative...also rescuer of children, apparently."

"I don't know what any of that means, but perhaps I'll find out later." Mrs. Bündenbender turned back to Beth-Ann and asked, "Where did you find that darling little puppy?"

Noodles snorted derisively. "I ain't no puppy, lady. I'm a grown-ass dog."

"Of course you are. Thank you. And thank you too, Herb."

"*Namaste*, Mrs. B." Herb flashed a peace sign to Mrs Büdenbender.

"Desist immediately!" Lovenight commanded. "Halt! Cease! Abstain from movement! You!" he said pointing to Simon. "You're Simon Callaway, yes? Simon 'the Pieman' Callaway?"

Simon looked confused and slightly afraid. "Yeah," he admitted grudgingly.

"You have a friend in Canada, named Cody. He's been a very bad boy, stealing his uncle's universal errata and hawking them to you in exchange for hemp, weed, chronic... whatever the kids call it these days. It's going to stop. Now. Understand?"

Simon regarded Lovenight with a puzzled expression, and then turned to Herb and asked, "How come the old dude is wearing your clothes?"

Herb shrugged and answered, "Dude was nude."

"Old dude?" Lovenight roared. "Old? Thirty-eight isn't old!" He waggled a finger at Simon. "No more tempting Cody to steal his uncle's incredibly dangerous bric-a-brac. Understand?"

"Fine. Whatever."

"Excellent. Good. Now, where the hell are we?" he asked, casting his wonderstruck eyes around the cavern, really seeing it for the first time.

"Looks like a cave," Herb said. "Same one we were just in."

"Moist-Jujubes said it was an allegory or something."

"Who's that?" Lovenight asked, his eyebrows narrowing. "Who is this...'Moist-Jujubes'?" Lovenight said the name as if he'd just discovered his mouth was coated in peanut oil.

"She threw me in the bonfire." Beth-Ann pointed to the small flame burning without smoke in the centre of the cavern. "It's not so big now, but it was huge the first time I was here."

"She what?" Mrs. Büdenbender shrieked.

"It didn't hurt. It kinda tickled."

"Today is getting away from me," Lovenight said to himself. Considering their circumstances, he felt there should have been a lot more panic and anxiety going around. Instead, everyone seemed to be reasonably calm. Lovenight's eyebrows arched in annoyance. "Look, you lot: don't you get it? Today isn't today. We're removed from all existence, you understand? From where we are, there is no way back and no time to get back to. We're outside all time-space."

"Cupcake is right," Noodles said. "There's no smell to this place. None. That could only happen in a place that isn't anywhere. Which means we're stuck in the pure inflation membrane, outside the universe."

"How can that be?" Beth-Ann asked. "We're still alive, we're still breathing so there must be air."

"We can still talk to each other," Mark added. "So there must be space for the sound waves to pass through."

"No, there isn't," Mrs. Büdenbender said sadly. Her head tilted to the side as she consulted the memories of the man in the black suit. She spoke slowly, checking each word for the appropriate meaning and context within the sentence. " The Inflation membrane is similar to dimensions smaller than Planck units, which is nothing. That's what this place is. A place which is no-place. A place where space has no meaning." She gave her head a little shake. "Dear me, I'm not sure I understand what I just said."

"Hey," said Simon, craning his head one way then another. "What happened to the entrance?"

"What are you talking about? It's right over there..." Mark began, then stopped.

The entrance into the cavern simply wasn't there anymore.

"What the hell?" Simon asked no one in particular.

The cavern rumbled. Every part of it, all the walls, ceiling, floor shook with a low intensity which vibrated the pit of Lovenight's stomach. His inner alarms became air raid sirens, blasting his consciousness with an unfaltering message: *You're in the shit now, mate.* And Lovenight knew he was in the shit, because he recognized what the rumbling was.

"What's going on?" Beth-Ann asked, her eyes darting around the cavern.

Lovenight answered, "That, my dear, was a chortle."

"A what?"

"A chortle. A throaty giggle, a chuckle, an expression of amusement. In this instance; an insidious, malicious sound of delight, presumably at our expense. I've been chortled at by many a villain, human and otherwise. I know when someone is chortling at me."

"Caverns can't laugh."

"No, but omnipotent beings can."

Another rumble struck the cavern, so strong it rocked everyone off their feet.

"Who's that?" Beth-Ann asked, getting up.

*That was Me.*

"Let me be frank," Lovenight said, dusting himself off. "I really don't like the question I'm about to ask, but I'm going to ask it anyway. Who are you, exactly?"

*I am the Gambrel. I will, thanks to those gathered in the allegory of the cave, be Everything. I am the space between spaces, the membrane between dimensions. I give space meaning, which gives the membrane potential. I flow behind all force. I am here at the beginning of heat and at the end. I am what is left over. I am what waits in infinity for infinity to end and begin again. I am the Cycle. I am what is beyond...and what is near. I will be Everything.*

"Trippy," Herb said.

Mark said, "You're the man in the black suit. We summoned you in my basement."

*I was. I am no longer.*

"You're one of the Seventy-and-Seven," Simon said.

*I was. I am no longer.*

Beth-Ann said to the Gambrel, "Moist-Jujubes said you would possess her and destroy everything."

*Not entirely accurate. I have already possessed the entity you know as Moist-Jujubes. However, by throwing you, Beth-Ann, into the fire, Moist-Jujubes deposited a fraction of Everything within you. I have possessed Moist-Jujubes, and I will now possess you. Then I will be Everything. Everything will change.*

Beth-Ann's face wrinkled up as hot tears streamed from her eyes. She tried to hold back the apprehensive sobs, which only caused her lips to tremble. Noodles, still in her arms, let out a single whimper and licked her chin. Beth-Ann said weakly. "Mom?"

Her mother moved toward her, arms outstretched, but did not get any closer. A puzzled frown twisted Mrs. Büdenbender's lips. She took another step but still did not get any nearer to her daughter despite clearly having moved her legs. Panic washed over her normally calm face. Mrs. Büdenbender strode towards her child, heaving one foot in front of the other, desperate to reach Beth-Ann.

From Lovenight's perspective, it appeared as if she was on an invisible treadmill, tromping towards her daughter yet remaining in place.

Beth-Ann screamed suddenly, her body stiffening, her head tilting back. Her eyes rolled backward leaving nothing but whiteness showing. She trembled violently.

"Noodles!" Lovenight yelled. "Help her!"

"Dip-twad! Can't you see I'm trying?" The pug simply looked stuck in the air next to Beth-Ann, his legs scrambling through empty space.

"Back up a second, evil guy," Lovenight said. "You said something about 'thanks to those gathered in the cave' you're now Everything? Explain yourself, damn it. I hate omnipotent beings who make outrageous claims to their captives and don't explain themselves. It's just annoying and thoughtless."

Many times Lovenight had gotten himself out of certain-death circumstances by enticing his antagonists to talk. As they talked, he had time to think, or blunder onto some flaw in their plan.

*You can't reason it out by yourselves?*

"We could, sure, given time. But since there is no time here, spill it. Gloat over your machinations. Revel in your unmatched genius. Go on. I know you want to."

*I'll give you a hint: follow the water.*

"Water? What water?"

"The man in the black suit asked for water!" Simon said. "Remember, Mark?"

"So?" Mark responded. "I gave him water, so what?"

"After he drank it, he handed it back to you and said, 'Don't spill it', which I thought was weird. He died right after you put the glass back on the table."

"Freaking hell!" Noodles yipped. "Fat Cheeks drank that water!"

"Oh wow," Herb said, eyes wide as dinner plates. "That's what I was seeing! Fat Cheeks was all wrong because, like, he was water-possessed!"

Satisfied with his deduction, Herb pulled out a cookie from his backpack and munched on it. The cookie was laced with hashish, a particularly potent strain developed by crossing Nepalese OG with Sour Diesel flown in from Amsterdam. It had been specifically grown and hand-pressed for him by an heirloom farmer in the micro-climate surrounding Niagra Falls. The cookie was his nuclear strike, his heavy hitter, his ultimate weapon. It turned his perceptive inner eye into an Ultra-dimensional Pana-scope in 12 D®, more powerful than a space-based intergalactic telescope, with finer resolution than a quantum-tunnelling scanner. Sure, it would leave him blotto-whacked, but for a few critical minutes, he would have an all-seeing eye.

Herb felt he would be needing an all-seeing eye very soon.

"Hey, Gremble or Gumbo or whatever the hell your name is!" Noodles yelled at the cavern. "Yeah, I'm talking to you, disembodied voice of a ball-licker. Tell us, what was in that water?"

*I was. It was the medium for My consciousness. It allowed Me to transfer from the vessel you know as 'the man in the black suit' to the dog-walker Fat Cheeks, and ultimately into the inflation-membrane through the slipway opened by the Amulet of Amon-zul. Freed, I returned here, to the gallery I had prepared for the entity known to you as Moist-Jujubes.*

"I get it," Lovenight said. "This 'gallery' of yours was a trap set for this Moist-Jujubes. Just an incredibly oversized version of a parlour assassin. You were going to lure Moist here and possess her. But good ol' Moist threw a spanner in the pudding when she tossed a bit of Everything to Beth-Ann, who then escaped. And we..." Lovenight fell silent.

Simon picked up on the insight. He said in a dire and regretful tone, "And we, very obligingly, brought her back here, to you."

*And for that, I thank you.*

"You putrid lump of cat vomit!" the pug yelled. "You pustulant, feces-eating, toilet raider! You killed Fat Cheeks! I'll gut you!"

*That, is improbable. Much more likely I will keep you here, for all eternity and a day, in one tiny gallery of My museum.*

They stood in stunned silence for a moment. The silence was broken by a Beth-Ann's quiet and terrified voice.

"Mommy? What's happening?"

# CHAPTER THIRTY-SIX

## -- EVERYWHERE, EVERYWHEN --

Beth-Ann glowed with the light of a billion stars. The brightness erupted from her skin, obscuring her face, transforming her into a luminous silhouette. Star-clusters swirled inside her. Strings of galaxies were nothing more than freckles on her cheeks.

"Beth-Ann!" Mrs. Büdenbender cried.

*She is Mine. I have possessed her. I will take her part of Everything and be Everything.*

"Let go of her, you cosmic bastard!" Noodles appeared to be mere inches away from Beth-Ann, stuck in midair. The pug scampered, nipping and twisting every which way, frantic to reach the girl. "What the hell is going on? Why can't I move?"

*You cannot help her. Nothing can. Look at her, each of you! She is the Navel of the Universe now!*

Mark's face wrinkled. "That term, the Navel of the Universe. It's how energy flows into the universe from beyond, or vice versa."

"She's the gateway!" Simon said. "The Gambrel has turned her into a gateway so all his galleries, those 'grains of potential' can leave our universe! We have to interrupt Beth-Ann, like she did when she stepped into the triangle-of-conjuration. That'll stop the possession."

"Shock the audience," Herb mused to himself. "Make a cool jump cut and exorcize that demon. Far out."

"Then get a lifeline to the girl, and reel her back to our perception of reality," Lovenight added. "What we need is a lifeline, something that has meaning for Beth-Ann on any scale."

"I don't understand any of this," Mrs. Büdenbender said stoically. She stiffened her back and held her head high. "But she's my little baby, and if she needs a life-line, I'm it."

Mrs. Büdenbender stomped her foot. It was no ordinary stomp, it was a *mother's stomp*, undeniable in its power and universal effect. Children all over the world dreaded that footfall, which meant *Stop what you are doing immediately and pay attention!* There was no sound, but the emotional force struck Lovenight in the gut.

"Beth-Ann!" Mrs. Büdenbender roared. "Come here this instant!"

Beth-Ann's starry form wavered, her features coming into focus momentarily. The colour of light radiating from her changed, making the star-fields in her cheeks quiver. The whiteness in her eyes rolled downward as her pupils came into view.

Noodles yelped, "Jesus Christ, are any of you seeing this?"

"Freaking me right out," Herb said.

*Mom, is that you?*

It was Beth-Ann's voice, but it resonated from everywhere at once. She sounded scared, desperate.

"Yes, Beth-Ann, it's mommy. And I need you to come here, right this instant!"

*Where are you mommy? I can't see you. I can't see anything.*

Mrs. Büdenbender said firmly, "You'll have to do better, Beth-Ann. Do you hear me? Do better. Follow my voice. Find me!"

*I hear you mommy.*

"Good. Find me."

*Mommy? Mom, you're everywhere at once but I can't touch you.*

"Beth-Ann! I'm here. I'm right here."

"Eureka!" Lovenight exclaimed, and spread his arms, gathering the attention of everyone except Mrs. Büdenbender and Beth-Ann. He paused for dramatic effect.

"Jesus-suffering-Christ, cupcake," Noodles berated him. "Get on with it!"

"This isn't a cave," he pronounced.

Mark, Simon, and Noodles all waited for Lovenight to say something more, but nothing more came.

"That's it?" Noodles growled, his ears flat against his head. "When this is over, I'm going to give you the same treatment I gave the mayor of Chicago."

Mark ignored Noodles and said to Lovenight, "We know that already. It's an allegory."

Lovenight shook his head. "Don't you see? We're in the inflation zone. Space and time have no meaning here. This was *terra incompleta* until the Gambrel arrived and made a trap for Moist-Jujubes. Now, Moist-Jujubes is gone and Beth-Ann is being absorbed, becoming Everything with the Gambrel. Which means it's our narrative now. We can change this space. Anything we want if we all perceive it together."

"How?" Mark asked.

"Heisenberg's uncertainty principle: the very effect of observing reality changes it. It's necro-quantum theory: 101. Try not to be such undergrads, will you."

"He's right, Mark," Simon said. "We just have to figure out how to bridge space and time and reunite Beth-Ann with your mom. That will break the possession."

"We can change this cave into whatever we want?" Mark asked. "Just by imagining it?"

Lovenight wracked his sketchy memory. What was it Niels Bohr had said to Reg? Time is an illusion. Space is an illusion. Perception is everything.

"Why not?" Lovenight answered. "It's just perception. People choose to believe in the most far-fetched, improbable, wackadoodle realities all the time."

"All right, I got this." Noodles said. "Everyone close your eyes."

They did. After several seconds the air felt different against Lovenight's skin, less humid and musty, more enclosed. Somehow the space seemed cozy. The ground beneath his feet softened.

Noodles said, "Okay, open your eyes."

They stood as they had before -- Mark and Simon on either side of Mrs. Büdenbender, Noodles next to Beth-Ann, Herb a few feet from Lovenight, except now the cavern had transformed into a dream living room for dogs, filled with sofas and half-chewed rawhide bones, the floor covered in luxuriant, freshly mowed grass. A white picket fence sectioned off part of the lawn, the sign hanging on it read IF YOU GOTTA GO, DO IT HERE AND PICK IT UP AFTERWARDS! A flatscreen monitor displayed a video of a large tabby leaping towards a screen door, only to have its claws stick in the mesh. It whined pitifully as it hung, trapped by its own misjudgment, its eyes swinging back to the camera for help.

"Cat-fail videos?" Lovenight asked.

Noodles chuckled. "Stupid cats."

Mrs. Büdenbender remained focused on her daughter. Beth-Ann's luminescent figure seemed more stable, harder around the edges, as it leaned toward her mother.

"Just how is this going to bring mother and daughter together?" Lovenight asked.

"What're you talking about? Everyone loves stupid cat videos! Pull up a couch and gnaw on a bone."

"And how, pray tell, am I supposed to pull up a couch when I can't move?"

A deep chuckle rolled through the canine-fantasy living room, jostling the widescreen monitor. *Run as you may, you cannot escape inevitability. That's what I've become: inevitable.*

"I got it!" Herb mumbled. "Connect Mrs. B. and Beth-Ann, followed by the biggest match cut of all time to release Beth-Ann! No problemo." He raised his hands and looked to each of them. Lovenight frowned. Noodles shifted uncomfortably.

Simon cleared his throat. "Herb, are you sure, buddy? You know how you can sometimes think something is a great idea when you're stoned, and the next morning you realize it's about as dumb as swimsuits for fish?"

Herb shook his head and smiled his half-baked smile. "No, man. I'm telling you, I got this."

Mark took in a dose off his inhaler. "Okay, I'm in." With that, he closed his eyes.

Simon shrugged as his eyelids shut.

Noodles panted rapidly. "Somehow's I don't think this is a good idea, but yeah, what the hell. Gotta scratch as much as you can outta life." He closed his eyes.

"It's just one existential crisis after another!" Lovenight sighed and shut his eyes. "Bugger it, I'm ready."

The change was instantaneous.

Lovenight felt different. He hunched slightly. His skull seemed smaller while his cheekbones had broadened. He resisted a tremendous urge to walk on all fours. The stoney ground warmed the soles of his feet with their prehensile toes. Bright sunlight blazed against his hairy eyelids.

Primal shrieks rent the air, like the bars had just been opened for the day at the monkey house.

Lovenight opened his eyes and found he was celebrating with the rest of the tribe.

He had become an apeman. A thick carpet of black hair covered every inch of his body.

"Ahhhh, that's why my skin is so itchy."

The other apemen gibbered and snorted, jumping up and down, waving their hairy arms under the African sky. Many brandished jawbones and femurs at a rival tribe of apemen retreating from a small watering hole, surrounded by several boulders. Two corpses lay at the edge of the muddy water. Members of Lovenight's tribe took turns beating the bodies with their scavenged weapons.

"What the hell is going on?" Lovenight asked, as he leapt onto a dusty boulder in celebration. He was completely naked, yet again.

Simon loped by on all fours, also naked, his face much more simian-looking with a pronounced brow ridge. "Herb!" he shouted. "What the living hell?"

Mark screeched and hopped around in a circle. "He put us in

*2001: A Space Odyssey*...as the apes!"

"Is this what's it like to be a primate?" yelled a retreating apeman whose face was remarkably pug-like. The pug-ape shook his hairy arms back at Lovenight. "I pity you poor bastards! There's no way you can lick yourselves."

300 miles above them, Herb-the-spaceship orbited. The metal hull morphed into Herb's features and said, "Being in a movie! Perfect to get Mrs. B. and Beth-Ann together."

"Except my mom's dead!" Mark yelled, and pointed to the corpse by the waterhole, a buxom female who appeared to be lying on top of a thin, sickly apeman. Their corpses formed a crude X shape.

"That's on me," Herb-the-spaceship said, his metal-face flushing.

*Amusing,* the Gambrel commented. *But ultimately pointless. Everything will change.*

"Where's Beth-Ann?" Mark asked.

"You mean this?" Lovenight yelled, and threw the luminous femur bone he was holding into the air. As it tumbled in the African sky, end over end, the bone shed clusters of stars.

"Quick, before we flash forward to space," Lovenight yelled. "Everyone close your eyes."

Deep in his brain Lovenight heard the chiding voice of Lady Montique yelling, *No cock-ups for you today, Donkey!*

The voice didn't bother him in the slightest. There would be no cock-ups. He had figured it out. He knew how to bridge the space between mother and daughter. Not just space, but time had to be factored into the reality as well. Niels Bohr had said to Reg, *Time was an illusion. Space was an illusion. Perception is everything.*

And if space and time are illusions, the past can be now, the future can be now, the past can be the future.

With their eyes closed, Lovenight bent reality to his will. Which wasn't hard: ignore a few uncomfortable facts in favour of a more self-satisfying viewpoint and you've got the general gist of how to change reality. Easy peasy. And more self-satisfying viewpoints were Lovenight's gospel. He didn't care if they fit conventional facts. It didn't matter if they made sense. What

Lovenight cared about was living, seeing another sunrise, drinking another cocktail; everything else was superfluous.

What mattered was life. That was the real connection between people, especially a mother and her child. All he needed to do was bring them to a time when mother and child shared life. This wasn't about space. This was about time.

And time was something Lovenight molded like putty.

"Okay, open your eyes," Lovenight said.

Noodles, Mark, Simon, Herb, and Lovenight floated in liquid, completely immersed, but able to breathe. They all glowed a beautiful, bioluminescent green, like algae in a tropical sea. The liquid was warm and comforting. They were sandwiched between two titanic membranes which stretched away into darkness, the surfaces perfectly smooth.

A pounding, rhythmic thumping thundered: the unmistakable beating of a human heart. Not the dry, sterile thump heard through a stethoscope. This heartbeat was squishy and wet. It rocked them gently.

"Jesus Christ," Noodles said, examining a fleshy tube snaking between the two membranes. "I think I preferred being an apeman."

Simon reached out his hands and felt a warm, elastic give where the cavern walls once were. Gurgles and burbles sounded nearby, just beyond the membranes. "What the heck is this?"

"Where's mom and Beth-Ann?" Mark asked, a tinge of terror evident in his voice. "I don't see them."

"Well, actually," Lovenight said. "You do."

"I swear to god, cupcake, I will mess you up!" Noodles yelled. "Just where the hell have you put us, and where's the girl and the mom?"

"They're right there. Connected." Lovenight pointed to the two membranes.

One of the membranes shifted causing a rip current in the fluid, pulling Mark forward and slamming him into Simon. Noodles cartwheeled past as the flow took him, narrowly missing their heads. Herb, unperturbed, tumbled passed sitting in a cross-legged lotus position.

"Just go with it," he offered as advice.

"Hey, we moved!" Mark said. "We touched."

"What was that?" Simon demanded to know. "That shifting?"

"Not entirely sure because I don't have a good vantage point," Lovenight said. "But I think the baby just kicked."

"Baby? What baby?"

"That baby," Lovenight said, pointing to the shifting membrane. "Beth-Ann the fetus, ready to be born."

Mark's mouth sagged open and his eyelids stretched back. "You mean, I'm in my mom's womb?"

"The amniotic sac, to be more precise, but, yes." Lovenight nodded. "Absolutely the perfect *space* and *time* to bring mother and daughter together, before they were separated, when they were one. "

On hearing he was back in his mother's amniotic sac, Mark bent forward and wretched uncontrollably.

# CHAPTER THIRTY-SEVEN

## -- UMM, I'D RATHER NOT SAY --

*What have you done?* The voice of the Gambrel resonated through every bone fissure and blood vessel contained in Lovenight's body. It reached into crevasses he didn't know he had. It rattled organs and squeezed airways. It chilled Lovenight's blood.

"Why, you spiteful little deity," he replied merrily. "Something the matter?"

*What have you DONE?*

The universe, which at this point was the amniotic sac carrying the unborn Beth-Ann, shook as the Gambrel's voice thundered across it. Shockwaves tossed Lovenight, Noodles, Herb, Mark and Simon about as they struggled to ride out the seething anger of the Gambrel.

"Hey cupcake!" Noodles yelled, grabbing Lovenight's attention. "Try not to piss him off."

*What is happening to Me?*

"You're losing your godhead," Lovenight explained. "You're

being absorbed into your old body through something called N.P.P., or Necronominal Probability Placement. Even you have sub-subatomic particles making up your existence. Those particles want to be where they were when you were alive, or dead, or something like that -- I can't remember what Reg said exactly. Regardless, the point is N.P.P. is now ripping you out of the fabric of the universe and putting you back into your dead body, the one still fused to Mrs. Büdenbender. Necro-science can be an unforgiving bastard."

As he spoke, Lovenight noted the galaxy clusters traveling along the umbilical cord. They pulsed in time with the omnidirectional heartbeat.

*Stop this!*

"You wanted to use a little girl as the fulcrum of your universal takeover," Lovenight sneered. "Quite gauche, if you ask me."

Noodles bared his teeth at Lovenight in disgust. "Have the decency to smack-talk in American!"

"Put a muzzle on it, stick-breath! Can't you see I'm talking with the decaying entity who tried to take over the universe?"

"I get that. What I don't get is why you have to use froo-froo words that would embarrass a poodle."

"Are you mocking me for having a vocabulary?"

"I'm mocking you because you're a cupcake!"

"I'm going to neuter you with a pickle-fork, you vile, bug-eyed excuse for a canine," Lovenight snapped. "How about a smidgeon of gratitude for saving everyone and everything!"

"Shut up, both of you!" Simon yelled. "Help me with Mark! He's in shock!"

Mark hung limp in his mother's amniotic fluid, gaping at the two massive cliffs of universal-flesh surrounding them. Simon gripped him under the arms and frog-kicked closer to Noodles and Lovenight, towing his friend along with him.

Lovenight cocked a sympathetic eyebrow at the insensible college student. "Can't say I'd fair any better, back in mom's womb after being evicted. That's gotta be weird."

"Eww, eww, eww," Mark said weakly.

*Ooooooohwereeeerre!*

A gnarling, gnashing wail of despair and feral anger thundered through their bodies. Without warning, flashes of deep darkness -- complete and utter shadows -- rushed by in a torrent. One engulfed the five of them. It felt oily and unhealthy on their skins, like being encased in warm lunchmeat. An unseen force ripped it away after a few seconds, its few remaining void tendrils dispersing as quick as ink drops in water.

When it passed Noodles shook himself and said, "What the hell was that?"

"It's the Gambrel, struggling to stay part of this universe." To the blackness surrounding them Lovenight yelled, "You can't beat necro-science, you immense philistine!"

"Could you please stop shouting and figure a way out of here!" Simon demanded. "Now! Look what being here is doing to Mark!"

If there was some possible way Mark could have drooled while submerged in fluid, he would have.

Noodles shook his head. "I'm no shrink, but I'll bet the boy's going to have serious mommy issues after this."

"An Oedipus complex at the very least," Lovenight agreed.

Vibration -- sheer oscillating energy, a thunderhead of it -- rolled over them suddenly. The membranes of mother-universe and daughter-universe squeezed together, squishing Mark, Simon, Noodles, and Lovenight against one another like commuters on the Tokyo subway.

When it finally relaxed Noodles yelped, "What in the name of God's succulent asshole was that?"

"Oh no," Lovenight said.

Simon fixated on Lovenight, glaring at him with wild, accusing eyes. "'Oh no'? What 'Oh no'? 'Oh no' is bad, isn't it?"

"I think the shock of reabsorbing the Gambrel is sending Mrs. Büdenbender into labour. That was a contraction."

"Jesus-suffering-Christ!" Noodles bellowed and turned to Herb. "I swear by my swollen left nut, I'm going to piss up and down your leg for getting me into this!"

Herb did not have time to respond before a strong current swept them up and carried them away. The fleshy cliff walls rushed by. They clung together as the current banked around a corner, then the membranes fell away and they tumbled in vast darkness -- a wide-open nothing -- continuing in the direction

Lovenight thought of as downwards, all the while accelerating. It was like drifting in a deep ocean current where sunlight never reached.

"This is pissing me off!" Noodles cussed as he sped along. "I feel like a turd flushed down a sewer."

"Not a bad analogy," Lovenight said. "I think the universe's water just broke."

"Just go with it, man," Herb advised. "Flow with the flow, ride the ride."

"What about Beth-Ann?" Simon asked.

Lovenight yelled, "Beth-Ann's coming with us whether she wants to or not."

Ahead, golden light split the darkness, folding outwards and separating the void into two distinct halves, until the warm brightness dominated the universe. The wide, wild torrent bore them straight towards the centre of the light.

The proverbial 'light at the end of the tunnel', Lovenight thought. Odd to see it from this viewpoint.

Turbulence buffed them as they shot into the brilliance. What each yelled at that moment was quite telling:

Lovenight: "No one should have to go through this twice!"

Mark: "EWW, EWW, EWW!"

Simon: "I've always loved you, Mark!"

Herb: "What a long, strange, head-trip this has been!"

Noodles: "I've been through worse."

# CHAPTER THIRTY-EIGHT

### -- YOU WOULDN'T BELIEVE ME IF I TOLD YOU --

Lovenight opened his eyes.
Lightning encased him, forking and twisting around his body, forming a web, which was actually quite comfortable he was surprised to find. It was like laying in a hammock, an electric hammock sure, but a hammock nonetheless. Carefully, he extended his arm. There was a slight resistance which gave way almost immediately as the lightning web stretched with him. Somehow it was reassuring, comforting; even if it did make the hairs on his forearms stick up.
Mark and Simon floated nearby, while Noodles and Herb bobbed just below Lovenight's feet, all of them suspended by electrical nets of their own. Looks of astonishment dotted their faces.
Good, Lovenight thought. I'm not the only one who hasn't the faintest idea what's going on.

They bobbed in the cleanest, whitest cloud ever imagined. It was so dense Lovenight could not see more than twenty feet in any direction through the heaps of billowing water vapour. The cloud was pristine, perfect. There was no wind, no sound, no discernible movement aside from the wisps of vapour. It was a child's vision of Heaven -- minus the white-haired grandfather figure lounging about in a toga and dispensing halos to passersby.

"Hey, look!" Simon exclaimed while pointing in a direction Lovenight assumed was up.

Beth-Ann floated above them encased in her own blue-white lightning hammock.

"Beth-Ann!" Simon called. "Are you okay?"

She looked startled for a moment, then looked down and saw the lightning webs below her. "Yeah, I'm fine, I think. Where's Mark?"

"Over here!" Mark shouted, and did his best to swim towards her, but all he succeeded in doing was stretching the lightning web around him into odd shapes. It bounded back as soon as he stopped flailing about.

"Where are we?" Noodles yelped. "And what's with the cloud and this lightning blanket I'm trapped in? It's making my ass itch."

Herb shrugged. "That's life, really. Aren't we all trapped in mental blankets of our own making?"

"Stop that!" Noodles shouted. "No freaking existential bullshit! You wanna know why? Cause I just came out of a freaking human vagina the size of a planet, that's why!"

"A what?" Beth-Ann asked. "What're you talking about? What's going on?"

"It's all right," Mark said. "I'll explain everything."

"Noodles, chill" Herb said, a wide relaxed grin on his face. "Don't you recognize this place?"

"No Herb, I obviously don't or I wouldn't have asked the question!" Noodles barked. "And don't tell me to chill! I hate it when people tell me to chill. It makes it impossible for me to chill. God, why do you have to be such a calm, peaceful dude? It bugs the shit outta me sometimes. Just spill it, where are we?"

Herb just smiled. "Who do the electric voodoo, so well?"

There was a moment of silence and stillness before Noodles

said stoically, "I'm going to need more therapy."

"Listen!" Lovenight hissed suddenly. "Do you hear that?"

Faintly, the sounds of a choir could be heard singing "I Shall Be Released". It was a joyous, hopeful sound, filling the ears and the hearts of all who heard it.

"Bloody hell, what new horror is this?" Lovenight asked.

The lightning hammocks intensified, brighten, pulled together forming a tight-knit circle. The individual webs merged, became a giant electric net surrounding them, which contracted, pressing them together like packaged spaghetti, nose to nose.

Noodles jumped back into Beth-Ann's arms.

"Hey, you feel that?" Lovenight said. "Gravity's back."

"And we're going down," Mark said. "Fast. Very Fast. Too fast, really."

Herb grinned. "Yeah, groovy."

The cloud thinned below them. The forms of trees and sky and hydroelectric towers coalesced out of the milky whiteness. The entire horizon opened up, green and lush, with subdivisions curled up against hills and hollows, and roads cut through the landscape. Fluffy white clouds cast long shadows on the earth below. It looked idyllic from high above.

The lightning flared, blinding them momentarily as they continued to descend.

"We're slowing down," Simon said.

Noodles shifted uncomfortably. "Watch where you're putting your hands, cupcake. We ain't that close."

Without warning, they landed with a solid, metallic thunk. The lightning sped off, releasing them. Lovenight blinked away the afterimages. After a moment he could see once again.

A blind man stood next to Lovenight, a huge grin stretched his lips, dark sunglasses obscuring his eyes. In his hand he held a hacksaw. He giggled like a kid.

"Ahh, yeah!" he screeched. "This is going to confuse the hell outta Preston!"

Lovenight had no idea what the blind man was referring to and at the moment really didn't care. What held his attention was the high-voltage power lines buzzing a mere metre from his head. All the hairs on his forearms rose up and waved to the mammoth voltage. Goose bumps pebbled his arms.

Below them on the ground someone was shouting.

The concept stuck in Lovenight's already overwhelmed mind. He considered it again: someone was shouting from below -- on the ground. But how? Hadn't they landed? A thought nailed him square between the eyes: look down and get more information! So he did.

Lovenight wished he hadn't.

All five of them -- plus the blindman -- were about seventy-five feet off the ground in the fully extended bucket of a bucket truck. A crew of electrical workers stared up at them with shocked faces. Some pointed, while others ran to the hydraulic controls. A supervisor wearing a yellow hardhat and appearing apoplectic, yelled, "Earl! What happened? Are you okay? Earl, answer me!"

The blind man giggled. "Stay away from the wires, y'all. Those makeshift lightning suits I fitted you with are gone now." The blind electrician cocked his head toward the pug. "Hey ya, Noodles. How y'all been?"

"Jesus Christ Earl, you blind bastard! I could lick your whole face then go in for sloppy seconds! How the hell did you pull us out of there?"

"Been watching the whole electromagnetic-paradisiacal spectrum since Herb dropped by last week. Knew something weird was coming down the pipeline. Just had to watch for it. Sure enough, things got really psychedelic about an hour ago. Every radio station started playing Santana. I knew it had to be Herb. Hey ya, Herb."

Herb nodded to the blind electrician. "Owe you one, Earl."

"Sure do."

"Look," Lovenight said, "I don't mean to interrupt this jolly reunion, but we're in a bucket. Next to wires. Very dangerous wires."

"Relax y'all. The boys will get us down."

As he spoke the bucket lurched. The hydraulic arm hissed as it slowly lowered down to the ground. The Episcopalian choir burst into "Oh Happy Day", arms raised and voices loud, their white and gold robes vibrant in the sunlight.

The electrical crew helped Mark, Simon, and Beth-Ann as they climbed out of the bucket. Mark hugged Beth-Ann, who still cradled Noodles. He then turned and gave Simon the warmest, most heartfelt hug of his life. Simon melted into the embrace.

Noodles appeared resolved to stay right where he was, pressed close to Beth-Ann. And for her part, Beth-Ann seemed dead set on keeping the pug with her. She had settled on him, and he had settled on her, and that was that.

Herb walked slowly on the soft earth, carefully placing one foot firmly on the ground before taking a step with the other. He probed the area for slippage. Satisfied everything was stable and in order, he nodded to himself and said, "Good job."

Preston, the supervisor in the yellow hardhat ran over, his eyes tight and small and fixed on the blind electrician. It took him several moments to relax the muscles around his lips in order to get them to form coherent words.

"Who...who're these people? Who're you people? How did you get up there? And what was that light? Earl? Was that a major systems failure? If it was, you have to tell me, I'm your supervisor! Are we going to have news crews here asking questions on why the entire Southeastern grid is down?"

Lovenight stood tall, placed his arms akimbo, and struck a pose reminiscent of MacArthur in the Philippines. The effect was somewhat diminished by his clothes. Herb's *The Good, the Bad, and the Ugly* t-shirt and sweatpants didn't really convey the gravitas he would have liked, but he struck the pose regardless and hoped his bravado would carry the day.

"Who're we? What a question! How dare you step forward and demand answers from we, the weary heroes whose deeds are destined to be unsung." He pointed towards the blind electrician. "And this man is a saviour, rescuing us from certain death, after we, of course, rescued all of existence from non-existence."

Preston, bewildered, turned to Earl. "How, how did you do that, Earl? How? The cloud bank, the lightning ball, these people. How?"

"Preston, baby, if you got the jazz, you got the jazz. You know?"

"Excuse me," Beth-Ann said, stepping up to Earl and asking.

"Where's my mom?"

Earl looked puzzled and concerned. "Your momma, baby? Ain't no one else in there. Believe me, I checked."

Beth-Ann's chin wrinkled, tears dripping down her cheeks, as she looked to Mark and asked again, "Where's mom?"

# CHAPTER THIRTY-NINE

-- LONDON, ENGLAND. SIX MONTHS LATER THAN THE LAST NOW. --

    Lovenight and Herb stood next to each other in Room 10a of the British Museum, studying bas-reliefs taken from the North Palace of Nineveh, an Assyrian city located in present-day Iraq. The reliefs depicted a lion hunt by an Assyrian king around 800 B.C.E. Lovenight and Herb peered intently at one particular relief, depicting King Ashurbanipal holding back a charging lion with one arm while thrusting a sword through its belly with the other.
    Herb and Lovenight tilted their heads.
    "I don't know," Herb said, his disincorporated form rippling in the gallery's solid-state lighting. "Maybe without the beard."
    "Definitely without the beard." Lovenight adjusted his ascot and straightened the sleeves of his double-breasted plum jacket. He had several invitations later to after-party parties, and wished to make sure this detour didn't make him look all rumpled. A thought struck him. "She never had a beard, right?"

"Mrs B.? No man. Not that I ever saw. And look, what's the thing sticking out behind the guy...?"

"The scabbard for his sword?"

"Yeah, it kinda looks like a leg, and the tail end of the skirt he's wearing looks like the other."

Lovenight cocked his head slightly, trying to see what Herb was seeing. He nodded slow. "Yes, I'll buy that. Far many more things have been bastardized by so-called artists taking so-called 'artistic license'."

"And the thing coming out of the guy's side, behind his arm."

"I think that's supposed to be the lion's paw reaching for him."

"Perspective, man. It's the same spot the Gambrel's head came out of Mrs. B. I'm telling you that's her! That's Mrs. Büdenbender! She's sending us a message." Herb took a hit off a small pipe, coughing for a moment before exhaling. The disincorporated pot smoke dissipated quickly leaving no scent.

Lovenight took a step back and sat on the row of benches running the length of the gallery. "Why would she send us a message? What good could it possibly do?"

"Maybe give some sense of an end, you know, so Mark and Beth-Ann don't have to worry."

"How are they?"

"They're getting by, and Simon's helping, but anytime you lose your mom it's hard. Having Noodles staying with them helps. He's become very protective of Beth-Ann."

"You'll tell them about this?"

"Sure will." Herb nodded, then indicated the bas-relief. "It'll give them hope. It's symbolic."

"Symbolic of what?"

"You know, the king defending his people from whatever threatens them."

"So, you think Mrs. Büdenbender is sending us a symbolic message in a 2500-year-old bas-relief? You think she's trying to tell her kids she's watching over them? A fundamental pillar of the universe is protecting her progeny?"

Herb shrugged. "I just think the universe owes us one." He paused a moment. "You find your friends?"

Lovenight opened his mouth to speak and found words failed

him. He had been about to say 'they're my colleagues, not my friends', but couldn't. Instead, he just shook his head. For a dangerous moment he felt empty, ready to cry. He shook it off.

"You never did tell me what happened?" Herb prodded.

"Simon's flat had been ransacked. Reg was nowhere to be seen. The Stout Scarab was demolished, the front passenger door ripped off its hinges, Lady Montique and John H. Smith both missing. Turns out those weren't just rats. Someone was trifling with me, and I didn't see it."

"You want help finding out what happened?"

"Thanks, but...maybe. Yeah, I think."

"All right. You let me know. Hey, you found us in an inflation slipway, then rescued Beth-Ann."

Lovenight smiled. "*Via con dios*, Herb. Whack the pug on the snout, for me."

"Later, Lovenight."

Herb dissipated, leaving Lovenight alone amongst the Assyrian reliefs. He sat for a long while, staring at the ancient carvings, his mind back at Simon's flat the last time with Reg, his thoughts as heavy as the stones around him.

He shook himself, dissipating the melancholic fog forming in his brain. What mattered now was finding Reg and Lady Montique and John H. Smith, and hopefully, rescuing them.

Only one person possessed the means and resources to capture them.

His trip to Mexico had yielded several relevant facts: the secret lab destroyed in a mudslide, the private airstrip bulldozed over, the coconut stand abandoned, the Governance gone, Baroness Zamora vanished. The trail went cold right there.

Somehow, now, he had to pick it up and keep going.

Before that night in Michigan he was ready to quit the Outliers. No more operative work for him. No more missing parties because while searching for a Long-Term Care Facility in the middle of an October night. No more hyper-evolving into a cockroach and tasting floor. No more being digested in the stomach of a pan-universal assassin. No more torture at the hands of the sadistic self-interrogators. No more tea tests.

But then Reg, damn his moustache, had become -- what? -- his friend? Yes, his friend. Reg was his friend, as was John H. Smith, and -- as much as the thought soured his stomach -- so was Lady Montique. He would find them. He would rescue them. He owed them that.

Lovenight sat musing, looking at the ancient Assyrian king and the lion with the sword through his belly and the bevy of arrows sticking out of his neck. It was then he noticed he was alone, which was unusual for the most popular cultural attraction in the U.K., boasting close to 7,000,000 visitors per year. Working on statistics alone (assuming 4 hours per visitor per visit) there should have been 266.32 people in the Assyrian Gallery. In fact, it was more than just unusual. Lovenight would go so far as to say *highly* unusual. Adding to the unusualness was the silence -- complete and utter in nature.

Something skittered. Or more precisely, something *nearby* skittered.

His inner alarms began ringing so loud his head felt like a bell tower.

He twisted around and there they were: the two rats. The brown one sitting on a bench, the mink-coloured directly behind it. The brown one regarded Lovenight for a second, its polished eyes drinking him in with a certain relish.

"You're trifling with me," Lovenight said. "I know you are."

The rats transformed. In microseconds they grew in size and stature as waves of purplish brilliance beamed off them. A shockwave crashed into Lovenight, hot as the outflow from a blast furnace. The brown rat's face changed into the austere visage of the baroness, while the mink-coloured one turned into Ned the Glaswegian coconut seller.

Ned shuddered and said, "Anyhow, that was horrific."

"Mister Lovenight," the baroness said with a purr. "Delighted to capture you again."

He peered at her intently for a moment. "We've met before, haven't we?"

The baroness smirked. "Little cockroach, you escaped my interrogators."

"Oh, that's right. You're Lady Montique's estranged homicidal daughter. Love the shoes, by the way."

"You're such an odd creature. Feigning ennui, tossing off blunt statements designed to shock, then changing tactics in an attempt to unbalance me. *Tres transperent*."

"Sorry, no. I'm nowhere near that calculating. I just love the shoes. Why're you trifling with me?"

"I don't like leaving things incomplete."

She waved her hand and the room shivered. Sparks pinwheeled and burst in the air as a slipway manifested. The fireworks dissipated, revealing Lady Montique, Reg, and John H. Smith, all shackled together with what appeared to be bondage restraints purchased at an adult sex store; their mouths ball-gagged, eyes wide with anxiety.

"Interesting and disturbing at the same time," Lovenight commented.

"Try shopping for that shite," Ned added. "You won't believe the number of times my arse was pinched."

"A trifle outré, I must confess, but when it comes to embarrassing my mother there is no length I will not go to." Baroness Zamora pointed a cruel finger at Lovenight. "You will complete my Outliers collection."

"No thanks. Sorry. Really not interested."

"You don't have a choice."

Lovenight slipstreamed, or tried to at least.

The welcome sign, posted on the psionic wall surrounding him, this time read, THE BARONESS ZAMORA IS DELIGHTED TO ONCE AGAIN WELCOME YOU TO HER EGO CITADEL. HAVE A NICE IMPRISONMENT. Lovenight strained, trying to pry through the psionic distortion. Punching a path through a twenty-foot wall of pudding would have been easier.

He felt her trans-kinetic fingers wrap around the arteries leading to his heart. It was like someone had slipped tourniquets around each vein and held the ends taunt, ready to pull and cut off the supply of blood to the pumping organ.

"Look, can we discuss this like normal adversaries? You know, dashing chrono-operative to despot shadow-ruler?"

"I think not. I don't bargain with my collections. You and these other Outliers will witness the eternal subjugation of the human race. Even now, in tens of thousands of fertility labs and clinics worldwide, our obeisance gene is being virus-spliced into the DNA of humanity. Soon everyone will be beholding to me and my progeny, forever! Order! Consistence! Ten thousand years of peace! That's humanity's future! And I--"

A low growl interrupted her.

Not the beefy growl of a Rottweiler or a Mastiff. No, this growl was small in stature but large in intent. This growl meant business. The baroness, Ned, and Lovenight couldn't help but turn towards it.

In the doorway of Room 10a of the British Museum stood a twelve-year-old girl holding a pug in her arms.

Beth-Ann wore a white linen suit, impeccably tailored with turned up cuffs and a mandarin collar. She wore no shoes. There was something different about her since Lovenight had seen her last. She stood ramrod straight, as if she'd been practising yoga daily for a decade, calmingly petting Noodles who looked ready to tear and rend flesh, glaring at the baroness with utter contempt.

The baroness tensed. Muscles in her neck bulged and strained. She pressed her fingertips to her temple. Her lips thinned and blanched. Beside her, Ned stiffened like he'd stuck his finger in an electrical socket, his halo of frizzled hair completely apropos for once.

"Won't work," Beth-Ann said matter-of-factly to the baroness. "You're stuck. And your invisible fingers can't touch me so don't even think about it." She nodded toward Lady Montique, Reg, and John H. Smith. The bondage shackles immediately loosened, fell from their wrists to clank on the floor. The ball-gags popped off.

"What have you done?" the baroness asked, the fury in her voice unrestrained. She remained transfixed, unable to move even the smallest of muscles.

"Stopped you," Beth-Ann said. "You were going to hurt everyone, even yourself."

"How have you done this?"

Noodles cocked a bulbous eye at her, snorted, and said, "Let's just say the universe is her mother."

Lady Montique walked over to Lovenight, smiled, then

backhanded him across the shoulder.

"Oww!"

"Donkey! How many times have I told you? Have tea waiting for released hostages!"

For a moment Lovenight considered putting the ball-gag back in her mouth, but decided against it only because too many people were watching.

"What do we do with the maniacal despot bent on ruling humanity for all eternity?" Noodles asked.

"Eliminate her," Lovenight offered, and received a wrap on his ear for his efforts. "Eewwow!"

Lady Montique stepped forward and in a calm voice said, "She is a maniacal despot bent on ruling humanity for all of eternity, but she is also my daughter. And every mother knows there is a time when you must let children make their own mistakes. It's a hard lesson, I am well aware. But it's also the truth."

"What do you suggest? Give her a good spanking?" Lovenight asked incredulously.

"Nothing of the sort," Lady Montique said. "Let her go."

"Let her go!" Lovenight shrieked. "After all this, after all this we simply let her go?"

"No freaking way!" Noodles roared. "Her kibbles are mine!"

John H. Smith cleared his throat and waved. "If I could offer a suggestion at this point?"

They all turned. The paragon stared awkwardly back at them, shuffled a bit, readjusted his glasses, and said, "Give her to me. I can confine her within my office, for a time, until you feel she has reconciled her debt."

It was too much for Lovenight. He said in a monotone as dry as toast, "You're going to imprison an egocentric despot with nearly inexhaustible resources and wealth...in a cubical."

"Not exactly imprison. What I can do is load her down with paperwork, block her exits with bureaucracy, fetter her with protocols. She is an important part of the overall balance. Eliminating her would be catastrophic, causing even more universal errata to surface. Much better this way, you see?"

Lady Montique sighed, then nodded her head.

"Cool," Beth-Ann said, and turned to go. Reality wobbled for a moment, then rebounded with a clerical vengeance.

The Paragon of Realty offices appeared untouched. Same cubicles, same desks, same motivational posters of 'Don't Gimme No Sass' Bear. Everything in its place, all perfectly normal. The electronic hum of computers and laptops crescendoed as if the office equipment was eager for someone to start using them.

Lovenight swung his head around warily. "What just happened? Where is the British Museum and why am I not in it?"

Beth-Ann stroked Noodles' chin and said. "Mr. Smith had a good idea. So I brought us back to his office."

"Ah, well, that's new." Lovenight bristled and turned to the Realtor. "Pray tell, Mr. Smith, just where is the homicidal megalomanic?"

John H. Smith motioned for everyone to follow him into the copy room.

The baroness stood beside a humming copier, a mighty frown on her lips, her complete attention focused on deciphering the user manual. A stack of documents several feet high teetered beside her. She appeared completely oblivious to their presence.

"What's she doing?" Noodles asked.

"Trying to clear a paper jam," John H. Smith explained. "She's trapped inside her own ego citadel. In order to escape, she must fix the machine and then finish her copies."

Ned the Glaswegian entered the room carrying a stack of files. Lovenight thought he appeared surprised to be there, judging from the sharp glint in his eye and the perky spring in his step. The white collar and paisley tie wrapped around his throat look tight enough to strangle the hardiest accountant. His frizzle of white hair bobbed as he plunked down the files on the machine, then robotically stalked off for more.

"The longer she takes to fix the machine, the more documents accumulate waiting to be copied" John H. Smith explained. "Oh, I forgot to mention. The machine jams every ten copies."

"An existential bureaucratic nightmare crossed with Greek morality myths," Lady Montique observed. "Fitting."

"Is that even possible to finish the copies?" Lovenight asked.

"Theoretically, yes."

Reg breathed out sharply and whispered, "The horror."

Lovenight nodded approvingly. "Tantalus, Sisyphus, and the baroness. A moral tale for our times, Reg."

"And what's the moral, sir?"

"Stay the hell away from water, boulders, and copiers."

"I'm hungry," said Beth-Ann, looking at Lovenight, Lady Montique, and Reg. "Can we eat before we get started?"

"I'm afraid I don't know what you mean, child." Lady Montique said. "'Start what?"

"I'm joining the Outliers!" she announced. "You still have to deal with the genetic plague Baroness Zamora introduced into humanity's gene pool. Noodles and I need..."

"Friends?" Reg offered.

"No," Beth-Ann said sharply. Too sharply, really. "No, we want to help."

"Young lady, you're quite correct. Welcome to the Outliers." Lady Montique glanced at Lovenight. "Cancel any plans you might have, donkey. The genetic plague awaits!"

Lovenight looked around him, scanning their expectant faces. It occurred to him he was surrounded by people who cared for him; Reg and Lady Montique, the pre-teen and the pug, John H. Smith. It stirred something inside him, something he hadn't felt for a long time, maybe as far back as when he was a child. He searched for a word to describe the feeling, something that would encapsulate the moment and bring it into a sharp, insightful focus.

"Bugger," he said.

THE END.

# ACKNOWLEDGEMENTS

Special and heartfelt thanks to Eli and Sean, Rich and Gord, Emily and Cassandra, Jessie and Dave.

# ABOUT THE AUTHOR

Nicholas de Kruyff's short fiction has appeared in The Magazine of Fantasy and Science Fiction, On Spec, and Parsec. A relentless optimist, he lives in Toronto, Canada with his amazing wife and sparkling daughters and far too many books. Slippery Times is his first (published) novel. To learn more please visit www.nicholasdekruyff.com or check out his profile at www.storywellpublishing.com.

CPSIA information can be obtained
at www.ICGtesting.com
Printed in the USA
LVHW031908290821
696400LV00015B/425